David Ashton was born in Greenock in 1941. He studied at Central Drama School, London from 1964 to 1967, and most recently appeared in *The Last King of Scotland* and *The Etruscan Smile*. David started writing in 1984 and has seen many of his plays and TV adaptations broadcast — he wrote early episodes of *EastEnders* and *Casualty*, as well as the *McLevy* series for Radio 4.

You can visit the *McLevy* website at www.inspectormclevy.com

and discover more about the author at www.david-ashton.co.uk

MISTRESS OF THE JUST LAND

New Year's Day: Through the misty streets of Victorian Edinburgh, an elegant female figure walks the cobblestones — with a certain vengeful purpose. Jean Brash, the Mistress of the Just Land, brings her cool intelligence to solving a murder that took place in her own bawdy-hoose (the best in Edinburgh, and her pride and joy). A prominent judge strangled and left dangling could bring her whole life to ruin, and she didn't haul herself off the streets to let that come to pass. The search for the killers will take Jean back into her own dark past as she uncovers a web of political and sexual corruption in the high reaches of the Edinburgh establishment, but she has little time before a certain Inspector James McLevy comes sniffing round like a wolf on the prowl . . .

Books by David Ashton
Published by Ulverscroft:

SHADOW OF THE SERPENT
FALL FROM GRACE
A TRICK OF THE LIGHT
NOR WILL HE SLEEP

DAVID ASHTON

◆

MISTRESS OF THE JUST LAND

A Jean Brash Mystery

Complete and Unabridged

CHARNWOOD
Leicester

First published in Great Britain in 2016 by
Two Roads
An imprint of Hodder & Stoughton
Edinburgh

First Charnwood Edition
published 2018
by arrangement with
Hodder & Stoughton
An Hachette UK company
London

A catalogue record for this book is available
from the British Library.

ISBN 978–1–4448–3735–3

Published by
F. A. Thorpe (Publishing)
Anstey, Leicestershire
Set by Words & Graphics Ltd.
Anstey, Leicestershire
Printed and bound in Great Britain by
T. J. International Ltd., Padstow, Cornwall

This book is printed on acid-free paper

To
PATRICK RAYNER
who started the ball rolling

1

The cattie sits in the kiln-ring
spinning, spinning,
And by came a little wee mousie,
rinning, rinning.

Her bare feet hurt on the sharp cobblestones as
the young girl ran for her life through the
gnarled and twisted wynds of Leith.

A memory of the old woman, bent backwards,
mouth agape as if trying to deliver a last word,
burnt into the girl's mind — a candle throwing
pointed shadows on the wall as she had tried to
shake some life into the dead body.

But Margaret was gone. The old woman was
gone. On the table a bottle of cheap White Dog
whisky lay on its side, last dregs soaking into the
rough wood. It was Margaret's custom to send
the girl early to bed, then mumble her memories
over a chipped glass before slumping into her
own recess to snore the night away.

Jean Brash usually lay upon a thin mattress on
the floor. Hers was a lonely, restless sleep, but
this night jumbled dreams and desperate
emptiness — a private emptiness she fought to
keep at bay; fought to keep any unwanted tears
from sliding down her cheeks to dribble salty
drops into the corner of a mouth — all that had
been arrested by a crack like a bone breaking.

1

She sat up in an old dress, yellow now that had once been white, to see Margaret had jerked back, a baleful, harsh croak shooting out from her chapped lips. Dead as a doornail.

* * *

Where to now? Jean was running blind; the wynds she knew so well had been left behind and these wormy, slimy clefts, with a cold, dark Edinburgh night, the east wind driving a sharp, cutting rain, were unknown territory.

She stumbled and crashed up against the rough wall, scraping some skin on her bare arm, but there was no going back. With one fierce action, she had burnt her boats.

'Buggeration!' she shouted, and then told herself off for such. Bad manners to swear and Margaret had tried to instil some manners into the child of her keeping.

She had also managed to teach Jean the rudiments of spelling and numbers, for Margaret, as the old woman never tired telling, once worked as a housekeeper for a wealthy Edinburgh family and had been taught the bare bones of learning and kitchen craft. Margaret never said why she had lost the position, only that the family had moved from the city, leaving their faithful, loving servant behind.

They were both a cut above the riff-raff that swarmed outside their grimy tenement, pronounced Margaret. But that was not so. The old woman drank like a fish and Jean ran wild with the feral street-children.

Though she always held something back. The boys called her Queen Bee. They caught the other girls and had their wicked fun and games, but not Jean.

She never ran. Just stood her ground. And even Dirk Martins, who shook his mop of flaxen hair and grinned his grin, and then wee manky Jeb Summers like a rat up a drainpipe — a pair of dirty devils — hesitated to shove a questing hand where there might be plunder.

They had tried it once, mind you.

Only the once.

She attracted men and she could sense it. Even at her eleven years, she could sense it. Red hair, porcelain skin, green eyes, thin as a rake — but she attracted.

Jean could smell it coming off them like a dank spoor.

And on she ran, a small figure in a dark landscape, the faded yellow dress flapping like a broken wing.

★　★　★

She wrenched open the door of the tiny, cramped room and fell out into the narrow landing of the tenement, calling for help. No one answered. All the families, ten or more to a room, were asleep or pretending to be so. There were many screams and cries at all hours of the night up and down the landings, cutting through the thin walls, and it was better to pull a ragged sheet over your head and render the outside world beyond sight and sound.

3

One door opened. The one she did not wish to see. Alexander Moncrieff stuck out his head. A cadaverous lank figure, his age was hard to guess: about thirty or so but he seemed older. As if his blood ran thin. Cold and cruel.

Moncrieff ran the tenement, collected rents for the landlord, had the one swivelling eye and a habit of licking his lips incessantly. It was said he had once been in the army and he affected a military bearing — straight back, instant obedience — which went down well with those in command. In fact, he had recently been offered a better position at another establishment by the landlord in recognition of his many virtues, and he was puffed up with the resultant power. No one ever saw the landlord — he was like God in heaven, hidden in the clouds.

The man shoved past her into the room and leant over the remnants of Margaret Brash. She had given Jean her name but was not kith and kin.

There was no mother, no father, just a procession of the dead. According to Margaret, Jean's mother had died at birth and her father had been up to no good and nowhere to be found. Jean had sensed a lie in these words, but the old woman would not be shaken. Now she was still as the grave.

'Well,' said Moncrieff. 'That's a peety. Drink is a terrible curse. I rarely touch the beast.' He turned and drew back his moist lips in a liverish smile that froze her to the bone. 'Nevertheless — the rent is owing and will have tae be paid. All things must be paid. One way or the other.' A

4

hand was held out, palm up. 'Have you the money?'

Jean shook her head.

Moncrieff moved forward till he loomed over her. 'I can take care of it. I can take care of you. I can take care of everything.' His large, raw-boned hand came to rest on her shoulder and she could feel its heat through the thin material.

'I am your lord and master now,' he declared, his one good eye boring into hers like a demon in the fairy tale. 'I am your lord and master.'

For a moment Jean felt something inside twitch in response. It must have shown in her face because Moncrieff grinned and his hand tightened, the fingers digging into her flesh like claws rooting her to his beck and call. Would she have been lost? Swallowed whole, like the child in the evil legend?

Then her leg swept up and a hard, bony shin hit into his groin like a hammer.

In all Jean's life to come, no matter what hardships and dangers were dealt, no matter the evil on hand, this feeling would never leave her. A voice that said 'Wait for your moment, then strike the blow. There will always be one moment — one chance to take — don't miss. One chance.'

Alexander Moncrieff yelped, hunched over in the most excruciating pain and when after some time he looked up again, the room was empty save for him and the corpse. The girl was gone. The agony, however, was only too blindingly present, and his eye swivelled wildly

5

to signal such condition.
One chance. One blow.

★   ★   ★

As she stumbled onwards, the breath catching raw in her throat, Jean could see some slivers of lamplight up ahead, faint in the mirk. Perhaps a street of some kind — she would be safe there.

Safe? Something had slid deep inside her when Moncrieff had spoken, an evil, insidious imprint that would always be there, waiting for a sign of weakness.

The devil's calling card, and many men take on his countenance.

Her bare foot slipped on the slime of the cobblestones and Jean fell headlong, jolted face first, wind knocked out of her body. Through the buzzing in her ears she could hear footsteps coming towards where she lay.

Was it *him*? Or some other fiend from hell?

Two women looked down at Jean. One sported a bright scarlet feather boa to disguise her wrinkled neck, skin stretched like parchment over the sharp bones, and the other had flat features, almost primitive, with jet-black hair and a jaunty emerald-green bonnet perched perilously on the back of her head.

Both wore garish cheap gowns under nondescript shabby coats, one a bright blue, the other faded pink set off by a slash of livid orange.

Faces painted white like masks, red markings like a signal in the dark.

6

Nymphs of the Pavé, Fleurs de Nuit whose petals often opened at night, cowclinks in Edinburgh's coarser tongue. Their names were Jessie Sheridan and Nan Dunlop.

Jessie was the older — men had passed below her like froth under the Bridge of Leith. Like paper boats.

From her and Nan's point of view, they saw a small figure crouched like an animal on the stones — hard rain beating down to soak deep the thin, discoloured dress.

'How come ye're running wild, wee girl?' asked Jessie. 'Have ye cut a throat, maybe?'

The figure shook its head, auburn hair plastered to the skull.

'Where are ye going in such a hurry, then?'

An answer came finally.

'Nowhere, thank you.'

Nan grinned, revealing wide gaps in her teeth. Unlike Jessie, there was a primitive, unstable quality to the woman, eyes dark and shiny like a mongoose. She was yet young enough that her body still cradled a sensual challenge and invitation.

'And whit are ye leaving behind, my wee chookie?' she asked, green bonnet dancing with the movement of her head in the cold, damp air.

'Nothing.'

The women looked at each other. A story would emerge eventually but this was not the time — it had been an unproductive night, the rain was getting heavier, and in Jessie's case the beginnings of a consumptive cough were already stirring in the fragile casing of her chest.

7

They could leave the girl to the tender mercies of rats and bigger beasts — or take her in hand — yet what had they to offer?

Only a profession that ran out of hope, like water down the drain.

The girl scrambled to her feet — feet that were bruised and bleeding from reckless flight — and faced them with a spirited defiance undermined somewhat by the shivering in her body.

'Whit is your name, wee girl?'

'Jean. Jean Brash. And I am a Queen Bee.'

Nan let out a roar of laughter at this response to Jessie's question, as the older woman smiled thinly.

'Well, we better take ye tae the hive, then.'

Jessie and Nan shared a room and had done so for the past two years — they could squeeze her in somewhere.

At least she was skinny, Jessie surmised. Maybe she could sleep standing up.

There was an element of calculation in Nan's eyes — if the lassie filled out, she might yet pay her way.

Everyone must pay their way. In this world, whatever you have to offer is always for sale from the moment you're born.

The girl stepped between them and the trio turned to go with the women leading in front. As they walked on, Jean, impulsively, put slim, delicate hands into theirs.

And so the three figures departed, moving towards the glimmering rain-streaked lamplight ahead, like ghosts disappearing from view towards an uncertain future.

2

This is the way the ladies ride,
Clippety clop, clippety clop.

The New Year bells clanged resoundingly from various pious pulls as Jean Brash shifted in her sleep. She had stumbled into bed in the early hours of that morning after her palatial bawdy-hoose, the Just Land, had entertained what seemed like half the professional ruling classes of Edinburgh city.

The medical and legal gentleman's clubs, having drowned their sorrows at the passing year and then greeted with appropriate conviviality a new arrival from the loins of Old Father Time, had descended upon the Just Land with appendages aquiver.

They joined forces with a number of Bristol businessmen who were up to finance a deal with the powers that be of the city council and, having haggled with some success but not quite enough, had called it quits for the moment, thrown caution to the wind, and led by a merry but totally bald round-faced fellow, Sammy Deacon, and his equally boisterous but taller, more handsome and fully thatched colleague, Joseph Tucker, had brought some of the more adventurous councillors along to slake their carnal thirst.

Who knows?

A satisfied man faintly redolent of a smudge of French cologne might look more kindly upon funds and figures. Satisfaction is a fine financial bedfellow.

A wild party had ensued where many a purloined legal wig had decorated many an unveiled evidential body, and the magpies for their part knowing by rule of thumb that medical men tend to strive longer than advocates who are all talk and no great pith, clove to choice of profession in accordance with their preferred or pecuniary desires.

The Bristol boys would no doubt be a mixed bag of sweeties as men inevitably are — dip your hand in a brown paper poke, trust they don't stick together, pop it in and hope for the best.

Amongst the gathering were also a number of wild young bucks of a more artistic bent, one, a sculptor, Jack Burns — a handsome devil whose high cheekbones set his face in conflicting sharp planes — had leant over Jean and most earnestly requested that he might immortalise her naked form in an innovative version of Pallas Athena.

'You see, Mistress Brash, a woman unclothed is the most powerful weapon of any artist,' he asserted, eyes blazing into hers part fuelled by creative intent, part by a fairly decent champagne. 'I would consider it a great honour to mediate between your earthly flesh and the immortal goddess. Athena presided over the finer elements of man. Courage, strategy and heroic endeavour.'

Jean nodded at this deific description, aware at the same time that one of the artistic champagne guzzlers was staring at her from the corner of the room.

She indicated the onlooker, who for some reason was dressed as a dusky-hued Arabian prince — many of the artists had affected exotic display, two had even come in extravagant ostrich plumes.

'The small, dainty fellow from the Mysterious East: who is he?'

Jack smiled briefly. 'Solomon Baines. Shows promise.'

'In what?'

'Portraiture.'

Jean inclined her head in a friendly fashion towards Solomon, who managed a jerky bob in response, then she and the sculptor got back to business. It could not be denied that a certain attraction was in the air along with the cigar fumes and aforementioned cologne. Art is a great leveller.

'And how do you see the goddess in human form?'

The sculptor took a deep breath. 'Lean-flanked, fertile-breasted,' he ventured. 'A long, slim body.'

'Was she not also virginal?' asked Jean. 'I fear that might compromise me somewhat as a model example.'

Her green eyes were open and candid — for a moment Jack felt a tickle at the back of his throat.

The woman before him was in her prime. Indeed fertile-breasted as far as he could see from her discreet décolletage, red hair lustrous in

11

the glittering candlelight, green eyes with a mocking glint echoed in the smile of her full lips, a porcelain complexion — all contained in a complex, withheld quality that radiated an almost feline powerful attraction.

But don't mistake magnetism for invitation, that would be foolish.

'Just give me the chance,' he said hoarsely. 'I will uncover your essential innocence.'

'That's what worries me,' replied Jean, aware that music was stirring once more in the background as their one-eyed fiddler, Finlay Craigie, laid down his drink with a deal of regret to loose ancient fingers for other matters.

'And once your garments are thrown to the four winds, it's a devil of a job to gather them back up again. A *devil* of a job.'

She smiled at the sculptor suddenly and Jack felt a spasm of masculine response that had little to do with artistic leanings.

Then the music began, she had disappeared into the throng and he was left cursing the fact that champagne is, now and again, not quite such an all-embracing aid to seductive strategy as portrayed in fiction. It may oil the tongue and fire the blood, but does not necessarily provide sufficient speed of verbal response.

Jean turned in the sheets, smiled in memory at the man's impudence and regarded her image in the long mirror beside the bed — red hair tousled from sleep, skin clear and innocent as a newborn babe.

In fact, was it not James McLevy, the thief-taker himself, who had muttered over a cup of the finest Lebanese coffee, 'Tae look at you, Jeannie, ye'd never guess what you've done and where you've done it.'

Always wanted to be a muse, she thought. *But I might end up as a mere plaything.*

And yet she could not help but notice the strength in the sculptor's hands, blunt powerful fingers that would no doubt exercise a strong and steadfast grip and a rough-hewn physicality that might have its own unclothed attraction.

Like Hercules unchained?

Certain licentious images were put carefully to the side but not completely forgotten as the Mistress of the Just Land reviewed the rest of that evening.

Couples had sped headlong for upstairs rooms to reappear later happily replete upon the fruits of Venus — a slippery goddess at the best of times — and then revelled in impromptu reels and jigs while the fiddler stamped his boots and big Annie Drummond shifted plump but dexterous digits over piano keys as if toying amongst so many cream buns.

While smooth legs emerged from flounced chemises and an exposed bare foot flexed itself in the dance, it would have been a cold fish that did not feel the blood-heat.

But hot blood can lead to hot deeds. Like murder, for instance.

A bang of sorts and then the bedroom door burst open to reveal Hannah Semple — Jean's right-hand woman, keeper of the keys of the Just Land, old as the hills, with a basilisk stare that might arrest many a rampant satyr.

13

But now her eyes were wide open in shock.

'Mistress, there's a deid body in the cellar, hinging over the Berkley Horse, a big knife in the back!'

The New Year bells kept ringing.

Ding-dong.

Ding-dong.

3

Robin-a-bobbin
Bent his bow,
Shot at a pigeon
And killed a crow.

The cellar of the Just Land was, to tell truth, a somewhat mildewed dungeon-like affair; however, that suited to a noteworthy extent its given purpose. That of bodily chastisement. The dank walls were festooned with whips of highest quality Spanish leather and there were many other implements of applied agony to hand, even the odd giant thistle if the season was in full bloom.

Nature is a generous soul.

Men of power, who spent their lives in complete mastery of others, whether as benign despots or harsh taskmasters whose very frown might set limbs atremble amongst the slaves who toiled in their offices, laid down meek as the lamb gratifying a perverse wish to experience the pain their decisions inflicted upon lesser mortals.

They groaned and yelped in a physical mortification that their employees would devoutly wish them but had little idea could actually take place.

Such are the ways of might and money. Only those who inflict suffering can afford to buy it as well. Of course a man can always get it for

15

nothing, but then the suffering may not stop.

At one time the cellar had been the domain of Francine, an elegant angular French girl who dressed in the manner of an Egyptian priestess and could calculate precisely where and how to hang, how far up to haul, and then proceed to lay down stripes like a tiger. However, she had returned to Paris to resume her art studies.

Now the welts were dished out by Maisie Powers, a local lass, broad in the beam, strong in the arm, lacking a certain sophistication but aided and abetted by little Lily Baxter — Francine's former lover, a sunny-natured soul, deaf and dumb, with the clear complexion and rounded body of a comely milkmaid, which was, to be precise, one of her fundamental functions.

Maisie laid it on.

Lily filled the pail.

Both were clasped in each other's arms upstairs as the cellar door burst open and Jean arrived, as if shot from a gun, with Hannah trailing behind, grimly holding on to her lit candle because the passageway and dungeon itself were pitch black, now and then illuminated with torches to add an inquisitional atmosphere.

What you cannot see may terrify all the more.

What you can see is not to be sniffed at either.

The old woman had not been mistaken — a long knife was stuck into the man's back as he slumped over the Berkley Horse — an apparatus that had cost Jean a pretty penny, designed to spread-eagle and manacle the willing participant, not however, to be a framework for murder.

The corpse lay face down.

'Did you touch anything?' asked Jean.

'Certainly not, Mistress,' was the offended reply. 'I jist came down early doors tae make sure the place was intact, these girls are gey scattered at times. One look at him was enough thanks. My touching days are over.'

They moved closer to the shrouded figure and Hannah's eyes narrowed in recognition as she did so.

'That's one o' my kitchen knives,' she announced with fierce indignation. 'I cut the Sabbath roast wi' that — stuck right intae the handle. Damn cheek!'

Jean reached out to the shoulder of the recumbent slumped corpse. Sticky to the feel, the material of the dark jacket inert and clammy, as if also moribund — some spread of blood but not a great deal. From her experience of blood, she would have expected more.

Slowly under Jean's prising fingers the head swung round, with a grating noise to accompany the movement.

A pale snouty face, eyes wide and staring, gazed vacantly at them in the flickering light of the candle.

'God Almighty,' Hannah breathed as if afraid to wake the sleeper. 'It's Judge Abercrombie.'

The face swung away out of vision and went back to the contemplation of eternity.

Jean bit her lip. Hilton Abercrombie had indeed been in the place last night, sitting to the side as usual, sooking at his glass of whisky. He paid a visit once every year and perched by the

17

fire with a face like a sore backside, watching his legal colleagues cavort out of court. He had never once taken part in the roistering, merely wet his thin lips and sooked his whisky.

And yet, despite his apparent disapproval, Jean sensed an element of voyeurism and cruel sadistic bent that was reflected in the harsh sentences he meted out to the poor devils found guilty in his court; a particular pleasure being to don the black cap that signalled a one-way passage to the hangman's noose.

Hilton was not a popular man but he was one of the most eminent and scholarly judges in Edinburgh city.

And now he was dead. Or, to be more accurate, murdered, since it is well-nigh impossible to stab yourself in the back with a large carving knife.

Jean whistled tunelessly through her teeth, a habit of hers when deep in thought. A habit she had picked up from Inspector James McLevy. It had become second nature.

This was bad.

This was *very* bad.

4

On looking up, on looking down,
She saw a dead man on the ground;
And from his nose unto his chin,
The worms crawl'd out, the worms crawl'd in.

Four women sat in the kitchen of the Just Land and three of them looked at their mistress.

Maisie and Lily had been roused from sleep and questioned as regards their activities of the previous evening. A shameful admission followed.

In the main, the girls were left to their own, as it fell, devices — trusted by Jean to perform without interference, length of abrasive activity being variable depending on the clientele.

Some had skins like the leather itself, some required pampering, then powdering like a baby either before or after, and some howled the place down, the cellar walls being thick to purpose.

The chief recipient last night had been one of the head surgeons at the university who, as a valued client, had to be decently indulged. Nonetheless the operation involved Maisie in the guise of a rather hefty Little Bo Peep while Sir Archibald Snoddy, for such was his name, enacted the part of a recalcitrant mehhing lambkin.

Normally this was a fairly long drawn-out

19

process, but this particular farmyard ritual had finished somewhat abruptly when Lily, as adjacent shepherdess, decided to waggle forth her darting little tongue at Sir Archibald while Maisie brought down a punishing crook.

For some reason, the waggle brought proceedings to an abrupt and premature cessation. Off stalked Sir Archibald, while Maisie reprimanded Lily as an impudent wee bugger. But then came the shame.

Under Jean's steady gaze, the girls confessed that — instead of sweeping up woolly hair of all kinds, washing the floor, polishing leather and generally making the place shipshape for future trade, plus, if time decreed, slipping up to the main salon and if not to cavort, then in Maisie's case, keep Annie Drummond supplied with cream buns, and in Lily's, pour out the champagne with a beaming smile — the reason for the projection of her fleshly organ was a sudden desire to welcome the New Year with a certain relish and Maisie, once informed of this, was very much in favour as she found Lily irresistible.

So, off they'd crept to pastures new. And — as a result — the cellar had been left empty.

Hannah was about to launch into a remonstrative tirade when an upraised hand from her mistress stemmed the ride.

'You saw no one as you left?' asked Jean.

Two heads shaken, but Lily had a memory that she did not dare to disclose.

★ ★ ★

20

Later that night the party still at full blast, she felt the floor vibrating with the thump of feet and wild music from below. Of course, Lily could not hear this world, but something had woken her. Or was it a dream? Her dreams were often so vivid she found herself in other rooms and stairwells, tears running down her face till Maisie sought her out and brought her gently back to bed.

But Maisie was asleep. There. Lying. Sated. A happy smile on her full lips.

Lily rose from the bed, walked to the window and looked out onto the garden. Then she blinked and tried to clear the unruly curls from falling over her eyes. A tiny scuttling figure moving in Lily's silence, cowled like a monk, crouched over, swift, shifting like a ghost across the grass from the lower reaches that led to the cellar door. For a moment it looked back and Lily flinched as if a shock coursed through her.

The face was pure white, eyes black holes in the ashen visage; whether man or woman she might not even tell. Yet though she could not make out the features, there was an impression of some particular identity. Like an imprint of malignance. A stamp of evil.

But it could not have seen her, surely?

The entity turned sharply and disappeared into the darkness.

Of course, and this was something else they had concealed, both Lily and Maisie were occasionally given to a tincture of opium, which added fragrance to their entwining limbs. Was it perhaps the cause of her wild dreams? Was this

21

moment itself a dream? For now the garden stood empty and the only things moving were clouds sailing past the crescent moon in a clear night sky.

Once before in her life Lily had witnessed a killer in action — one Alfred Binnie, who had poured acid over a woman's unprotected back and then, finding out that Lily had seen him, tried to kill her. The terror she had felt had paralysed her then and benumbed her now.

What she had seen was a dream — a nightmare.

She crawled back, laid her head on Maisie's firm no-nonsense breast, the nipple of which perked up even in slumber, and drifted off to sleep.

★ ★ ★

Lily looked at her mistress's face in the cold light of day and kept this frightening vision to herself. If not real, then leave it be.

Jean had been silent since the question but her mind was buzzing with consequence. The silence grew and Hannah found it difficult to bear.

'Whit're we going tae do with the body? It's still on the bliddy horse.'

'No rush. It won't be going anywhere,' said Jean.

This thoughtful utterance jolted Maisie into a sudden burst of laughter, more to do with a release of tension than any discovered humour.

'Sorry, Mistress,' she blurted. 'I just don't know what tae do with myself.'

'I'll give you something,' muttered Hannah. 'Don't worry, my girl.'

She looked grimly at Lily, who hid her head.

'I'd expect better from you, Lily Baxter. If it wasnae for the mistress, you'd have been hung, drawn and quartered on the streets. Long since!'

Maisie flushed and opened her mouth to defend her love, but Lily laid a warning hand on her arm. All this time she had been aware of Jean's eyes fixed steadily upon her. Lily could lip-read well and understood most of what was said, but Jean's mouth did not move. Like the eyes.

Did the mistress know she might hold something back?

Yet whatever Jean may have been secretly considering was, for the moment, subsumed under a welter of practical and unwelcome thought. She suddenly banged her fist upon the table, the sound shockingly sharp in the silence.

'We could *all* end up on the streets.'

A flat statement that brought the rest upright.

'If we report this,' she continued, 'James McLevy will rip the place apart. It's his job.'

She fell silent as her memory brought a sharp image into focus.

★ ★ ★

Henry Preger leant his giant form back against the bar of his tavern, The Foul Anchor, and looked at the young constable who had blundered into his lair. One of Preger's men, Patch Wilson, had cut a love rival in the street

23

and run for shelter. The constable had followed close, only to find himself isolated within a hostile crowd and facing a man who was feared throughout Leith for his unremitting violence.

Preger also ran a low-class bawdy-hoose, the Happy Land, and treated his women with the same cruel ferocity. His present pet wagtail stood just behind him, young, red-haired, green-eyed; she was in thrall to her master — or so Preger believed. He had put his mark upon her. A deep imprint; a brand on milky skin; the Devil's calling card.

A heavy bruise, but it would heal. However, the darkness in her mind was quite another matter. Now she watched him inflict a different violence.

The fight was hopelessly one-sided, the crowd jeering as they kicked and shoved at the policeman while Preger's granite fists beat a tattoo upon the young man's countenance, the assailant's slash of a mouth curved up in an evil smile.

Finally the constable slumped to the dirty floorboards and through a blood-haze watched the iron-tipped boots of his opponent move towards him.

The crowd stilled and shifted back as Preger stopped to put his hands on his hips. 'No one interferes now,' he announced grandly. 'This scraggie will be kicked intae the boneyard.'

The target looked up and saw, as if the haze had parted, a clear vision of the young wagtail at Preger's elbow, red hair alight in the dirty tavern smoke. She smiled, and then winked at him.

24

James McLevy came off that floor like a man berserk and battered his enemy from one end of the tavern to the other. No one made a move to interfere. As instructed. At the end, Henry Preger was a crumpled, crushed heap. No longer a figure of dread.

McLevy grabbed hold of his quarry, Patch Wilson, and marched him out of the door without a backward glance.

Jean Brash looked down at the man who had ruled the Happy Land with a fist of iron and became conscious of a voice within: 'There will always be one moment.'

★ ★ ★

'We could jist get rid of the body.'

Jean emerged from memory and shook her head at Hannah's words. The constable was an inspector now but some things never change.

'That would make us accessories; if McLevy found out, and he has a knack for just that thing, matters would be a damn sight worse.'

There was something deeper and darker behind her words, and whatever it was brooked no argument.

Although Hannah, to give the old woman her due, tried.

'We could keep it secret, Mistress.'

'There's already four of us know. That's three too many. Plus whoever it was that killed him. Too many.'

She cut a beautiful figure sitting there in a silk-frilled dressing gown, red hair loose on her

25

shoulders, but the eyes resembled icy-green chips.

'That wee room at the back of the cellar, where we keep the cheese sometimes. How cold is it?'

'Lik' a morgue,' said Hannah.

'Good. We can hold the corpus there for a while. That should give us time.'

'Time for what?'

'To find out who did this.'

A stunned silence followed the statement.

'I don't like,' said Jean calmly, 'folk using my house as a trysting place for murder or indeed applying my kitchen knives for the same purpose. So I intend to find out the culprit and act accordingly.'

'How the hell do we do that?'

'That's a very good question, Hannah. And I intend to give it my full consideration.'

Jean Brash leant forward.

'Now, you might rustle me up some coffee. I have a deal of thinking to do.'

5

Who caught his blood?
I, said the Fish,
With my little dish,
I caught his blood.

The white rat sniffed with caution at the morsel its master had thrown to the ground. The offerings were many and varied; some with blood, which the rat preferred, some with fragments of bone, which was also welcome, but some were squashed and hard-shelled, oozing with a slimy trail of innards, which was not enticing, even for a rat.

This object had a curious texture and smell. Another sniff. A tentative bite. One more circle.

'It's Dundee cake, beastie,' said Jeb Summers. 'Rich pickings.'

His laughter echoed round the womblike cave that he shared with many crawling creatures, though the white rat was his preferred company.

Jeb was also of the same hue — his skin had a chalky, pallid, near translucent quality, the eyes pale and hooded, hair that framed the face long and surprisingly clean, though with a thin, wispy quality as if it might fall off the skull at any moment.

His chin curved up and the nose curved down, like a nursery book witch-woman, but he considered himself a handsome fellow and the rat was in full agreement.

Handsome is, as handsome does.

Jeb wore a rough brown blanket fashioned into the shape of a monk's garment with a covering cowl; his clothes underneath the cowl, though threadbare and dusty, were not covered in dirt. Fastidious. What he could not wash, he scraped, even unto the whiskers.

As he observed the rat groom itself, so Jeb followed suit — a pair of swells.

His feet were covered with a pair of old shoes, too large but stuffed with newspaper and wrapped round with rags. Yet he could move like a scuttling scorpion in them — silent and poised, fangs at the ready.

White as a sheet. He rarely saw the light of day, moved through the city at night, kept to the shadows of the back streets and wynds, sometimes mistaken for a child, a figure that could disappear in an instant.

Albino. Though Jeb would not have recognised that appellation — he had been called many names, none of them to flatter. A stunted, warped creature, legs bowed with rickets, lucky to reach four feet in height — once he had run away from the Charity workhouse, life on the streets had not been easy without his boon companion who had been taken away, Dirk Martins. Until that first cut.

A razor sharp stone had done the trick. Gash down the side of a face and the tormentor had run away howling for his mother, gang trailing behind.

Jeb did not have either luxury, but from then on he had been left alone and that suited him just fine.

'Jist fine,' he muttered. 'Eh, beastie?'

The rat had discovered the delights of Dundee cake and twitched its long tail in response.

In the dead of night, after he had choked and plunged that bastard judge and then grinned goodbye to the Smiler, he'd slid off into the dark of the garden — unseen except maybe by a female face at a window, but that had disappeared quick enough and who would credit whit they saw when whit they saw was Jeb Summers?

After that, with the fireworks and flames lighting up the city, Jeb had made his usual round of the midden bins. Often there was food to be found — scraps of meat, pot scrapings, tattie peel, a carcass of some fowl — but the killing had brought him luck and in the heavy metal bin behind a big bakery in Commercial Street he had scooped up the cake.

True, it had a fur of mould, but only skin deep.

Mould, like murder, is easy scraped away.

Especially with long fingernails. Jeb was proud of his; they curved like talons, but were clean, strong and razor sharp. A natural weapon and also a fine lockpick.

He could insert them into many a metal orifice and tickle the mechanism into surrender.

Nature is kind to those in need.

He had returned to the cave last night, slept like a dead man and woke with a fine hunger.

Now it was satisfied and he had a work of art to accomplish.

Jeb took out a small chisel he had found on a long-ago excursion, the point sharpened to a deadly fang, and began cutting an image into the soot-grimed bricks of the wall, his pale eyes intent with purpose.

He had many hidey-holes but this was his favourite — in the catacombs that ran below Salamander Street, where, further on up the slope of that thoroughfare, the slaughterhouse lay in waiting for cows, pigs and sheep.

All God's children.

If he moved a distance further along the gouged channels here he could scramble up through the hidden grating, forewarned by the bellowing of the fearful animals, and sneak a look from the narrow deserted alley to see their hooves strike sparks on the rigid stone of the main street itself.

At first he had drunk in that terror but then he had begun to feel sorry for the beasts; their plight was not unlike his own.

Outcasts.

Sometimes, when he travelled through the underground tunnels, he might also try his luck at spearing a quick glance up a woman's skirt if she passed over the bolted gratings of the road above, but there was little to see and he had no real interest.

Especially now that he had discovered a better thrill. Now that his friend had returned.

As he concentrated on the image to be cut into the wall, his fingers like pinions around the chisel, Jeb's mind set back to the previous night.

★ ★ ★

The Smiler had kept his word and brought the judge down the stairs to slaughter.

Jeb was already waiting. He could break into any back-garden premises, and had found a coal chute that he could scramble through easily enough. Being a dwarf had its benefits.

As the target turned to the Smiler, expecting promised information on civic corruption, Jeb leapt up on the man's back, passed his wee thick wire line round the scrawny neck of Hilton Abercrombie and choked the life out of him. It did not take long — the man had no great gusto.

They could have left the corpse there or hung it high like the first kill, but he had reconnoitred earlier, watched the lassies leave with arms entwined, had seen their lair and the contraption. The Smiler knew its usage and they both thought it a rare laugh to hoist the man up astraddle. And then?

Jeb found a knife in the kitchen, big and sharp — he lifted it up and looked the Smiler in the eye. The man had not been so eager at the first killing, but they had sworn in blood, and blood must be kept. Yet this time, Dirk nodded. Keen this time. That was good. He was getting a taste for it.

Up went the knife and down it plunged. Once more for luck. Up to the hilt.

Jeb had sliced deep a few times before but

only to defend himself. This was better in execution. And before that, as the cord bit deep and his hands pulled tight, he took judicious pleasure in the frenzied thrashing that gradually diminished to an eerie calm. The knife crunching in through inert flesh and bone added the final touch of icing on the cake. And one in the eye for that bitch Jean Brash — she owed him a reckoning.

'We have pronounced a verdict.'

To this solemn statement from the other, Jeb Summers made reply. 'Next time it's your turn. Why should I have a' the fun and games.'

They laughed together at that. It was like old times.

★ ★ ★

Gouged now into the wall was an image — a man bent over, big dagger sticking out of his back. A child could have done it but Jeb was proud of his artistry.

Next to the standing man, another previously etched image showed a figure hanging on a rope.

Three more in prospect.

Jeb grinned and gnashed his sharp little teeth together. The rat looked up, groomed itself to a close, and twitched its whiskers.

What other delicacies had its master brought home? Alive or dead, it made no difference. Feeding time.

6

Snail, snail,
Come out of your hole,
Or else I will beat you
As black as a coal.

'Whit a bliddy caper, eh?' grunted Hannah Semple as she and Jean lugged the corpse, chastely wrapped inside a slate-grey winding sheet, through to what had formerly been the cheese room but was now converted into a rind-ridden, curd-odorous mortuary.

The mistress being especially fond of stronger-smelling delights such as Brie and Roquefort, it had a tang that might well be useful as the days wore on and the flesh fragmented.

Not, Jean reflected, that there was very much time to spare — at the most, given the period of year, probably three or so days before Hilton Abercrombie's absence was officially remarked upon and his last known appearance brought to mind, sooking at his whisky in the Just Land.

They dumped the body on a long table, and Jean celebrated the first day of the New Year by gingerly parting the sheet to gaze upon the dead, waxy countenance of the said Hilton.

Hannah had previously wrenched the knife from the man's back, the old woman bitterly cursing such a lack of finesse in the usage of her domestic implement.

33

She had plunged the thing into a scalding basin of hot water to get rid of the blood and various shreds of flesh, but whether it could ever be used again to carve up a succulent joint of ribbed beef was open to question.

Before the wrenching and the scalding, however, Jean had carefully examined the man's back.

Two stab wounds, the second delivered with fearsome force, but the cellar was, of necessity, gloom-ridden, and the cheese room offered a better chance for her to survey the ruins of what had once been a respected pillar of the community.

How to begin?

God knows, James McLevy had drummed her ears back often enough with his long harangues upon forensic science and the art of detection. If she could just remember some of the dissertation, trouble being that her mind had so often slid off to more interesting topics as the man blethered on.

She carefully parted the stiff collar, trying not to catch the bloodshot staring gaze. Hannah frowned.

'Should we no' close his keekers, pennies for his eyes ye ken? Otherwise it's bad luck.'

Jean forbore to mention the lack of good fortune so far in this affair but pressed the tips of her fingers over the eyes and the gummy lids stuck together with a satisfying little squelch.

'Thank God for that,' commented Hannah, and indeed it was a relief not to have the frozen vacant face looking up at them even though it was seeing little that could provide testimony in court. Or anywhere else.

In the main, the dead are not welcome guests at the feast. A stone in the new-baked bread.

Back to the collar and there was an unexpected revelation. Across the man's neck, behind the stiff collar, in a neat straight line, ran a savage deep crease in the flesh.

'I wondered why he bled so little from the stab wound,' murmured Jean. 'Just a trickle.'

'Never had much blood, that swine,' Hannah replied.

'He's been choked first. See?'

Hannah bent over. 'Right enough. Whit a weasel, eh?'

'And that could have been anywhere,' mused Jean. 'I wondered at such, for Abercrombie would never approach the Berkley Horse. He was not of that persuasion.'

'Somebody stranglet him like a pig, stuck him wi' a kitchen knife and then hoisted him up there?'

'Uhuh.'

'Why do that?'

'Damned if I know.'

They both stared down at Hilton as if he might suddenly spring to life and, in the manner of all judges, pronounce a sentence.

Jean, though far from enjoying herself, was beginning to warm to the task.

'Abercrombie was a miserable specimen, was he not?'

'I never saw him crack a smile once,' Hannah responded. 'Face lik' a duck's arse.'

'Could this be some kind of . . . joke?'

'Joke? The man's been murdered!'

'Uhuh. But if ye had a wee twist to your mind, ye might think it funny. A judge. Him sitting there. Laying down the law.'

While Hannah shook her head doubtfully at that notion, Jean undid the man's jacket and began searching through the pockets.

Nothing much of interest: a pocket book, an unpaid bill for provisions with the judge's name and address upon it, a ring of house keys, oddly enough a wee fancy poke of liquorish sweeties that the man had not offered to share with the merry company of last night, various odds and ends but nothing of import until . . . Jean slipped two fingers discreetly into the top pocket of the jacket.

She had a certain skill in that respect from her days and nights at the Happy Land. Fingers that fondle may flutter into a money pouch.

The digits emerged with a crumpled, faded old playing card. On its back was a faint floral design of loops and whorls. On the front, it showed a Jack of Spades. A knave. The Trickster.

As she held it up before Hannah's puzzled eyes, the door to the room burst open. Both women nearly had a heart attack but it was the flushed, anxious face of Maisie Powers that intruded.

She and Lily had been sent to the kitchen to find a home for the various cheeses in the cupboards. For some reason, however, the big lump had come running back again.

'Whit the hell do you want?' Hannah

36

squawked. She meant it to be a roar but somehow the sound had changed timbre.

Maisie's frightened eyes were fixed upon Jean; however, the voice also choked in her throat.

'Mistress, there's somebody at the back door,' she spluttered. 'Somebody we don't want tae see. Never!'

7

Punch and Judy
Fought for a pie;
Punch gave Judy
A knock in the eye.

Inspector James McLevy dipped the crisp offering into a steaming cup of best-quality coffee and then slid the object into his mouth like a holy wafer.

'There is an art tae eating a sugar biscuit,' he announced, not for the first time in Jean's memory and most certainly, unless she was arrested and sent to the Perth Penitentiary, not the last.

'If ye wait too long after immersion, the body will decompose, burst asunder and contaminate the brew, but if you judge it correct?'

Jean and Hannah had slammed shut the cheese-room portal, locked it fast, planked the key by the lintel, and then bolted somewhat comically towards the back door only to find the bloody man already poking about in the kitchen, the tall lantern figure of Constable Martin Mulholland loitering uneasily at the rear.

Maisie had shot past the constable and disappeared to seek out Lily, who had unwillingly led the police in and then also ran for her life, still holding on to a wedge of Orkney Cheddar that had not yet been found a home.

38

The place seemed full of hurtling female bodies.

Luckily the kitchen knife, amongst its fellows in a drawer left neglectfully ajar, did not shriek out, 'Ah've done a murder, Inspector, arrest me quick, my conscience is troubled and my guilt manifest!'

But it was bad enough just having McLevy's presence in proximity to a recently used lethal weapon plus, on a not too far distant table, its miserable victim. The mistress had had little option but to set Hannah to whipping up another pot of coffee as she lashed out the biscuits, all the while wondering why the man himself had turned up at such an inopportune moment.

It could of course be an accidental coincidence, but it was never a good idea to assume any innocence of fate as far as this dangerous bugger was concerned. He had a nose for crime like a bear for honey.

Or a wolf for a lamb that has strayed far from the flock not realising this might be its last gambol.

So Jean made small talk, Hannah whipped up while Mulholland loitered, and the upshot was that the inspector had just swallowed a perfect sugar biscuit.

Seated at table, he could have easily been mistaken for an ursine arrival new woken from hibernation — wrapped up in a thick, dark overcoat, low-brim bowler rammed square on his head, eyebrows abristle and his gaze everywhere.

He reached out a surprisingly dainty paw and

helped himself to another wafer. In it dipped, out it came, and in it went past the oddly lush lips as McLevy beamed to one and all.

'There we were wandering about in the bitter cold, on the saunter, Mulholland doing nothing but complain about his lot in life, and whit did I think?'

'Please enlighten us,' said Jean wishing she could make the man vanish like a snowball in hell.

'To pay the Mistress of the Just Land compliments of the season!'

'Tae scrounge some coffee, ye mean,' grunted Hannah, finding it difficult to keep from rushing shut the knife drawer, which for some reason had been left open.

'That as well,' agreed McLevy. 'I did hesitate a trifle thinking ye might be still in your scratchers but Mulholland would have his way. Aye looking for a refuge!'

The constable was in fact only drinking water and shook his head in mute denial of the sins so far thus attributed to him. His face was open and fresh, blue-eyed, clear-skinned, and that innocent Irish visage had tempted many a criminal to think him an easy mark.

Nothing could be further from the truth. He and McLevy might have seemed a strange pair — the inspector grizzled and unkempt, Mulholland neat as a well-kept lighthouse — but they were a deadly pair of thief-takers.

The tall fellow had a hornbeam stick, fashioned by himself, that would fell a charging ox, and James McLevy possessed a reservoir of violence that shot constant and abject fear into the criminal fraternity.

Plus the fact that, besides his forensic capacities, the inspector had a knack for putting himself into a wrongdoer's psychological shoes, thence worming his way towards a sharp intuition that reaped a rich harvest of corruptive corn.

He would himself have made a fine malfeasant but, luckily for the powers of justice, had taken another turning. Mulholland was more straight-forward but through the years had developed his own insights. In short, what one missed, the other jumped on.

'Are ye going tae scoff a' thae biscuits?' Hannah remarked tetchily of the inspector as another was dipped daintily into the coffee.

'This is the last. I know my limitations.'

With this sage observation, McLevy leant back in his chair and whistled tunelessly.

He and Jean had been eyeing up the opposite, not at all unfriendly, each just conjecturing what the other might have on their mind.

They had been through many adventures together, sometimes on the same side, some-times opposing, but never, she thought, never as far apart as they were now. Thank God she was the only one of the pair who could have knowledge of such.

Or was she?

'Ach it's a sair fecht,' McLevy announced genially, 'here I am with a murder case and not a clue how it came about or how to solve the beast.'

Jean kept her gaze steady while Hannah finally shut the knife drawer before anything popped out to join in.

'A mystery right enough,' Mulholland agreed. 'Though mind you the man wasn't popular — anyone could have done it. And this time of year thoughts are dark. Fell deeds abound. Devil on the loose.'

'Who was he?' asked Jean, sipping her coffee with an air of genteel unconcern while McLevy noisily sucked at his brew though stubs of teeth.

'I'll come tae that in a minute,' replied the inspector, wondering at the slight air of tension he could sense — mind you, he had been fully expecting to have the door slammed in his face it being early hours and also being Jean's firm practice to close the bawdy-hoose for a few days around this time to let the magpies visit family.

He supposed it gave her a chance to draw in breath and prepare for the sins of the coming year.

Mulholland and himself had risen with the dawn and rousted up some erstwhile acquaintances of the dead man that they had missed on the first trawl, but with little success and had met no end of curses from the hitherto unawakened, awoken by unwelcome battering at the door.

The fellow had lived solitary, there were few cronies, and he was rarely in the taverns. His door was heavy with locks as if he feared something. That same door had been left wide open, which had alerted some of the other tenement dwellers.

One of them had ventured inside to discover a

42

grotesque pendulum swinging to and fro. But more than that could not be found except that there was something about him that made the flesh crawl. Folk avoided the fellow like a bad case of the pox.

One old gadgie described it thus: 'Something in the way he looked. Like a belly snake. I aye felt like stamping on him. I didnae like the way he gawked at the wee girls. A scaly bastard, aye drippin' at the mouth.'

On an impulse and a memory of something Jean Brash had told him many years ago, McLevy had decided to stick his proboscis into the Just Land.

That plus, of course, the aromatic brew.

Lebanese. From *L'oriente misterioso*.

'Alexander Moncrieff,' he announced out of the blue. 'Ye remember that name, Mistress Brash?'

Jean's eyes widened — she had once confided to the inspector a little of her childhood.

A long time ago and though dark elements of that past were still alive in her soul and would always be so, she might have thought him to have forgotten the story. Should have known better.

Now and again she had caught word of Moncrieff.

He had ended up in charge of a charitable workhouse for streetboys, seemingly trusted by the authorities, and then the place had been closed down some time later. She had gathered little more of him after that until a rumour that there was some scandal in another children's home, involving a young girl.

43

After that, nothing to be heard.

But now Jean *had* heard. It was like finding a dirty taste in the back of her throat.

'Long, long ago,' she replied calmly. 'What of him?'

'We found him hanging from a rafter in his room,' was Mulholland's quiet incursion. 'At first the thought was of suicide.'

'But then it took a wee foozle intae murder,' said McLevy, and smiled at Hannah, who kept a perfectly blank face. 'Murder is more of an interest.'

'No great loss either way,' Jean responded.

'Ye've heard nothing on the streets?'

Her network of informers and petty thieves was still thriving despite the fact that she had renounced certain criminal pastimes as she grew more respectable — such as, if you believed the stories, poisoning, forgery, arson and assorted chicanery.

At least, that was as far as the stories went; there were probably more crimes lurking in the underbrush.

In fact, McLevy observed, she cut quite a demure figure at the moment, in a plain working gown. Obviously been clearing up the debris from the night before. Even without make-up or other wee jingle jangles, Jean Brash still looked beautiful. Porcelain and steel, he thought, as the full red lips formed an answer.

'I've been busy. New Year is busy. Everybody wants to celebrate. Happy times just around the corner.'

'Not for Moncrieff,' was the inspector's

response to this ironic statement.

'I didn't even know the man was dead. But as I said, it's no great loss.'

'Nevertheless, murder cannot be condoned. Justice cannot pick and choose.'

With that sententious response, the inspector had taken a last slug of coffee, then levered himself up, and seemed prepared to depart.

Part of Jean was much relieved; so it wasn't the judge that had brought the inspector calling — Hilton Abercrombie could rest undiscovered under his grey sheet — nonetheless she was curious.

'How did you know it to be murder?'

'A wee thing,' replied McLevy breezily. 'The man had already been strangled before he was strung up.'

'Garrotted,' offered Mulholland as he unfolded his lanky body and put his empty glass neatly on the side of the sink. 'A nice clean job. One deep line across the throat. Near professional.'

'A thuggee, perhaps? Dab hands at the stranglin'.'

To this suggestion of his inspector, Mulholland shook his head. 'With that cold east wind, you wouldn't see many of them in Leith.'

'Right enough, they'd stick out a mile.'

The policemen nodded at each other as if stumbling upon a universal fact.

Hannah and Jean looked on and tried not to breathe too hard at what had just been revealed. Then the old woman broke what was becoming an interminable silence.

'Why string the bugger up afterwards, then?'

'That's the mystery, Hannah,' replied the inspector. 'It is also my supposition that there were at least two men involved. Hauling up the body would be no small job. And there was one other thing.'

With the air of a conjuror he swooped his hand into the inside pocket of his overcoat and produced a crumpled piece of thin cardboard.

'We found this stuffed into his top pocket.'

It was a playing card. The Ten of Spades.

Hannah's hand instinctively went to where a cut-throat razor was kept concealed behind her apron, while her mistress was still as a statue — Pallas Athena or not — carved in stone.

McLevy replaced the card and tipped his hat.

'Thank you for the sugar biscuits and the coffee, Jeannie,' he said. 'Happy New Year.'

Mulholland offered similar sentiments and the two visitors departed the scene.

The women waited while the door closed to the back garden and the footsteps of both policemen faded out of hearing. Hannah then took a deep breath.

'Whit a bliddy caper, eh?' she muttered.

Her mistress made no reply. She was putting together in her mind what had just been disclosed. The deaths must surely be connected, but how?

'Ye think McLevy suspects a thing?' asked Hannah.

'Who knows?' said Jean Brash. 'But I have my own investigation to pursue.'

What might have given both food for thought was an exchange between their two unwelcome

46

guests as, the deep pool of Jean's exotic fish having been skirted, Mulholland closed the ornate iron gates that guarded the back entrance to the gardens of the Just Land.

A handsome building in the high reaches of Leith, it bore no evidence of the occupation therein although many a respectable citizen hurried his spouse past lest some familiar face should call from a high window.

'Any thoughts?' asked his inspector as he glanced up into the sky. White clouds in a wintry blue sky of the newly forged year. Birds skittering in the firmament. God in his heaven.

'The place seemed very . . . active?' came the careful response.

'Uhuh. I was expecting a bucket of water, gardyloo, thought they'd a'be dormant. Beauty sleep. But no. Busy as your bees, Constable.'

Mulholland was a keen apiarist. To be truthful, he much preferred insects to human beings.

'The hive is quiet at this moment,' he replied. 'The Queen Bee sleeps.'

'Well this one was wide awake. Like a cat on hot coals. That makes me curious.'

'You're forever curious,' observed the constable as they walked down the hill. 'It's your given nature, sir.'

McLevy pondered. 'Jean told me the once that Alex Moncrieff tried tae harm her when she was a wee lassie.'

'So you say. But that was long ago.'

'The pain of memory never fades.'

'You surely don't suspect her of anything to do with the man's death?'

'She could have hired an assassin.'

'Why? And why now? Why wait all this time? That doesn't make a lick of sense!'

At this hefty dig from his constable, McLevy shook himself like a bear emerging from a snowdrift.

'Aye, you're most probably and definitely right, but I sense something. She's up tae something.'

'That something could be anything.'

A black crow flew overhead and croaked loudly as if agreeing with this observation.

McLevy came to a decision.

'Since the present is proving so unfruitful, let us return tae past history, Mulholland. Back tae the past.'

And off they went. On the saunter.

8

Old father Long-Legs
Can't say his prayers:
Take him by the left leg
And throw him down the stairs.

A key turned in the lock and the front door to Hilton Abercrombie's narrow house opened with a doleful creak.

Jean slipped inside, heart pounding. She was wearing nondescript clothing and had trudged through the streets of the city trying to look most unlike her known self but, rather, like some dowdy, less salubrious relative.

Before leaving the Just Land, and not by her easily identified cream carriage accompanied by the hulking form of Angus, her coachman — packed off some days ago for Aberdeen to celebrate, if such a word can be used in connection with the grim inhabitants of the Granite City, this coming year — Jean had instructed Hannah, Maisie and Lily to recall and record all the events of the murder night. Especially those in connection to Hilton Abercrombie, but in fact any unusual happening that had struck their recollection.

Neither Jean nor Hannah had noticed the man leave his nook by the fireside, but anything could have happened in that whirling, hectic throng. Once the dancing got going, it was like a madhouse — both Jean and the old woman, other than one wee break in the kitchen, had been hurtled off their feet.

Hannah was also commanded to quiz the magpies about any unusual events — before they set off for a few days' rest in the supposed bosom of their families — but of course to say nothing of the reason for questioning. The girls were still lying late in bed after the previous night's exertion.

Any detail, no matter how small, might be a key to the mystery.

It seemed an eternity had already passed this day but in fact it was still only eleven o'clock, Jean having been roused by Hannah at seven of that morning.

Four hours of murderous mayhem.

The old woman had been anything but pleased that her mistress was setting off alone to try her fortune at the Abercrombie domicile, like Orpheus in the Underworld.

'Whit if there's a servant man? Or a great big twa-heidit jowler of a dog that would bite the living daylight out of you?' she demanded.

Her mistress had replied loftily that Abercrombie was too mean to have live-in domestic staff and no dog worth its salt would share residence with a hanging judge.

But despite the dismissive words, while she moved through the streets Jean had felt oddly exposed — as if she were parting company with a familiar world and moving into a strange and unreal other existence.

As if she was somehow living in a dream, in a

different time, and as a pencil might poke upwards through a piece of paper so some event might rupture the tissue of what passed now on this plane of reality.

Edinburgh seemed strangely out of joint as she walked over the George IV Bridge, heading for Niddry Street where the judge's house was located.

The excesses of the night before lay like a misty hangover on the city, the populace striving to rediscover and refurbish respectable modes of conduct — the bridge itself seeming oddly insubstantial, as if swaying like a matchstick edifice under her feet.

It was as though a layer of Edinburgh had been peeled away, leaving a raw inflamed surface at the mercy of the wintry elements.

Of course, Jean knew that almost all of this was a product of her own mind — she was the one out of joint, an insubstantial wraithlike figure. But the notion still clung to her like a spider's web.

What was it in all this that was so troubling? Of course, a dead body in the Just Land on a New Year's Day was no small matter, but there was something else — something much deeper. A darkness from her past that she felt was spreading once more into the present.

Evil never dies, just sleeps. And then it comes to life.

As she walked onwards, an actual mist, a light sea haar of sorts, had suddenly descended, turning everyone into ghostlike entities. She was out of her world and in another domain. Leith

51

behind her, the Grassmarket ahead.

Jean had ducked her head to avoid the glance of any passing pedestrian, and as she did so she had noticed that her hasty disguise was betrayed by footwear. An elegant pair of fashionable boots stuck out defiantly from below the old-fashioned shapeless coat, borrowed it must be said from Hannah Semple.

The sight cheered her. She was still Jean Brash, and the Mistress of the Just Land would never wear undesirable footwear. As clothes maketh the man, so footwear defines the female of the species. Nature cannot be contradicted.

The sea haar had now seemed more friend than enemy, providing a welcoming blanket cover — the judge's street before Jean to the left, Abercrombie's heavy house keys in her hand and a small derringer in her right-hand pocket.

In, she had entered and here she was.

Fine if her heart was pounding — all this might signal was Jean to be alive and raring to go. The derringer loaded. Two bullets: peas in a pod.

The judge's house inside was just like the man himself, mean, narrow, gloomy, the furniture sharp-edged with disapproval as she inched her way down the hall. No Janus-headed dogs sprang out; no ancient retainer lurched forth to confront the visitor.

Jean turned the first door handle she came across and seemed to have struck lucky.

The judge's study by the looks: a small, cramped room dominated by a heavy, plain desk with a high-backed chair before it, and on the walls a number of portraits of the male Abercrombie ancestors bearing the same disapproving nose and thin lips. Men of lore and learning.

'A rogue's gallery,' she muttered and hesitated a moment.

Hannah had stomped along with her to the back-garden gate and the exchange had proceeded thus.

'Whit're ye going tae accomplish, tell me that?'

'I shall investigate.'

'Ye're no' a bliddy policeman.'

'Well I'll just have to assume the mantle, Hannah.'

'Can we no' jist dump the bugger in the ocean?'

'I've already given wherefore against that.'

But beside her statement as regards McLevy's potential for finding out this proposed action, Jean had another reason. She had dumped a body once before in the ocean and once was quite enough to carry in memory.

★   ★   ★

After his beating by the young constable, Henry Preger had lain in his bed and abruptly died. Of course, it could have been the after-effects of his hammering, but he had also been fed a thin neep brose made by the delicate hands of his young wagtail.

He complained about the pungent taste but was in no condition to refuse and besides turnips can be bitter. However, when he expired, the

53

symptoms bore a strong resemblance to that of arsenic poisoning.

The poor young wagtail was caught in a dreadful dilemma. What if the authorities investigated and found it was indeed the easily purchased toxin to blame? Bought usually to kill vermin, Henry Preger being well qualified.

And as regards the culprit? While the gruel was cooking anyone could have added a heartfelt farewell, for Preger was hard hated by all the women under his command. Too many magpies might have spoilt the broth.

So, with the help of a pair of young street keelies who were a mite unscrupulous at a price, and more importantly men who could keep their mouth shut, she had found no option but to arrange that the high seas receive a deep diver.

Over the side of the boat Henry had gone; the wagtail watching him slowly sink out of sight by dint of his attachment to a pair of large dowie stones, deposited in Scotland during the Ice Age but still useful in the present day. She observed carefully while he gurgled his way to a watery grave, and as the keelies rowed back for shore, she could not repress a shudder, whether of delight or dread would have been hard to tell.

But death leaves its mark, and once was enough.

★　★　★

'Do as you're told, Hannah Semple,' she had said quietly. 'That's my last word till you hear another.'

54

And now, hesitation past, in the study of Hilton Abercrombie, Jean Brash got down to brass tacks. The pursuance of detection as channelled through a bawdy-hoose keeper.

There was a back window to the room and when she twitched the dusty brown curtain aside, some pale grey light crept in through the sea haar, at least sufficient for Jean to begin her labours.

She had explained to Hannah the conclusions so far.

Very well.

No man is killed without reason. If nothing on his person can provide a clue then you must travel to the next best destination.

His den, his dunghill, his hidey-hole, where a man would stash all he desires never to be revealed. Or, to be more prosaic — his Presbyterian lair.

The desk was an obvious starting point. It had a slatted wooden flap, which unfolded upwards to reveal a series of small cubbyholes and narrow slots, crammed with various bills, folds of paper, a few letters of law — detritus and of little interest.

The lower drawers were no more useful — legal scraps, old case notes, everything you would expect from a judge and nothing that would supply a motive for homicide.

The bookshelves groaned with official tomes of heavy authority — they could possibly have been employed to brain someone, perhaps, but were of no more use than that. The law as a blunt weapon.

Jean gave it up and decided to move further into the recesses of Hilton Abercrombie's kingdom.

The kitchen and pantry were of little interest as well, being mainly, as far as she could see, filled with jars of porridge oats and oatmeal biscuits.

Dry provender for a withered man. Liquorish sweeties would seem to be his one exception. The whole place reeked of a crabbit bachelor and the upstairs bedroom put the tin lid on such.

A museum to repression: the bed like a tomb, the hangings as if enclosing a mausoleum.

Again she had pulled the heavy curtains aside to let in some light — a peek outside to see the street below. Save for the sea haar and a few random passers-by, it was mercifully empty, but so, it would seem, were her hopes of finding anything.

She had stretched her arm under the bed to find nothing but layers of fluff and a pair of moth-eaten drawers that his honour had obviously forgotten were lying dormant below. Thrown there perhaps in wanton ecstasy but more likely they had crawled under for sanctuary.

Jean wondered for a moment what stories they could have told. Hard to think that they may once have been fresh and white, hoping to clothe a healthy body withal. And see where they ended up?

No mercy.

Better move on.

The bedside cupboards were filled with

medical jars and evil-smelling ointments, mostly for haemorrhoids and various pustular complaints, all of which might have explained the miserable swine's penchant for such severe sentencing.

A sore arse is a terrible thing.

Nothing in the wardrobe, only judge's robes, starched white shirts, dark suits; she half expected to find John Knox rigid on one of the hangers, glaring out at her.

For some reason that thought amused her.

But nothing personal, nothing secret, nothing that would aid a bawdy-hoose keeper on a murder trail.

Jean stepped back and walked to the centre of the room. Something McLevy once said had come into her mind.

'I forever look for a wee thing out of place, Jeannie,' the inspector had remarked. 'It can be a hair, a fingernail, it can be a spilt coffee cup, or a crack in the mirror — if it doesnae fit, there is aye a reason.'

The man was full of wind but now and again he made sense. Her breathing slowed, body stilled itself, eyes concentrated as she looked around the room.

It was here. She could feel it now. But where? The dull contours of the place sharpened under her gaze, belatedly coming to life.

There!

A painting above the bed. One highland cow in a brown field. The cow looked morose. Out of place. Horns pointing nowhere. But why?

Why have a painting just above your bed?

What if there was an earthquake and it fell upon your head? Why this poor unfortunate animal catching its death of cold and what might it be hiding?

She knelt over the bone-hard mattress and pulled the painting aside to reveal a neat, sturdy iron safe recessed in the wall. A solid proposition but it had a lock and on the house-ring in her pocket, she had noted a stubby iron key of a particular shape — heavy in her fingers now.

In it went, and turned easy as pie. Mind you, the judge was not anticipating being murdered, so a certain laxness of security was understandable.

Amongst the various papers, share certificates, bonds and wax-sealed legal documents inside, was a large brown envelope. For some reason she hesitated, as if it might spit up in her face, before opening and pulling out the contents.

Photographs. Women. Naked. Under a cruel lash or gripped hard by various instruments of pain; mouths agape, splayed in agony; whether feigned or not, it made no difference. White bodies against the dark metal. But it was the faces that cut into Jean's heart.

Bruised. Without hope. Teeth bared in a meaningless smile.

One of them, an older wrecked soul, bore a frightening resemblance to Nan Dunlop.

After Jenny Sheridan died by coughing herself into a consumptive eternity, Nan had taken up with Henry Preger in the Happy Land and dragged Jean along with her.

Preger had picked out the girl for himself; Nan

58

became fierce jealous, and the man had booted her back out on to the streets.

Hard, simple words. Hard, simple facts.

Jean had been given no option; Preger would have taken her life. She had never seen Nan again. But was she looking at her now? Her hand opened limply and the photographs fell about her feet like so many dead leaves.

Though was she not a bawdy-hoose keeper, part of the same corruption? Did Lily and Maisie not dish it out? Yet these men went home — smarting maybe — they had consented and paid for their pain.

These chained and manacled women had no choice.

And no one harmed her girls. The magpies of the Just Land were protected; any man who laid a wrong finger upon them was kicked out, if necessary from a high window, and never came back.

No one harmed her girls. A strange family but the only one Jean had ever possessed.

This other was an abomination.

She bent down, placed the photographs back in the envelope and shoved the packet inside her coat pocket. Now she knew one of Hilton Abercrombie's dirty secrets, what else was on hand?

The safe was full of other documents thrust aside as she delved, but at the back Jean found a folded piece of paper that had, from the looks of it, lain there for a long time.

As she opened it out, she had the same weird feeling of excitement and dread.

A list of names in what Jean could now note was the judge's crabbed handwriting.

Five in all. One, Abercrombie's own; one below that she knew personally, the next two by social happenstance; the very last, she recognised only too well — *Alexander Moncrieff*.

A sudden hammering on the door startled the wits out of her, and Jean darted to the window to look down. A man's figure below, shrouded in the mist but unmistakable for all that.

Jack Burns.

She pulled back in case he looked up.

Another loud rat-tat-tat and then silence. When she glanced out again, he was gone.

Jean took a deep breath. Time to go home.

9

Three blind mice,
See how they run,
They all ran after the farmer's wife,
Who cut off their tails with a carving knife,
Did you ever see such a thing in your life?
Three blind mice.

The trio of young callans waited in the darkness, each trying to encourage or bait the other conspirator.

Johnny Finch was the leader, a hard, nuggety boy, sharp featured, with a wicked sense of humour. He enjoyed tormenting Jeb Summers, the smallest, the runt, but did not realise that his wit, at times, might be not so much funny as downright cruel.

As a whip might land on the same spot, so it strikes all the more deeply.

The middle of the trio was Dirk Martins, the Smiler — he was aye put in front when it came to blame. He could play the innocent like a Jew's harp, with a mop of fair hair and the open, blameless countenance of a born liar.

Now they were about to embark on the most daring venture yet. If it went awry, they would suffer a most severe and terrifying punishment — beyond even Jeb's wild imagination. But if it went right, if successful, in their own eyes they would be magnified, and everyone in the home would know that they were top dogs.

The workhouse bore the grand title of Charitable Institute for the Lost Children of the Streets, but it was not a large building, housing about two dozen or so young boys, feral, abandoned, living on their wits by theft and deceit, who had been rounded up by the officers of the charity and were to be taught some rudimentary skills before being moved on to a bigger establishment. The theory was that they were too vulnerable to be thrown to the hungry beasts in the larger den, and needed education of a sort to learn the rules.

A harsh regime. Step out of line and a sharp cane would welt till blisters stippled the skin.

Such is Christian charity. Under the sun. Rise at seven, to bed at eight o' night and in between give thanks to God for your bounden labour.

They were forced to clean, scrape and pick like so many monkeys looking for fleas. Their small, nimble fingers worked over leather, unfastening rope, sack-making, lungs full of dust and dry fragments — all this would serve them well in the glorious future of the senior workhouse. Praise the Lord.

For that they received three meals a day, each worse than the other, and were told to count themselves lucky.

The master of all this was Alexander Moncrieff — a savage skew-eyed swine but stupid as a lumpfish. Our three boys could run rings round him and indeed were kings of the lost children. They were relatively the oldest, the smartest, and now they were going to have some

62

fun and retribution. Retribution for sure; fun provided you were not caught in the act.

Johnny Finch punched Jeb sharply in the arm. 'Ye ready?'

The smaller boy winced a little and nodded. They were stationed atone of the wynds that had a wooden arch of sorts stretched across the entrance. A remnant of better days — the structure still holding together. Rickety as a skeleton.

The other two hoisted Jeb on high so that he could scramble up a drainpipe to the arch and perch far above them — they also had a small iron bucket with a piece of heavy twine attached, and threw him the rope so that he might carefully pull up the container inside which some liquid slopped from side to side.

They had all solemnly peed into that bucket; it was flaked with rust and had been found lying in the streets by Jeb, a born scavenger.

Dirk Martins grinned up at Jeb, who was struggling to steady the bucket on a shaky strut of wood.

'Don't you drop that on us,' he called softly. 'Ye daft wee mongrel. Johnny'll kill ye.'

'I cannae keep it at peace.'

The plan had been to balance the bucket securely, for Jeb to shin back down, then wait for the target to approach, pull on the rope and run like hell. But all plans can misfire.

Every time Jeb took his hand away, the bucket slipped to the side so that he had to grab it again. A nearby church clock struck eleven and this meant time was short.

Johnny Finch was losing patience.

'Ye're a useless wee bastart, Jeb!'

'No' my fault,' Jeb wailed in reply.

'Ye'll have to dae it yerself. Stay up there,' announced Johnny decisively.

'Whit about efter?'

'Ye scrape doon. And run!'

'Whit if he sees me?'

Jeb had a point; his pure white hair and ashen skin stood out in the dark night like a beacon.

'He'll be too busy.'

Dirk had ventured a little way out into the street and now he hissed back softly. 'Moncrieff. He's comin'.'

Johnny shook his fist at the marooned unhappy figure of Jeb teetering above.

'Don't you let me down now,' he warned. 'Or I'll cut yer smelly face tae ribbons.'

The other two retreated quickly into the depths of the wynd where they could watch from a safe distance.

Dirk giggled nervously but Johnny's face was set — he had a score to settle. Moncrieff had leathered hell out of him for some misdemeanour hardly worth a candle and now it was his turn. The scabs on his back and buttocks where the cane had sliced were a painful reminder.

The Master loved dishing it out. Licked his lips. See if he could take it, eh?

The gaunt figure of the man showed in the faint, wavering lamplight. They had tracked his movements and he aye came back at this time and by this route. Moncrieff had not long ago

64

been appointed and every Friday week he made his report to the governors, kissing their fine backsides, no doubt, before returning home.

As the footsteps came closer, marching to a military rhythm because Moncrieff fancied himself as a soldier of the Queen, Jeb shivered above. He was terrified but knew that worse would await should he fail in the appointed task. Yet under this fear there was a harder edge forming: one day he would rule a kingdom like Johnny Finch. Jeb would make the jokes.

So, he gritted his teeth and as Moncrieff passed below, emptied the bucket with a swift lunge.

The man wore a hat of sorts but even then, his neck, face and shoulders were soaked with a noxious mixture of rusty amber urine. As the drenched figure let out an outraged roar, Jeb slithered over to a side-wall, shinned down its iron drainpipe and hurtled off in search of safety.

He ran till his lungs burst and he could run no more, but as the boy jolted to a stop, a pair of hands fastened round his throat.

'Got ye!'

Jeb near wet himself in not quite such a glorious cause but it was Finch's fingers that choked in at him.

'Ye did well,' said his leader while Dirk Martins winked approvingly. 'Come on!'

They yelped and howled like a pack of dogs, racing through the streets till they got to the back of the workhouse where there was a small cellar chute that Jeb could squeeze through and then unlock the rear door.

In quick. No danger of discovery since the other two custodians were older men who, in Moncrieff's absence, couldn't wait to snaffle some whisky from the cupboard, have a quiet game of cards and then be well out of the way asleep by the time the master returned.

The callans followed suit. They slid into the long, narrow dormitory, clothes off, their rough, dank nightwear on, and then dived under the thin sheet of the lumpy single bed. The other boys knew something had been going on but nobody wanted to cross Johnny Finch.

The king himself looked over at Jeb.

'Ye did well,' he said, and then added. 'For a dirty wee greasy freak.'

Jeb flushed with pride though his fingers dug their long nails into his palms as pleasure and pain kissed lips.

He looked the other way to see Dirk's smile.

A moment of triumph that in time to come would bring a brutal reckoning.

10

Here come I,
Little David Doubt;
If you don't give me money,
I'll sweep you all out.
Money I want,
And money I crave;
If you don't give me money,
I'll sweep you all to the grave!

The Smiler had walked himself near to exhaustion as he tramped up the barren wintry hillside of Arthur's Seat. The slopes rose from the Palace of Holyrood where many monarchs had sat their royal arses to possibly remind such potentates that time is inexorable and one day their bones would be extinct as the volcanoes that had formed these gradients many million years ago. Just so much dirt in the wind.

Even Queen Victoria would crumble to dust.

The rocks curved around and climbed to a height that had they embedded eyes of stone, they could have ranged their sights all the way to Edinburgh Castle — one massive pile of rock face glaring at the other like two lions about to spring into battle.

The climber shivered in the bitter cold.

Happy New Year's Day.

His mind was a welter of fear and excitement, one vying with the other as the mist that had settled on the peaks lifted now and again to show the way ahead.

Jagged crags of what seemed prehistoric rock had been exposed and eroded by the movement of glaciers — themselves slow moving beasts of ice and mineral — then these crags split and sundered to stand there like grim sentinels that marked a deep convulsion.

He had been unable to sleep in the hotel, not so much from the noise and excitement of the firework celebrations that echoed through the streets until the early hours, but from that one terrifying moment in the Just Land.

★ ★ ★

Jeb Summers had perched like a malign homunculus on the man's back and, as the cord pulled tight, the Smiler watched life drain from the judge's face with a sick but hungry fascination. Like a nightmare summoned from his own depths.

It had been easy to entice the man downstairs — a hint of civic corruption, a secret to be told against a covert rival, and then Jeb had struck.

A moment when their eyes met and the Smiler had nodded both permission and collusion. A thrill ran through him like a private spillage. The person he had constructed over the years; that completed careful edifice had crumpled with the one gesture.

In the first killing he had been merely a witness, but now he had crossed the line. He had informed Jeb that the judge would be at the Just

68

Land that night and a kind of madness had seized the dwarf. Would it not be a rare laugh to have the old bastard die in Jean Brash's place — the snooty wee bitch would not allow them finger room. Kicked his balls near out of sight. In the old days. On the streets.

And even funnier — she would not know Dirk, said Jeb — he had changed. Beyond recognition, his voice, his looks, his whole person — even Jeb had struggled to put the man he had known as the Smiler to this new image.

A foreign body.

The dwarf had pointed at this altered sight, howling with laughter, and Dirk had caught the madness.

After the killing he had returned to the salon above and cavorted around with the magpies, priapic with death, safe in the knowledge that, other than Jeb, no one really knew him. Not even himself, it would seem.

★   ★   ★

He stopped for breath, the fresh cold air harsh in his lungs at the effort of the climb — too many flat city streets and business meetings. Too many civic suppers where roast meat and bribery passed with the salt and a conspiratorial smile.

A family passed by on the way down, their small dog yelping with pleasure as it was chased by a little boy, mother, father and bigger sister looking on indulgently.

How the hell had these people managed to get so far up the incline in the first place — were they mountain goats?

The boy had found a stick and threw it. The dog chased after, barking in pursuit. Innocence that he would never know. Not now.

Ever since he had had come back to Edinburgh, the past had pulled him in like a fish on a hook back to his childhood haunts.

★ ★ ★

Salamander Street — if the albino dwarf had found a refuge it would be near there, he had thought. A narrow, enclosed alley off the street for the scaffie men to run their carts through, a small relief grating hid behind a ruined door.

The grating looked solid enough but it was easy shifted, and easy put back in place. It led to the catacombs — they had found it by chance after Johnny Finch died. It was their underground kingdom. Jeb and the Smiler.

Dirk had ingratiated himself with Moncrieff and been given various 'messages' to deliver in the city with Jeb to accompany. Perhaps the master was afraid of what they might know or say about Finch's death, so he let them loose for a while and the boys thought they were in clover — but the sly bastard had a plan up his sleeve — a treacherous strategy of which they were unaware.

When out on the loose, Jeb and he had reacquainted themselves once more with some of the remaining feral children and had their fun with girls who ran fast but not fast enough, yet all the time the clock was ticking.

Tick-tock.

Tick-tock.

And then Dirk had been taken away to another life. That had been their plan — the ones who sat in power. Four plus one. Moncrieff, the one. They had gathered in a room and signed a paper. Signed away the Smiler's future. For his own good, he was told. A new life in another country. Hidden away. Just as they had hidden away the death of Johnny Finch.

As the carriage rode off that day, Dirk saw Jeb's blighted face looking out of the window of the Home. Betrayed. Abandoned.

The Smiler had promised to come back and they had already sliced a blade through the skin of their palms to seal a pact in blood, but all these years later it was Fate that had arranged his return.

He would have forgotten the past. Buried it. He was good at burying things behind a smile. But back he had come — and money was the other hook. In fact he cared for money more than anything — money could buy you the world.

Salamander Street. Smell the slaughterhouse wafting down, flesh on the bone. Take a deep breath, eh?

He was back and curious. No more than that, just curious. Yet everything else had followed so quickly. He had called out in the half-lit catacombs.

'Jeb? Jeb Summers? It's me, Dirk. Are you there?'

A white rat scuttled across his feet and he instinctively aimed a kick at the beast.

'Leave it be,' said a voice in the gloom. 'That is my good and faithful friend.'

Laughter unseen in the dark.

'Pit on the flesh my friend. I wouldnae know ye.'

'I could not say the same,' replied Dirk quietly, as Jeb emerged into what passed for light. 'Uglier maybe.'

Jeb laughed again, a harsh sound like broken glass scraping under feet. He held up the palm of his hand towards Dirk. On it was a jagged scar, long healed but livid yet in the white, cracked skin.

Dirk slowly lifted his own hand. It bore the selfsame scar but it had almost disappeared into the folds of soft living.

'Vengeance,' said Jeb Summers. 'Not before time, eh?'

The little man's laughter echoed once more in the dark as the rat sniffed round his feet and looked up at the Smiler with pink, unblinking eyes.

★　★　★

But two murders later, had Dirk really been looking for vengeance?

Walk on, walk on.

His feet slipped a little on the grass and gravel that made up the path leading to the side of the steep hill. Above he could see a thin, dangerous, narrow fissure, which reached to the very top.

72

A seagull screamed in the mist and the sound startled him. Higher up he could see some sheep grazing, oblivious of an impending slaughter-house.

Moncrieff deserved to die, no doubt. He had killed Johnny Finch. Or caused the death. But that was so long ago. Did Dirk remember straight?

Anyhow, Jeb had known where to find the man — his long talons were cunning with the lock and had gained them entrance in the dead of night.

Somehow it had been like when they were callans together, up to mischief, a bucket of piss, a running girl caught and pinned up against the wall, steal where you can and where you like. Dog eat dog. As before they had jabbed each other on, but then it got real. Or was it more like a bad dream?

*   *   *

Moncrieff had been asleep as Jeb gently looped the leather cord round his neck, then pulled it tight like a flesher with a chicken neck. For a moment the eyes bulged open, one of them still aslant, the mouth gaped and shot breath rank as the devil's armpit out into the room.

Out but not in, and that creates a problem. A body needs air unless extinct, and Moncrieff was no exception to this rule.

His last act was to loosen his bowels. Between that and the foul breath, it was not a fragrant departure.

73

Jeb's idea was to hang him there as if an execution and then the dwarf had flicked out something from his monk's garment and showed it with pride to his companion. A playing card. The Ten of Spades.

'I've kept the pack a' these years,' he said and his sharp teeth had chattered together in laughter.

★ ★ ★

Dirk Martins began to climb the steep heights but the images climbed with him. The first killing had seemed like a dream, the second like tasting blood and the third was to be his own doing.

So far he had only witnessed. Now it would be his turn to kill.

He could run away, turn his back on it all, leave the company, make his excuses and vanish. But besides all this, there was something else — if he could pull it off — it was big money. And as testified, he loved money more than anything else in the world. It was his god.

The haar had covered his face with an oily film and Dirk giggled suddenly for no reason that came to mind. Unless. Unless it was a memory of when Johnny Finch gobbed in Jeb's face and made the wee squit stand there while the saliva dripped down.

Just a time after they had dropped the piss on Moncrieff, Jeb thought he was quite the man and Johnny decided to teach him otherwise.

Finch had thought this funny. Jeb had grinned

as well, teeth bared.

The three of them had howled with laughter.

Dirk turned round and from this high vantage point he could see the church steeples and high chimneys of Edinburgh poke up through the mist like spars of a shipwrecked fleet.

Like a graveyard.

No matter how high he climbed, a man would still have to come back down.

And face the music.

11

Lady-bird, lady-bird
Fly away home,
Your house is on fire
And your children will burn.

Five names. Two of them already dead. Three more to go, or was the murderer's name already looking up at her?

Then again, there could be no connection at all, simply a coincidence of separate murders, though that might be hard to swallow — coincidence being a random collision you start to believe in when you've run out of better ideas.

What was the reason for death, and why had it happened now? She knew that a certain police inspector always set great store by the precise time of day of month of year that murder took place.

'What has changed?' he would announce to the world at large. 'Circumstance may inform ye of many things.'

Jean sat in the shelter of the gazebo in the garden of the Just Land, staring down at the paper list while Hannah Semple trundled towards her with a full tray.

At this moment neither particularly wanted to reside in a deserted bawdy-hoose with an inert member of the judiciary for company, and as the old woman dumped the tray on a table in front

76

of her mistress she sat herself down heavily.

'That's your third pot this day,' she warned. 'Ye'll be jumping about lik' a horny toad.'

The cautionary words were ignored as Jean poured out and in fact the old woman grabbed another cup as well. No sugar biscuits though, in case they invoked the reappearance of James McLevy. One horny toad was enough.

They had brought each other up to date as far as possible, though there were a few loose ends yet to tie as Jean had returned only just in time to wave goodbye to the departing magpies and it had all been a hellish rush.

For some reason, many of the girls were in tears as if never returning — but in a bustle of hansom-cabs and carts, off they all went, bright-coloured coats and gowns striking a vivid contrast with the greyness of this day.

Like so many birds of passage.

Off they travelled to families, old lovers, ancient neglected aunties or perhaps even a sailor-boy or two, for tarry breeks and magpies are attracted to each other like redshanks to a bed of oysters.

The Dalrymple twins, who had been much in demand to satisfy the duality in the Scots psyche at this occasion of year, were heading for Aberdeen to join their father Angus, Jean's coachman, who had departed earlier — he would no doubt by now have half a cow twisting over a huge fire — the twins, despite their slim semblance, had ravenous appetites for meat on the bone.

Life can often be divided into those who like

to gnaw a bone and those who prefer a more unctuous slider. An oyster, for instance.

Big Annie Drummond had a cousin Mamie who ran a sweetie shop in the Grassmarket — Mamie was equal in breadth to her hefty kinswoman but rather less in height — and both would settle into a kinder, more upholstered world for a few days. A warm oven with puggy buns and petticoat tails lights the way to a buttery bliss.

Amongst the tangle of the leaving party were Lily and Maisie, both, for different reasons, glad to quit the place for a few days and bury themselves in the family bosom of Maisie's large, squabbling, tribal gathering.

Her younger sister Jessie had just returned from a long and, in Maisie's opinion, totally unjustified visit to the Perth Penitentiary for the lifting of a wedding dress from a high-class but heavily scrutinised department store — a mistaken act of self-generosity that had been sadly discovered and disclosed to a certain police inspector. Can folk not mind their own business?

The fact that the sister was heavy with child and needed to get married in a hurry had registered no weight in the scales of blind justice.

The babe was born in prison, passed over by the authorities to Maisie's mother, the sister had served her sentence and, none the worse for the experience, it would seem, was coming back this very day to cuddle her bonny wee potential shoplifter.

The father, unhappily, had lumped a longer sentence for the reception of stolen goods.

Lily, who had no family of her own, was doted upon by the assembled clan.

The deaf and dumb girl had tried to keep out of Jean's way as far as possible during the extended leave-takings for fear that her mistress might see straight through her and act accordingly.

That weird, stunted image from the garden with its past attendant memories still haunted Lily's thoughts and she welcomed the idea of normal life for a while — if you could call Maisie's family normal.

So off went the magpies in a flurry of excited laughter and for a moment you might forget there was the dead body of a judge lying on the cheese table.

Maisie had the enviable knack of putting out of her mind situations about which she did not desire to give consideration. She had a childlike faith in Jean Brash — the mistress would sort it out; she ruled the land.

That just left Hannah, Jean and the corpse. Two drank the coffee, the third stayed put.

Jean had communicated most of the events at Abercrombie's house and the offensive envelope with the vile images lay on the table.

Hannah had looked at them and spat on the ground.

'Poor buggers,' she said, fingering where the cut-throat razor lay within an easy cross-reach just above the hip. 'If I found the man that took such, I'd slice him up lik' a blood pudding.'

So the two sat and drank their coffee, while in Jean's ornamental pool the large exotic fish dreamed of warmer climes and kept a wary eye out for passing herons. Long beaks may signal a short life for the unwary.

Jean's equally ornamental peacocks lay inside their large cage and shivered their feathers with the cold, as opposed to the same motion that attracts the opposite sex. The eyes in the feathers supposedly hypnotise the female — well, at least, that's what the males are led to believe.

'Barton Laidlaw,' said Jean thoughtfully. 'He was present here last night.'

The name below Abercrombie's on the list.

Laidlaw was a big wheel on the city council; a corpulent bachelor with his fingers in many pies. Rumours were rife that he pocketed more than his fair share of the civic purse, but he had an affable, conniving manner that gave the impression of a gentleman at peace with his bank balance and the world in general.

'The man's a bliddy twister,' said Hannah.

'He's on the council. What else do you expect?'

'I cannae see him plungin' somebody wi' a knife, though. And him and Abercrombie were thick as thieves.'

'How is that your conclusion?'

'Had their heads thegither a fair time of last night.'

Jean nodded thoughtfully. She had caught a glimpse of that through the whirling limbs before events became too chaotic to register anything at all.

Though, as she had observed from her carriage horses, when heads came together and

80

they whispered in each other's ears, it was often prelude to warfare.

Whatever Abercrombie's twisted sexuality, he was a stickler for the rule of society and Laidlaw was not of the same persuasion.

What had been going on under the breath?

Hannah had laboriously scrawled out a name call of the revellers of that evening from her memory, and that of the magpies. It was a depressingly long catalogue.

'We need to narrow this down,' Jean muttered. 'I could be on this quest for an eternity.'

There were the great and the good of law and the healing profession, the Bristol boys, the deviant band of artists and then a few stray town councillors — a motley crew that would now be scattered across the city. No. The obvious place to begin was the list from the safe.

Upon it lay Barton Laidlaw and two other names. One, a tobacco importer, Gavin Young; the other, a man of God. Of course, it is always possible that God smokes — she was a great reader, especially of the opposition works, and the Bible is full of divine emissions, Mount Sinai, for instance — but Jean did not grasp an immediate link to the Reverend William Baines.

Young she had met at a few social events. The man had a wife twice his size and ran a swanky tobacconist emporium in George Street. Seemed a timid enough soul, but who is to know what a man does or thinks secret? As any politician may testify, there's no art to finding the mind's construction in the face. Especially their own duplicitous visage.

Baines was minister of the Old Greyfriars Kirk that had been destroyed by fire, rebuilt by the faithful, and, apart from the oddly flamboyant advent of stained-glass windows, was a severe strong-hold of Presbyterian thought. A widower, with a daughter Jean had never met but assumed to be as respectable as a tombstone, Baines always assumed a grave air of the devout, but appearances should never be taken for granted.

As she well knew from the Just Land, when a minister drops his breeks, the devil rises up. The annual General Assembly in Edinburgh city was one of her busiest times of year — hectic with flying collars.

Back to the list.

What might connect them was nothing that sprang to mind. Though she did know a man who might help. Sadly he was a drunkard, dope fiend, embezzler and often lost to the sentient world at large. But beggars may not be choosers. She swiftly copied the names on to a piece of paper and handed it to Hannah Semple.

'The Rusty Nail tavern,' Jean said.

'A den of iniquity!' was the indignant response from the old woman, conveniently forgetting the times she had crooked an elbow in that very place.

That was when she was heading straight for hell and a third looming visit to the Perth Penitentiary, until a heavy bunch of keys had crashed on to the tavern table and she had looked up to see this elegant, perfumed creature plus a very different future.

★ ★ ★

'*I plan to open the best bawdy-hoose this city has ever seen,*' *said Jean Brash.* '*And I need a Keeper of the Keys. You have been recommended.*'

'*Who by?*' *Hannah asked.*

'*By whom?*' *came correction.* '*Never mind. Jist pick them up if that's your desire.*'

★ ★ ★

From that moment the old woman had never looked back, though she never did find out who had made the recommendation. Some mysteries are best left unsolved, though it niggled away at her sometimes. Who knew her well enough to make such an appraisal?

'I agree, Miss Semple, it is not for the faint of heart but gird your loins,' Jean said firmly. 'Thomas Drayton. Show these names and buy him a drink.'

Hannah sniffed. 'Drayton is a wrecked ship. I wouldnae take his word for damn all.'

Jean gave her a look. Hannah shook her head.

'Can I take the carriage?'

'If you can drive it.'

Another shake of the head and the old woman disappeared indoors to find adequate weather cover while her mistress pondered.

Drayton had been of good family, a mover in high circles, clever as they come. But he had a fatal weakness for alcohol and hashish. All very well if you're a French poet, not so clever otherwise.

She had even read a few in translation. Rimbaud and the like. Wild Rovers.

Jean had a smattering of French from a former lover, a cheerful young chef in one of the big hotels, but he, like Francine, had returned to Paris and the mother country. To tell the truth, she was quite relieved — she was getting too fat on his gateaux.

Back to Drayton.

The bold Thomas had embezzled a goodly sum from the British Linen Company, and though his family had found the money to keep him out of jail, they had disowned him simultaneously.

His father was a dentist and there are only so many teeth you can pull.

But Thomas had a memory seemingly unaffected by substances ingested and an encyclopedic knowledge of the tendrillous connections and hidden history of the world that had turned its back upon him.

Though Hannah was right. He was a wrecked ship.

The old woman came back, struggling into the coat that Jean had so recently and gladly discarded.

'Are ye coming along?'

'No.'

'Where are you going, then?'

'Not rightly sure.'

As Hannah picked up the list and slugged back the last of her coffee, Jean placed a fair amount of coin and notes on the table.

'I'm no' going tae buy the place!'

'Better safe than sorry.'

'Tell that tae Abercrombie.'

The very mention of the name brought the hard reality of murder back in the frame. The great difficulty that stared Jean in the face like a Galloway cow looking over a drystane dyke was that in order to investigate she had to ask questions.

All very well for the likes of McLevy lumbering about with a validated corpse, but she was stuck with the problem that anyone with any sense would be wondering: why was she asking about the judge in the first place?

That might be inconveniently remembered. Thomas Drayton wouldn't give a damn, however, as long as he had a hooker of whisky close to hand.

Jean could pass a cautious word to her network of informers but their world was of the streets, and this was a higher class. She was half tempted to go with Hannah, but oddly enough Jean was beginning to find a guiding instinct that had its own voice.

Seek and ye shall find.

'You didn't say.'

'Say whit?'

'The magpies. I asked you to see if they'd noticed anything that night, especially as regards the judge.'

Hannah shook her head but it was more in annoyance that in all the hurly-burly she had forgotten to report the task in hand.

'Nothing much. Two o' the Bristol men were full o' beans early on that night, chased the lassies up and doon the stairs, one fell over Abercrombie and near spilt the judge's drink.'

'I saw that.'

In fact Sammy Deacon and one other, Joseph Tucker, had been both life and soul of the party; Tucker a tall, handsome, fleshy type with a ready smile, and Deacon less attractive but a willing accomplice in the fun and games.

Tucker was slightly running to fat; Deacon had already got there and even tried a highland reel with the large stuffed bear Jean kept in the main salon — Septimus by name. For some reason the sight of it gingered up the clients, but the bear was not to be shifted from its niche in the corner so Samuel danced on alone.

It was Tucker who had stumbled over Abercrombie but it had ended amicably enough — a proffered whisky, a sour smile from one, a broad grin from the other. The Bristol man had rejoined the revelling councillors — all boys together.

Jean had been well aware that a deeper game was going on in that there was a big fat contract of work to be awarded as regards an additional dock extension in Leith, and many hats were being thrown in the ring.

No doubt there would be the usual skulduggery and rank deceit, but that was not her concern. A knife in the back was her concern.

'Oh, and one other thing,' Hannah remarked as she gathered the money into a large reticule and made sure her cut-throat razor was in place — Leith harbour at this time of year was not for the tender-hearted.

'Teenie Donnachie,' the old woman ended.

Jean sighed.

Teenie was one of the clumsiest humans God had ever put on the planet.

As a pleasure provider, she was a walking, or indeed supine, catastrophe. A timid, doleful, bovine soul, how she had been accrued by the Just Land was a mystery to one and all and the idea of her being able to offer anything of use was hardly feasible.

She had left this day with the other magpies and was rumoured to have a maiden aunt in Dundee, if there were any maidens to be found in that particular city — Teenie would sojourn there but always sadly found her way back.

'What has she done now?'

'Heard I was asking about Abercrombie and up she comes. Claims she saw him have sharp words wi' another at the party but who can believe her? The woman's wandert.'

'When and where and who?'

Hannah was now accoutred to leave. She pulled a shapeless felt bonnet out of the coat pocket and stuck it on her head. The effect was comical enough but the face underneath was haggard and grim. If they were depending on Teenie Donnachie, they were in a parlous condition.

'Late on, says she. A' these arty crafty buggers were drinkin' the place dry.'

Hannah had no time for the demi-monde of Edinburgh and certain of its more outré practitioners, but Jean had always nurtured a soft spot for louche vagabonds. Had not Robert

Louis Stevenson once sipped champagne from her silver slipper?

Well, that had been his story, anyway. And she was sticking to it.

'So what happened then?'

'One o' them faced up to the judge and Teenie saw him grab Abercrombie by the collar.'

'I saw nothing of that.'

'Neither did another soul but Teenie swears it so. It was a quick moment, she said, but hard. She was hoping for a fight — Teenie likes watching fights — but it didnae last. And not long after, the whole bunch left.'

'Who was the fellow?'

Hannah sniffed. 'Ye spent a fair time wi' him gawking down your front. Burns. Jack Burns. The Chiseller.'

With that somewhat disparaging description of the sculptural craft, Hannah departed for Leith harbour, leaving her mistress with much to contemplate.

For some reason she had not mentioned Burns turning up at the judge's dwelling to Hannah. In life it's always good to keep some things to yourself, like sugar biscuits for a good investigator.

Now her appetite had sharpened.

Outside in the garden, the ornamental fish had come to the surface with their mouths opening and closing. Hunger is universal.

12

Says the fly, says he,
'Will you marry me,
And live with me,
Sweet humble bee?'

Says the bee, says she,
'I'll live under your wing,
And you'll never know
That I carry a sting.'

Sarah Elizabeth Baines reclined near naked under the drapes of a goddess and shivered in the cold air of the studio.

'Don't move,' said Jack Burns sternly. 'You'll destroy the line. The line is everything.'

All very well for him, she thought bitterly, the only fire in the place was positioned right behind the man's posterior and his alleged muse therefore lay remote from any warmth the flames might supply.

She supposed Pallas Athena had been impervious to the elements if not actually controlling them, but Sarah was not a goddess. Nor did she wish to be one. Just an equal in a world that constricted her body and would contract her mind.

Her father was a man duty bound to deny her any rights except those of conformance, and if he had the slightest idea of what she thought, did, or planned to do in the near future, the minister would — as one of the old biddies she had persuaded by dint of promised whisky to sit for a portrait, might say — *die with his leg up*.

Especially if the Reverend William Baines witnessed her present situation, lying within thin folds of damask on a chaise longue with one bare outstretched arm, the fingers of which held a dried twig that Sarah imagined might be supposed to represent the laurel tree, nature as a whole, and a hunting bow to boot.

What an idiot his daughter had been.

She had challenged Burns to smuggle her into a stronghold of vice and lechery, never expecting that he would actually do so. But it had been at a price and now she was paying the bill in goosebumps.

Sarah caught sight of herself in a long mirror the sculptor used to display all sides of his subject; at this moment he was engrossed in a series of rough preliminary sketches that would be later translated to a shape in stone. He had, mind you, guaranteed that the face would bear no resemblance to hers.

The body, however, would be only too evident, although, as she had shivered behind the improvised frayed model's curtain into the drapes of the goddess and then taken her position on a lumpy chaise longue, Burns had muttered something to the effect that his ideal was longer-limbed and more fulsomely bosom-gifted.

Sarah was slightly built, gamine, slender like an elf of sorts, dark hair cut as short as convention and her father would allow.

Her fiery temperament did not endear her either to respectable kinswomen or members of his congregation and she had learnt to temper her rebellious ways so that she operated in secret — like a spy from another country.

So many women are agents of secrecy.

Although she despised fear, Sarah could feel it sniffing at her heels. She had much secrecy on her mind.

What if her plan went wrong?

What if no one turned up at the meeting?

What if word got out to her father?

What if — as was only too evident at this moment — she had bitten off more than was digestible?

'Keep still!'

This stern command from Jack Burns reminded Sarah that she was a mere symbol, a cipher, a representation to be copied by hand, and all this because she gained entrance into a haven of sin and had lost a bet at the same time.

★　★　★

It had been a most hazardous, exciting whirl. The wild men of their group had bundled her amongst their midst in the guise of an Arab prince, out of the carriage, into and through the bawdy-hoose doors.

The entrance of the Just Land. Where, according to righteous thought, the apples of Sodom turn to ashes in the mouth; or, to the sinfully inclined, taste all the sweeter.

91

Sarah had fleeting impressions of a flurry of movement as they hustled into the main salon — strong banks of perfume, laughter, a one-eyed fiddler sawing away in the corner while a big fat lady at the piano played strangely delicate melodies. All this reflected in the many mirrors that shot vibrant images to and fro between them, as if the world had nothing better to do than show itself to itself, as if there was nothing else but this moment, this life. Naked of propriety.

And the girls! The magpies, wagtails, birds of a feather. Dressed to the nines, their shoulders bare, hair unloosed, eyes glittering — more like forces of nature than pillow-wantons. They greeted the arrival of the artists with a certain delight but no great hope of material gain.

Her escorts having sneaked Sarah past the grim old harridan who opened the door, had dumped the girl in a corner with a glass of champagne, which suited her just fine and dandy. As she sipped, her eyes below the hastily wrought turban were alive and darting from image to image.

Some of the men she even knew from her father's congregation, where they lifted their pious eyes towards the granite gaze of the Almighty. Not quite so holy now as they lurched towards the nearest fleshly outpost. How could she keep her face straight in church from now on?

But the men did not really interest her. Men were predictable. Like dogs with a bone.

It was the women that held her regard, faces

alive and bold with a curious and striking independence. Their laughter was mocking at times, wholehearted, a bond between them at which Sarah could only guess — they flirted, teased and provoked as an advent of artists brought a new energy into the room.

But these whirling women knew only too well where their bread was buttered. Never lose sight of that. Wild young men might fill the room with dazzling light but their pocketbooks are, for the most part, empty and dark. Artists entertain but money talks.

Money can be painted, drawn, and even written about, but possessing the beast is quite another matter.

Supply and demand. A hectic mix of appetite and calculation. That which you desire rarely comes without payment.

Two sayings operate in this world. There's no justice — and — you pay for everything.

Sarah felt light-headed, giddy, careless, and, above all, hungry to depict what she saw in the glittering light. A matriarchal kingdom. Erotic and unlicensed. If she could only get them to sit before her.

Even the old harridan whose eyes never blinked, whose gaze Sarah swiftly avoided when some sixth sense made the old woman aware she was being observed. The lines on her face like an engraving.

To get them all on canvas!

Some of the girls were bold as the magpie itself and looked at Sarah in her guise, with open inducement. And what if she had revealed

herself — would the invitation still be extended?
And what would her response have been?

* * *

A hand fell upon her shoulder and the sudden shock brought her out of this stream of memory. Jack Burns adjusted the drapes so that a little more of her slender neck was exposed and grinned down at her.

'How does it feel to be a goddess?'

'Cold,' she replied. 'And far from immortal.'

His hand had stayed resting on her shoulder and she gave him a look that occasioned its hasty removal. All the men of the group were attracted to her but Sarah was like quicksilver, and her preferences were a dark secret.

Male or female, who might tell?

All roads lead to Rome.

She was wilful, hot-tempered, took offence easily but, luckily for Jack, stuck to her bets. However the wager was for one sitting only, so the sculptor went back to the task in hand and Sarah resumed Olympian detachment.

While he frowned over lines on paper and shot fierce glances from under his brows like so many darts, her mind wandered once more to the previous night.

* * *

As the evening wore on and it became impossible to ignore what was happening in the bedrooms upstairs, the isolation that Sarah had

94

initially welcomed began to chafe, especially when Jack spent an inordinate amount of time with a certain Jean Brash.

The woman, infamous or celebrated according to taste throughout the city, was like a still centre in the midst of this whirling sensual energy. At one point she had looked over at Sarah with a glint of amusement in her green eyes. A responsive glare covered up the fear of discovery — if indeed the Arab prince was to be revealed as a minister's daughter, it might be a hard disclosure to live down.

The observer, however, turned away and listened to Jack with a faint smile on her lips. Then as the music became wilder she had disappeared and Sarah — fearing she might be hauled into the fray — took the opportunity to leave with two of their company who were also adorned in bright plumage though not for disguise.

They had been prancing around for the amusement of some so-called respectable citizens, one of whom she recognised from her father's many committee meetings as Barton Laidlaw. But now the two had other venues in mind where brothers of the gusset might flutter together, and Sarah wedged herself between them like an obedient chick, to take flight before finding herself the target for some wild oscillation.

The last sight before she left was that of a duo of magpies, one bearing a startling resemblance to the other, hooking arms and whirling around like a two-headed female version of Janus.

★ ★ ★

Back to Pallas Athena.

A fierce draught of sorts sent a shiver down her spine and Sarah looked past the concentrating artist to discover what had caused such an unwelcome intrusion of an Edinburgh east wind into the place.

Indeed it did have a cause. A tall, elegant creature, dressed in the height of fashion, had found the studio door open, entered behind the absorbed sculptor and incidentally brought some cold air for company.

She seemed as surprised to see Sarah as was the opposite case. They stared at each other. The goddess meets a fashionable lady; one exposed to the eye, the other not so. Silence stretched like a worm hauled from frosty ground by a hungry sparrow.

The lady's eyes narrowed in recognition as the goddess scowled across the room. That scowl rang a bell.

'You were an Arab the last time we met,' said Jean Brash. 'Do you make a habit of these . . . manifestations?'

13

I had a little husband,
No bigger than my thumb;
I put him in a pint-pot
And there I bade him drum.

'It didn't take you long to find a new deity,' Jean murmured. 'But I suppose nature abhors a vacuum.'

As she gazed at the slightly sweating sculptor who stood in front of the log fire, a dark crayon still clutched in his fingers, the Mistress of the Just Land wondered about her real motives for being here.

Investigation or attraction?

Yet how can one be attracted to a man who changes divine beings in midstream?

And bangs out of the blue upon a judge's door?

Better stick to the case. What was it McLevy had pronounced once while stuffing his face with a mistimed soggy sugar biscuit?

'Always keep distance. The heart is a fine organ but it can be easy deceived.'

Not that Jean's heart was necessarily the only organ involved.

Having found out to her surprise that the barely sheathed goddess was the daughter of a clergyman, William Baines, in fact a name upon Jean's list — and how the hell would that tie in?, plus the fact that the girl was an Arab potentate on last viewing — Jean then watched Sarah as opposed to the previously alleged Solomon vanish into the other room in a flurry of damask folds and wondered what personage the girl might return as, perhaps Queen Victoria?

To give the lassie her due, she could have lied about her identity and either brazened it out or simply beat a retreat and vanished.

But despite a flush in her cheeks and no doubt a wish to better cover her maidenly charms, Sarah owned up to the person she was, and, with as much dignity as goose-pimples would allow, departed the scene to disappear behind the curtain, shed the goddess and resume humanity.

That left Jack Burns. To whom she had recently addressed the words *nature abhors a vacuum*.

'I thought you were worried about a lack of innocence,' he replied sturdily enough.

Jean had learnt the value of an enigmatic smile from Francine the French girl, who could calculate a man's weight to the nearest British pound before hauling him up on a complicated series of pulleys to receive a just chastisement — not that such a thought entered her mind about the sculptor as, smiling enigmatically, she moved past him to peruse the rough sketches.

At the same time and despite any personal pique over his slippery near immediate finding of another godly template, her mind was working at a rate of knots.

This might be a way in. Amidst confusion aye lurks opportunity.

'You have a certain primitive talent,' she observed blithely. 'Rough and ready does it, eh?'

Jack flushed, the high cheekbones each betraying a blotch of red.

'They are guidelines for a shape in stone, nothing more. Sarah is the one for fine lines.'

'Another artistic soul?'

'She has a certain talent in portraiture,' said Jack tersely, wishing they might change the subject.

'And why her desire to visit the Just Land? Is she looking for employment?'

'Sarah can inform you of that herself,' was the stiff response.

Jean traced the lines of the goddess's body with an idle forefinger.

'You seem to be . . . intimate colleagues?'

'Colleagues, yes. Intimate, no.'

She turned a page to a sketch that, while lacking refinement, was charged with a certain penetrative energy.

'Well, I suppose it's all in the eye of the beholder,' murmured Jean.

Emotions conflicted while her mind raced. Was that a wee hint of jealousy stirring in the bosom?

Stick to the case, Mistress Brash. Misplaced desire might create murder but it won't solve the beast. She shuffled the pages of the drawings together like a gambler with a pack of cards, and the subject was then changed to Jack's relief and Jean's potential benefit.

'Did you enjoy your visit last night?'

'I enjoyed our conversation very much but

then you vanished from sight.'

In fact, Jean had sneaked off to the kitchen where she and Hannah had shared a glass of the very best champagne to toast in the New Year, little knowing that death was also drinking up its own tribute.

'A woman's work is never done.'

With that somewhat bland rejoinder, Jean moved closer to the fire, which still had some energy to spare.

'And did you talk with anyone else?'

'I spoke to many. But then our party had to move on. Other venues.'

She sensed a growing puzzlement that might lead to an unwelcome curiosity, as in *what in God's name does this woman actually want here? Or, has my fatal charm once more wrought havoc in the female heart?* Nip this in the bud.

'You frightened one of my girls,' she accused equally out of the blue.

'What?'

'She told me this morning. Trembling like a leaf.'

'What?'

Jean was tempted to say *please stop repeating yourself, it's awfy tedious,* but kept to the straight and narrow, plus the fact there was the imminent possibility that her Royal Highness might return at any moment.

'An act of violence; shocked her to the core.'

'What?'

'That's the third time you've said such,' Jean remarked with apparent asperity.

'What act of violence?'

100

'Judge Abercrombie. She saw you near strangle the man.'

'That's — that is complete nonsense!'

'Is it?'

For some reason the simplicity of her response stopped Jack Burns in his tracks. His face showed a deal of confusion — either the man was a consummate actor or, unlike most men, he was about to tell the truth.

'I — I had a disagreement with Abercrombie, that is true.'

'Over what?'

For a moment it seemed Burns would say nothing more, but then he picked up a poker and shoved it angrily into the fire. As he thrust the metal with some violence into the charred wood, his face was averted but the words came out clear enough.

'Someone . . . I knew . . . Abercrombie had passed severe sentence upon him. He died in the Perth Penitentiary.'

'What was the crime?'

Another violent thrust sent the embers flying.

'A stupid, senseless one. But then Robbie never had much sense.'

Jack took a deep breath and then banged another log on the fire — a flurry of sparks from loose chippings danced around in the air for a moment and then vanished.

So are we to the gods: loose chippings.

'Robbie Osborne. A natural talent but no sense. Silly bugger.'

Jack let out a pained laugh while Jean watched closely.

'All he ever drew was fairy people. Claimed he saw them everywhere, even on Sir Walter Scott's monument one day. Most of our crew thought him to be an opiate hound, but I don't think he touched the stuff.'

A scratching noise in the corner startled Jean, but it was a large ginger tomcat that slunk insolently over to Jack, rubbed itself against his leg and then settled by the fire to match its yellow eyes against the flames.

'Robbie stole a leg of lamb in the Haymarket. He was hungry, he said. Caught. Up before Abercrombie. A sentence of ten years handed down.'

'That would seem severe.'

'He was of the streets, Robbie. A natural talent but . . . it never pays to steal property. Even if you're hungry. And especially if you have no advocate on hand.'

Jack smiled bitterly and cut a handsome figure against the flames. Beware an artist by firelight.

'The idea of ten years. It broke him. He didn't last three months. Hanged himself from the bars of his cell.'

'And you were angry with Judge Abercrombie?'

'Spilt over. Too much champagne.'

'It can lead to strong action at times.'

'I grabbed him by the collar and told the miserable swine that he had murdered by legal process.'

Jean said nothing but wondered what it might be like to be grabbed by the neck in Burns's strong hands. She could imagine the judge's flinty response. The man lived by the law. And may have died for it.

'I apologise if I caused one of your . . . damsels some distress.'

There was a hint of arrogance in the remark, no matter how sincerely intentioned, and it angered Jean Brash, even if she had made up this imaginary scenario in the first place.

Thus lies become truth in the twinkling of an eye.

'And did it end there?' she asked sharply.

'What?'

'You grabbed him by the throat. Did it end there?'

There was a lethal glint in her eye and Jack Burns was afforded a momentary glimpse of the fact that a woman does not become Mistress of the Just Land by plucking the odd buttercup in the meadow.

'*Did it end there?*'

The fireside cat blinked at the sharpness of her tone; Burns blinked also and said nothing in response, though there was a flash of anger in his eyes.

The side door opened and into this primal scene walked Sarah Baines, now all too human and dressed to depart, coat and bonnet already donned.

She was every inch the contained Victorian miss, a tribute to corsetry and muted colours, but had obviously been nerving herself up to make an announcement to Jean and so missed an edge of tension in the air.

'I have a favour to ask of you, Mistress Brash,'

103

she declared, only the slight twist of one gloved finger over another betraying some inner disquiet.

'And what might that be?'

There was something about Sarah that reminded Jean of a young woman she might have known a long time ago. A woman who faced up to a monster intent on her destruction and did not step back, even though she feared for her life.

Nerve and vulnerability. One to each hand; or foot, as the case may be.

'Your . . . ladies,' said Sarah.

'Ladies?'

'What would you call them?'

'My girls. But a lady is fine. I've heard worse.'

Jack Burns felt curiously ignored as the two women squared one to the other. As if he had been forgotten. Men often feel so when women face across.

But Jean had merely laid him to the side for the moment — he had yet to answer her last question.

'Your girls, then. I would like to — to capture them,' Sarah continued doggedly.

'For the zoo?'

'On canvas.'

Now it was Jean's turn to blink.

'Is that why you came in disguise?'

'No. I came out of foolish curiosity. But then I saw them. And I . . . found them inspiring.'

'Inspiring?'

'I can find no better word.'

As Jean contemplated this, one of the logs fell

from the fire grate. For a moment it teetered as if to crash on to the hearth, but Jack swiftly kicked the wood back where it belonged. The cat didn't move a muscle.

'I have my own studio,' Sarah continued. 'Your girls would be safe there.'

'I doubt they'd need much in the way of protection,' Jean murmured. 'Except maybe Teenie Donnachie. She's on the timid side, as Mister Burns here can confirm.'

Jack was way out of his depth and felt oddly threatened.

'I'll ask the girls,' said Jean finally. 'They can decide. When they get back home.'

'Home?'

'That's what they call the Just Land.'

Sarah nodded acceptance, inclined her head towards Jack in farewell and left abruptly.

'How did you get her to remove her clothing?' Jean asked unexpectedly.

'It is . . . part of the procedure.'

'Is it now?'

She looked around the studio. It was an untidy prospect with a rumpled bed stuck into the corner.

'Do you live here?'

'Sometimes.'

A couple of his works, neither finished, both on what would seem to be a mythological feminine theme, caught her eye. The curves lacked a little precision.

'I do not appreciate my respectable clients being roughly handled,' she remarked, hoping to provoke him into further response without too much repetition.

'I apologise once more,' Jack replied stiffly. 'I left soon after the incident.'

That left just one more question to be asked and answered: why had he called at the judge's house?

Jean looked at the cat. The cat licked its chops.

14

There was an old woman had three sons,
Jerry and James and John.
Jerry was hung and James was drowned,
John was lost and never was found.

The two young keelies had waited most of the day for an easy target. The weather had closed in again, and that was good for it is much easier to pikepurse when visibility is at a premium. The old woman who was muttering her way over the harbour cobblestones would be easy to shove over, whip the wee reticule she had clamped under her arm up and away, and then be lost in the mists of a New Year.

They had drunk helter-skelter the night before and were desperate to bombard their livers with more of the same; ram-stam beer and White Dog whisky.

Cheap drink, but it still cost money and they had not a penny between them. This would soon be rectified.

Neither were professional thieves, but thirst can make criminals of us all.

The auld biddy had not even raised her head, as if either she already knew her destination or did not know where she was bound — lost in the fog. The streets were empty save for a few faint figures. Perfect for felonious activity.

They jacked up their flashy-dashy collars,

pulled down the brims of their peaked caps, moved swiftly out to be on each side of her and spoke softly — no need to terrify the poor old wifie — you could easy knock her over with a feather and besides loud words might attract unwanted and unwarranted attention.

'Can I help ye, Granny?' said the smaller keelie with a winning smile on his dirty face. 'I'll take your bag, you take my arm. These cobblestones are fair skiddery.'

He attempted to slide his hand beneath her elbow but was shoved away with surprising force.

'I'll manage,' said the old crone.

The bigger man then stood straight before so that the woman was forced to halt. 'Give your money or I'll hammer ye down,' he grunted, raising one meaty fist to show violent intent.

The old biddy scrabbled under her coat and both men relaxed. Maybe her purse was inside the thing — that would make it all the easier.

God is good to those in need.

The smaller keelie smiled again to encourage the fumbling ancient figure.

'It's aye best to do whit you're told, Granny,' he grinned, revealing a remarkable number of bad teeth for one so young. 'Now jist you give me and I'll be taking it, eh? Then ye're on your way. All friends thegither.'

He offered forth a dirty hand with the palm outstretched and then howled in pain as the blade of a cut-throat razor sliced deep through the crusted skin just into the gathering of flesh below his thumb that is known in different circles as the Mount of Venus.

The old woman was just tall enough to get the same blade up like lightning to the other man's throat so that he could feel the sharp edge resting tight on the soft folds just under the chin.

Two stony eyes stared into his as the edge cut in just enough to make the giant realise that a deluge of his own gore was not a far distant prospect.

'Well my big mannie,' said Hannah Semple. 'Do you feel light of heart this day?'

The blade pressed in a little deeper and the large keelie swallowed hard while his companion made quite a lot more noise as he tried to staunch the flow of blood with a threadbare rag from his pocket.

'Get tae hell out of my sight,' said this demon from hell, 'before I change my mind.'

She whipped the razor back just enough that the keelie could see it glisten in the damp air and motioned it as if aiming anew at his Adam's Apple.

Both men ran off as if the devil himself were at their heels.

Hannah Semple sniffed a little in the damp air and looked across the harbour to where the Rusty Nail tavern lay amongst the other buildings like a dissolute next-of-kin.

'Damn cheek,' she muttered, and set off again.

A seabird watched the figure of an old woman shove open the tavern door and disappear inside. The bird was perched on the mast of one of the fishing boats in the harbour. This still being New Year's Day, the crew lay with kinfolk, and not a scrap of fish-gut was to be found on deck.

It was a herring gull known locally as a Pewlie Willie, and it let out a wailing cry to signal a loss of hope in this particular moment and the life so far.

15

When I went up Sandy-Hill,
I met a sandy-boy;
I cut his throat, I sucked his blood,
And left his skin a-hanging-o.

The barman in the Rusty Nail did not register the bird's complaint. He had worked in the place for near twenty years and watched the ebb and flow of life — the sappie-heids, spewin' fous, drunkards of many gradations, and then the tarry breeks, the harbour trallops all ages, shapes and sizes, all the human flotsam and jetsam that washed in and out of the tavern with the tide. His name was Hughie Garrigle, known to one and all as Shug.

Very little surprised the barman but he had been taken aback when Hannah Semple walked in. The old woman had once been a regular, aye kept herself clean and tidy but had few friends and — once she was too far past it for the game — seemed to be waiting for nothing but an empty hole.

But then she had linked up somehow with Jean Brash and never looked back.

Until now.

She had marched in, ordered up a wee dram for herself plus a big hooker of whisky for Tam Drayton, who was shaking like a leaf at a corner table from the hammering he gave it last night,

111

and then looked around the place.

'Hasnae changed,' said Hannah.

'Life is a hard road,' answered Shug.

She nodded, paid, wedged the handbag under her arm to collect her drinks, and marched off.

Now from where she sat, Hannah looked back at the barman. A small, wiry cove, with skin that had been hard steeped in whisky fumes and tobacco smoke, he had laid out many a bigger foe without much change of expression.

In mythological terms, he could have been Charon, the ferryman who takes damned souls to the Gates of Hell; but in this arena, he was just Shug the barman.

The tavern itself was quiet as the grave. Most of Leith was nursing an evil hangover the like of which caused Tam Drayton's hand to shake like a man with palsy as he lifted the glass, and the sight of which trembling had caused Hannah to avert her eyes.

Lest she catch the disease of self-loathing and a hatred for the weakness that had caused it.

Drayton was skeletal thin, with a straggly moustache, goatee beard, yellow-stained fingers, pale-blue eyes and tobacco teeth that were now like outposts in the desert.

Our Thomas had once been an elegant, fetching fellow — before the worm of corruption found a welcome home and hatched out more of the same.

He drained the hooker to half with one smooth swallow and smiled as the alcohol jolted him back into life. Fire in the blood. Addiction, his faithful friend.

'There is a God in heaven,' said he softly. 'And you, Hannah Semple, are his angel of mercy.'

In truth, he still cut a striking figure as a ruin will yet have remnants of what it might once have been.

For a moment there was a glint of pity in her eye but to pity an addict, as she well enough knew, is to pour from the empty into the void. Hannah dipped her reticule — stubby fingers prodding inside like a surgeon's cutter — and came out with the list Jean had given her, which she laid before him.

'The mistress desires tae know whit might connect these men. One tae the other; hand in glove.'

A cynical twist to the thin lips in response:

'Dear me. And I thought you, from the goodness of your heart, were here to see me. How disappointing.'

He picked up the paper and as he did so, almost absent-mindedly emptied the hooker at the same time.

'I shall need fuel for the boiler, Hannah Semple. Man cannot live by bread alone.'

She signalled the barman, who came over with a half-full bottle of whisky, poured out a large measure and was about to leave when Drayton plucked the container deftly from his hand.

'If you don't mind, Shug — what an ugly name. Let us call you by a proper appellation. Hugh. If you don't mind, Hugh, just relinquish the bottle. It will be happier here. Where it belongs. A *natural* habitat.'

The barman looked at Hannah who nodded

assent with some resignation and slid over coinage to cover the cost.

'I don't mind anything,' said Shug on his way back to the bar, jingling the money in his hand. 'So long as the coin rings true.'

Since the owner was not on hand, however, and paid meagre wage, the money would stay in his pocket. Charon needed an obolus coin put on the eyes of the dead as payment for the ferry; Shug was a little more expensive since there were not quite so many paying customers.

Tam Drayton smiled once more, took another long draught of spirit, fished out a pair of cracked reading glasses with a piece of tape holding it all together, and perched them on the end of his nose.

'My eyes are not what they were,' he murmured. 'Unlike the rest of me, which is . . . a picture of health.'

As he shook with silent laughter and bent over the paper, Hannah allowed her mind to drift back into the past. She had worked the harbour for many years. So many bodies, so many sailorboys, so many ships in passing. So long ago. Another life. Another woman.

It struck her with some force that the unsettled emotion in her breast was one of dread.

The Just Land had become her world. A home. A kingdom where she held the keys and Jean Brash ruled. But what if that world changed?

Hannah Semple was not given to sudden insights. Her feet were on the earth, her

Excalibur was the cut-throat razor, her reality had been fashioned against many rough walls in many side alleys.

Now, for the first time, she had something to care about — a life that had some meaning.

She had been sent twice to the penitentiary, once for common assault and the other for a razor stuck under the nose of a non-paying customer. The mannie had twitched his neb and had a chunk removed. Served him right, but sadly his father was a magistrate. McLevy came in as arresting officer and, give the devil his due, was none too happy because the assaulted man was a right snotter, but the inspector did his duty and Hannah did time.

A third visit and she would have been dead in the water — a habitual offender.

That was when Jean Brash made an appearance.

What if this murder — this killing of a judge — brought down the mistress? A stone thrown in water will send ripples that may reach out to the very edge.

For a moment a terrible cold fear almost paralysed her. What the hell was it that had gripped her like an icy, evil claw? *What was this terror?*

We are all gripped by fear waiting by the door, and though we may shut it out, it never leaves. You can no more lose your shadow.

Hannah jerked up her head, became once more the woman known to herself and the world at large, and then knocked back her whisky in the one fierce gulp to feel an artificial but welcome fire of life in the veins.

'Well,' she demanded of Tam Drayton. 'Whit's the verdict?'

The man had a guarded set to his face.

'What does your mistress want with this?'

'That's her business.'

'The implication being it's none of mine?'

'Correct.'

While Hannah had been pondering unwelcome thoughts as Tam hunched over the list, his hooker had emptied itself as if by magic. He swiftly remedied the fault by filling it up again with a magician's flourish.

And again Drayton drank deeply. The spirit seemed to cut more profoundly this time. His eyes closed and the face crunched up in reaction like a disappointed child.

Shug watched from the bar and remembered the first time Drayton had swaggered into the place, wild as hell, Jack-a-Dandy, a harbour wagtail on each arm.

Tall as a tree, he had bought drinks all round, money to burn — not his money as it transpired — and then announced to one and all that he was immortal. That would be the hashish talking. Delusions of grandeur. See where it gets you.

As soon as he lost the money, he lost all so-called friends and especially the women that had flocked around like hungry seagulls.

'Better off wi' a blood pudding,' Shug muttered, swiping a cloth over the counter. 'Any day o' the week.'

A bird screamed outside in the harbour and Drayton opened his eyes again.

'What says Baudelaire?' he murmured. 'We are all born, marked for evil.'

Hannah had never heard of Baudelaire. French by the sound of it. Cheery bugger.

'Whit's the verdict?' she asked once more.

'Of course it was a time ago,' he murmured. 'But I might point you in ... a possible direction.'

'Point away.'

'Moncrieff may link them. However, the man is dead, I hear. Not long dead?'

Hannah nodded. She had come to get information, not supply such. Tam Drayton was no more to be trusted than a heron by the goldfish pond.

'Moncrieff was appointed to run a charitable workhouse — for streetboys. In Leith. Then he moved on to Haymarket: another establishment. Boys and girls. There was a scandal. One of the girls. He had to leave.'

Hannah knew from Jean Brash of Moncrieff's slimy predilections but this told her nothing except that evil bastards don't change their ways. Was that whit this Baudelaire meant?

'Ye said a link between them. How come?'

'Ah yes, I did say that, didn't I?'

His eyes slid meaningfully towards her handbag and without hesitation Hannah delved in once more and took out a couple of silver coins, laid one out before Drayton but kept the other close to hand.

'Man cannot live by bread alone,' remarked Drayton once more, almost giggling as he slid the coin from the table into his pocket. 'The

117

Bible tells us all this verity.'

'Ye'll get another if I think it worthwhile, but quality is everything.'

Drayton removed the spectacles and pushed them carelessly into his jacket pocket. 'Who knows what you or your mistress might consider worth the while, eh?'

She had a feeling he was laughing at her somewhere or perhaps concealing something but kept her gaze steady upon his face.

Another swallow of whisky went down and the only sign of this was a slight slurring of his words.

'What happened in the Haymarket is not within my ken but . . . there was a rumour of a death in Leith. In the home. A young boy. Moncrieff the cause. A just chastisement that became . . . unjust.'

He stopped suddenly, face blank as if he had just lost touch with reality.

'Whit was the boy's name?'

Drayton came back to life.

'Finch, I believe. John Finch.'

The man held the near empty hooker up to the light and peered through the thick glass at Hannah, his face warped in a twisted image like a gargoyle.

He spoke from behind the tumbler so that the words had a strangely distorted resonance as if coming from some intestinal part of his being.

'All this I found because the workhouse funds were banked by the governors at the British Linen Company in Leith Walk, and I was a trusted employee of that fine establishment

118

. . . all this I found. All this was given.'

Drayton took out a shabby leather pouch, prised out some strands of tobacco and yellow paper, rolled himself a thin cigarette, sparked a lucifer into light and puffed contentedly as if the conversation was over.

He was a perverse creature and Hannah realised that if she seemed needy, like an addict, for instance, the man would hang her out to dry.

Also, there was a feeling that he was laughing at her, laughing at everyone because next to hating himself Tom Drayton hated the world even more.

And perhaps women most of all. For, as Hughie could have told you, all the wagtails and harbour girls had left him for dead once the money ran out.

They had helped him spend it quick enough but that was as far as their generosity travelled.

When what might have been a good man turns bad, he inherits a force for evil that is truly corrupt. *Deadly* corrupt. Perverse as Satan himself.

So she calmly poured herself another small dram, her companion a slightly larger measure, placed the bottle back to exactly where it had been before, took a genteel sip, and then folded her fingers together like a Presbyterian wifie on the Sabbath waiting for the sermon.

Drayton also took a genteel sip, the sight of the bottle still with a decent content having calmed his thirst. No need to swallow fast like an animal that fears discovery, and in his own twisted way he always tried to give value for money. The least a fellow could do.

'Very well,' he announced as if she had actually asked another question. 'The boy's death never made the light of day, the rulers of the workhouse saw to that. Some months later Moncrieff moved on to the Haymarket. A different set of governors. It was there he suffered disgrace and dismissal. But not in Leith.'

Hannah pushed the silver coin so that it lay precisely in the centre of the table between them.

Drayton pushed the paper back towards her and palmed the coin at the same time.

'The names of the governors of that Leith workhouse were the same as lie upon your list. Gavin Young, Barton Laidlaw, Reverend William Baines and Hilton Abercrombie.'

Hannah schooled her face to reveal sweet damn all and shot out another question.

'Whit happened tae the place?'

'Shut it up eventually. Building sold at a fine profit. Landlord was delighted.'

'Landlord?'

'Owner to be more accurate.'

He leaned closer so that she could smell the far from attractive mixture of whisky, tobacco and rotting gums. Something seemed to be amusing the man as if he could hardly contain a private laughter.

'Barton Laidlaw,' he almost whispered, and giggled like a child. 'Fingers in many pies.'

At the bar, Shug's face registered consternation as the tavern portal creaked to admit someone. He opened his mouth to utter words of

disguised warning, but as he did so, another voice sounded so that for a moment the barman seemed like a ventriloquist's puppet.

'Hannah Semple. Whit are you doing in this wee segment of hell?'

In the doorway stood Inspector James McLevy, beside him Constable Martin Mulholland — birds of ill omen.

16

There was a man in our town,
And he was wondrous wise,
He jumped into a bramble bush
And scratched out both his eyes.

The two boys lay in the darkness and shivered. Dirk Martins was the worst affected, his body jolting with fear, while Jeb Summers remained still and silent under the thin sheets.

Moncrieff had found them out, thought Dirk. But how? Could only be that someone had clyped, betrayed, pointed a finger, because they had lorded it too much, bullied, bossed, stolen a few trophies from the smaller boys.

Thought they had the rule, or rather, Johnny Finch thought such. Thought he was king. He had even treated both his confederates with a certain contempt; they were his creatures and while Dirk could smile and smile and take it, Jeb bore the brunt.

When Johnny's spittle slid down Jeb's face, the wee boy had grinned like a monkey while the other two shook with laughter; but Dirk did not think it was all that funny and wondered if he would be next.

Yet they were still together. All three. And when Moncrieff, his scaly eye bulging, shouted his way in to where they sat by their beds playing a game of cards with an old scabby pack that Jeb

had stolen from one of the younger boys — a pack that was quickly hidden — when he wrenched Johnny up, accused him of a dirty deed by pouring piss upon his master's head, and hauled the boy out of there — the other two were frozen like statues.

There was a back room where Moncrieff dispensed his rough justice.He had a selection of canes and strong rope that he used to make sure his victim was unable to move: thence to a heavy wooden beam, named by Moncrieff the Pole of Correction, that he tied them to like a flayed rabbit before he went to work. Licking his lips.

When his arm became tired, he would retire to his desk, survey his handiwork, and seat his bony haunches on a nice soft velvet cushion that was plumped upon his armchair. Then, thus refreshed, he would begin again.

They heard the screams much later when Johnny could not hold them in any longer. At supper they sat. The food tasting like pigswill, which indeed it was, but worse this time. Some of the other boys hid a sleekit smile: which one of them had tipped the wink?

As long as it's not happening to you, nothing else matters.

What Dirk could not understand was why he and Jeb had not been taken as well. Or was Johnny perhaps just the first in line?

The screams went on. And then they stopped on a final choked howl.

After a time, Moncrieff came back in. Sweating. He looked balefully at the line of bent heads.

'You will go to bed now,' he said, sucking at his dry lips as if he'd just had a plate of raw liver. 'And you will think upon your sins.'

He still had a cane in his hand and they could see smears of blood upon it. Moncrieff brought the cane down on the table with a savage swipe and every scratched, dented tin plate danced as if itself in pain. The two old gadgies who helped keep order were almost as afraid as the boys themselves.

'I will go back in the morning,' the master announced. 'And ye'll hear him again. Howling for mercy.'

And still Moncrieff made no move towards Jeb Summers or Dirk Martins. No smile now upon Dirk's face; his bowels were in an uproar and the boy was in terror of soiling himself in front of everyone. Had Johnny Finch taken all the blame? Or was the master playing with them like a cat does a mouse? What would happen?

Moncrieff left finally. Like a black shadow. But just before he closed the door, he looked back at Dirk and Jeb and wiped a hand across his mouth.

As if he had tasted blood. And wanted more.

A church clock struck two chimes that broke into Dirk's terrified thoughts.

The rest were asleep, grunting, snuffling, snoring and farting from the rancid supper fare.

'I'm goin' tae see,' Jeb whispered from the dark.

'Eh?'

'Johnny. I'm goin' tae see.'

There had been no sign of their king. He was

no doubt still in Moncrieff's room of severe punishment.

Jeb slid out of bed and sniffed the air like a rodent on the hunt.

'The door'll be locked,' Dirk warned.

'I'm good wi' locks.'

That much was true. The wee runt had a talent for such.

'Ask him —'

Dirk stopped, shamefaced at his cowardice. He should be worried about his comrade but all he could think of was his own fate. 'Ask him if he's told on us.'

For a moment Jeb hesitated. What was he thinking? Then he was gone, his white form a stunted, spectral pygmy in the darkness.

The boy in the next bed to Dirk, Archie Millar, lifted up his head for a moment and watched the dwarf leave. Then he buried it under the dirty sheets again.

'Archie?' Dirk whispered in a conciliatory tone. 'I'm sorry Jeb stole your cards.'

There was no answer. They had set themselves up as kings. And a king has no friends.

Dirk lay for what seemed hours. Every creak in the house sent a shiver down his spine. An owl hooted somewhere, the sound muffled and distant — a bird that sucks your blood and plucks out the eyes.

Thoughts kept running like spiders through his mind. Who had betrayed them? The smaller boys? He would have thought them too frightened of Finch's vengeance. And why only

125

Johnny? So far, that is. Only so far.

Something landed on his chest and Dirk started to scream but Jeb's other hand gripped hard around the mouth, the strength surprising.

The hand let go. The white face was above him.

'He's jist lying there on the pole,' Jeb hissed. 'I couldnae wake him. His back's a' blood. He's not moving. I said his name. In his ear. He didnae move.'

The owl hooted again. Like a funeral horn.

17

Little General Monk
Sat upon a trunk,
Eating a crust of bread;
There fell a hot coal
And burnt in his clothes a hole,
Now little General Monk is dead.

Of the three other names on that list, each man disported himself according to taste and habit.

Barton Laidlaw embraced corruption as to the manner born. He rolled a fine malt whisky round his large fleshy mouth and smacked lips in appreciation.

The two Bristol men smiled and looked around at the dark-wood furnishings of the New Club, a fine and elegant building in Princes Street to which they had been invited by the councillor. Normally full of the power possessors in Edinburgh city, this night it appeared less busy.

Oddly enough, the oak-panelled wood and red-leather armchairs might put a man in mind of a certain bawdy-hoose. Minus, of course, the other embellishments.

No bare feet flexed themselves in erotic invitation, and the severe mutton-chopped portraits interspersed with dreich highland landscapes that hung upon the wall were a far cry from the large painting of a gigantic octopus

127

dragging a scantily clad female to a watery doom, which loomed above the fireplace and was reflected in the salon mirrors of the Just Land.

A great favourite of Jean Brash. When asked why, she would simply reply that it was a cautionary tale.

However, Samuel Deacon, his bald pate shining in the discreet candlelight, and Joseph Tucker, a vibrantly maned opposite — tall and handsome if carrying a little too much ballast, whereas Sammy was round, cheerful and resembled a despoilt cherub — were here to do business. A tasteful endeavour — but business nevertheless.

Not to put too fine a point upon it, bribery of a council official. What form it would take was, as yet, a mystery, but they knew it would involve hard cash and not be a moderate amount.

They also knew they had a limited amount of applicable grease with which to slide Barton Laidlaw out of the hand of rectitude and into a more malleable position.

Sadly for them, the official below Barton would have been much cheaper and they were making splendid headway with the fellow, Forbes Crichton by name, but then the ubiquitous councillor had sniffed the fragrance of financial procurement and parked his fat backside exactly where undesired.

'A heavy responsibility,' murmured Barton, his hefty form settling back in the chair. 'This new addition to the Leith Docks will be a boon but also a *great* expense.'

A deeper harbour was to extend alongside the

existing ones. It would open up the port to more shipping and hopefully the revenue gained would help pay back a government loan.

The city council would ponder long and hard about awardance of this contract, but ultimately they would do what Barton slyly manipulated. He knew far too many secrets about his colleagues; indeed, had helped arrange a decent, or even indecent, proportion of them.

Keep it in the family.

Joseph Tucker took the lead. He had large teeth like a handsome horse, smiled in a flash of light, and was front man for the consortium.

'We have the expertise and will not waste a penny, sir. Not one penny.'

Unlike Deacon, who had a broad Bristol accent, Tucker possessed an actor's rhetorical flourish that chimed well with many clients, and though a few of the more Calvinist members of the council might find him a little overripe, he had the advantage of belonging to a strong Somerset lodge plus an immaculate Masonic handshake.

All of which seemed to strike a resonance with Laidlaw.

Or did it?

'I am sure your ... parsimony is to be commended,' said Barton, signalling for another glass of the most expensive malt from the waiter in the sure and certain knowledge that he would not pay the *compte rendu*. 'Yet there are many imponderable costs to be considered.'

Imponderable in this context meant undisclosed to the public at large.

What they do not know will not harm the poor souls.

'We would of course meet these costs,' Tucker responded judiciously.

'With open arms!' added Deacon with what seemed to his colleague quite unnecessary enthusiasm — to tell the truth, Tucker now and again regarded his fellow contriver with the merest trace of a faint disdain.

The hirsute often so scrutinise those without, as if desert above betokens a lack of cranial activity below.

Sammy often reminded folk of a puppy — bumbling, with stubby, unformed features — whereas Joseph Tucker had a fine profile — hook-nosed, stalwart-limbed and a manhood, as testified by his chosen magpie of the night to her companions-in-arms, 'lik' a barber's pole on market day'.

However, in fact, they were a shrewd combination: distraction by Deacon, decisive insertion by Tucker.

They were good. But were they good enough?

The drink set before him, Laidlaw inhaled the aroma like a pig over truffles, sipped and nodded wisely in appreciation. But then his face changed to solemn lines as if weighty thought had arrived with the whisky.

'I regret to inform you though, gentlemen, that much as I am in favour of your represented company' — here Laidlaw paused to unveil a long cigar from its wrappings, beckon the same serving-man over to supply a lighted taper, and afterwards puff with all the enjoyment of a steam train on an easy gradient — 'we have also received a more recent bid from a Liverpool consortium.'

Puff, puff.

In fact he received a free dozen of cigars every week from a certain tobacco importer name of Young — for services rendered. All friends together.

Both Bristol men had become stock still while the smoke wafted gently towards them.

'First time I've heard mention of this, sir.'

In answer to Tucker's questioning smile and response, Laidlaw sighed acknowledgement.

'It was agreed . . . to keep the bids separate. But now I am afraid that separation is no longer possible.'

The smile was still fixed on the face of Tucker, but so is a limpet to a seaside rockface.

As Laidlaw spoke further he rose from the table and gestured towards the club dining room, where the maître d' had appeared and bowed solemnly in their direction.

'Ah. Our table prepared for early supper. I can thoroughly recommend smoked salmon on anchor stock, the dressed sheep's head, especially with brain sauce, and an Edinburgh Fog to follow for a wee touch of pudding. The fare of Scotland at its finest!'

As the others sat and he stood, cigar plus drink in the one fist like a true cosmopolitan, with his free hand Barton Laidlaw tweaked a slip of paper from a top pocket to lay it face down on the table between the inert tumblers of the Bristol men.

'That, I delight to tell you, is the offer from Liverpool you must better . . . for the imponderables. I am sure that you will triumph!'

'And if we do not?' asked Tucker quietly.

'Then, I regret to tell you, the gravity of economics must have its way. Up . . . and down.'

There was a hint of beefy menace in his tones before the councillor laughed merrily and went on his way towards the dining room, a faint trail of aromatic cigar smoke following its master.

Those left behind looked at the slip. Finally Tucker reached forwards and turned it over. It contained no words, just figures. The prime numbers were not a problem until it came to the noughts that followed.

'He may be bluffing. To raise the price.'

Deacon's face was that of a sick sheep possibly about to lose its head, because both men had put their own reputation on the line. If this contract was gone, so, in many eyes, were they.

Tucker looked again at the figures as if they somehow might change. The maître d' shuffled restively in the doorway of the dining room; despite his title and formal persona, he was from Paisley and the natives of that city are not noted for their patience.

'The money will disappear into many pockets. But we can't raise this amount. Bluff or no bluff.'

Deacon still looked like an ailing ram.

'So what do we do?'

'Negotiate down. And hope for the best.'

Joseph Tucker was tight-lipped, and white with a barely concealed fury.

'And if he won't budge?'

132

'We try others in the council.'

'He *rules* the council, Joseph. Like a bloody emperor! If this offer is genuine, we're sunk.'

Deacon's Bristol accent had become more pronounced in his agitation.

'True. All we can do is . . . negotiate.'

'And if that doesn't work?'

'We find another way.'

'How?'

'I don't know.'

Into the leaden silence these three words produced came Laidlaw's call from the dining room.

'Gentlemen. I await your presence.'

A stag's head on the wall, shot by a certain Colonel Goodwillie on the Isle of Skye, looked on as the Bristol men picked up their drinks and departed the scene.

One way or another, we all become targets.

Eventually.

★ ★ ★

Gavin Young's supper was early also, but frugal and solitary. He cut a strangely isolated figure in the large, echoing vaults of his tobacco emporium.

His chosen repast was the mill bannock, a large, round oatmeal cake that was dry but wholesome, with a meagre portion of hard goat's cheese as company — for, to be blunt, Gavin was miserly by nature and had made the mistake of marrying a wife who was an exact opposite.

Martha Young would be at home with her

133

friends from the church congregation, all stuffing themselves with various fancy pastries; gibble-gabbling righteous slander to rend reputation and scald the scapegraces.

The couple had no children, unless you count appetite and greed as offspring.

Yet Gavin was happy enough with that, for it left him in peace and quiet. With his own pastimes.

The shop upstairs was neat, tidy and spotless, every accoutrement to the fine art of smoking arrayed in racks and every different kind of tobacco arrayed also. A treasure trove of inhalation. An orderly existence.

He finished eating, laid the bannock remnants neatly in some greaseproof paper, the cheese following in the same manner to be put into a cupboard for tomorrow night.

Mister Young belied his name, for he was a small, mousy-looking middle-aged man with a tight little trimmed moustache, a pair of wire-framed glasses that he wore near constantly, clothes neat and nondescript, shoes black and shiny, the fellow a perfect member of all the various committees that respectability dotted and clotted throughout Edinburgh city. He rarely had an opinion, always nodded with the majority and barely registered in anyone's consciousness.

A citizen who went to church, cleaned his nails, shined his shoes and otherwise might as well have been a furled umbrella in the hatstand.

Now he crossed to the vault safe, a large and strong construction that seemed oddly out of place amidst the sacks and barrels of stacked tobacco leaf.

The brass plaque upon it said *Cartwright and Sons*, and Gavin Young had paid a pretty penny for it. A most unusual act.

The key to the safe was hidden under a loose floorboard that lay under a heavy chest nearby, and Gavin grunted as he shifted the furniture to gain access. A man cannot be too careful.

Key in hand, he opened his treasure box.

The door to the shop upstairs was locked also. He was protected from prying eyes. No one could get in. No one could see him.

No one.

He brought out a large envelope and neatly laid it upon a workbench where his assistants scrupulously sifted various quality of tobacco leaf, the surface of the table retaining a scent like the plant itself.

For a moment he looked down as a priest might survey the relics on an altar — although Gavin was, of course, a good Presbyterian and would eschew any hint of Romanism.

He took the photographs out one by one and laid them face down flat upon the scented surface. Such a pity Moncrieff had died. The man was a splendid conduit for fine-quality merchandise, not unlike Gavin himself in some ways.

Even after the Haymarket, where, sadly, the fellow had fallen from grace — though no doubt the girl had led him on, women being such bearers of temptation — Moncrieff had understood that they could not protect him any longer, for they were not governors in charge of the place, but still he conveyed fruits of the lens.

Mind you, such fruit was no longer quite so reasonable in price, which grieved them both, but then the poor man had lost his other means of livelihood and John was a charitable soul.

Charity begins at home. And ends in exactly the same place.

Gavin wondered how the 'creator' of these beautiful images would manage without his beast of burden. And how would the originator know where to find his clientele?

No doubt time would solve this mystery. One day he might look up into a customer's eyes and see that the man had something to offer, rather than purchase.

Hopefully Moncrieff had left some note of his most valuable customers — and in fact just before this valuable beast of burden died, Gavin had requested a message be passed to the 'creator'.

That he might fulfil a secret dream one day to be there when the images were translated from life — of course, it might be disappointing (actual flesh might sweat, smell and weep blood) perhaps better to see it pinned and printed on paper positive.

Better, perhaps, that he was not exposed. Unlike the dripping negatives.

But no. Young would take that chance if such were offered — if Moncrieff had passed the message on.

He could only hope. Hope springs eternal. There was certainly little chance of such opportunity in the bordellos of Leith. Jean Brash for one had firmly set her face against such a prospect and, if the story was to be credited, had thrown a man bodily out of an upstairs window of the Just Land because he had dared to leave a mark on one of her girls. Poor fellow, an apothecary by trade, bruised sorely by the impact, but at least he would have had the ointments to treat his contusions. Ah well. No more of that.

Now to begin.

His wife had a loud voice; you could hear it everywhere in the house. These women were silent — a deserved discipline.

Now, the delight.

Young slowly at random turned over one of the photographs. Ah yes — the cagebird. How pretty she appeared. Mouth wide open but not in song.

As he wet his lips the tongue came upon a crumb from the bannock cake lodged in his neat moustache — this was brushed away with a deft forefinger.

Another turned at random.

How splendid — the slave in chains kissing a whip that had already left an imprint upon her. A worshipful handmaiden. What a joyful prospect.

A sudden rattle upstairs startled him for a moment, but it was just the east wind tugging at the window. A natural force but not allowed entry.

As he crouched there like a hobgoblin of sorts, a small tobacco beetle scuttled across the clean floor. Such insects were not encouraged here. Its

137

days were numbered.

So, as a matter of fact, were Mister Young's.

★ ★ ★

While the hansom-cab rattled through the damp, misty streets of Edinburgh, the Reverend William Baines looked sternly at his daughter Sarah and for the umpteenth time wondered what on earth was going on in the girl's mind.

She was spoilt, there was no doubt of that.

In fact, though some freethinking elements might consider him somewhat rigid and fixed by dint of his religion, William did not regard himself a cruel or punitive man.

At times no doubt Sarah thought him harsh of outlook but ever since his beloved wife Mary had passed away to a just reward, he had deemed it his duty to keep this child in check. For her own good, she not knowing decent limitation by dint of a wayward nature.

Mary had been far too soft, a mind affected by a succession of inappropriate books the woman read; this habit she had passed on to her daughter — pondering the holy books that populated the bookshelves in his study was as far as Baines allowed himself.

For when the ultimate truth was sought, were it not in the Bible then it wasn't worth a candle. The most radical William allowed himself to be was a slight preference for the New Testament, though he steered mostly a middle ground like Moses at the Red Sea.

Mary had wheedled him into allowing the girl

to have a painting studio near to Pilrig Street where they lived, and, given the poor soul's state of health, he could scarce refuse — she had always been of fragile disposition and virulent influenza had then taken her to the bosom of the Lord.

He had also, at her urging, persuaded the committee of the church to install stained-glass windows. Mary loved the colours as the far from frequent sun shone its light through. She loved colour — like her daughter.

It could not be denied that Sarah had talent, but as he had remarked to his good friend Lieutenant Roach after both had struck fairly decent drives on the Leith Links golf course, the subject matter that his daughter chose to portray would be a better fit for the police cells than on canvas.

No doubt, however, Sarah would have been happy to sit in Leith station and paint through the bars.

Old women off the streets who had never seen the inside of a holy dwelling in their lives; thank the Almighty, his daughter had at least seen sense and not attempted their male equivalents.

He had threatened that had Sarah done so, the studio would have been barricaded with his own hands. And padlocked to boot.

If she had only been a boy, his life would have been so much simpler. There was a disturbing undercurrent amongst young women now, not all but some, and he feared Sarah might be a victim of this infestation. God had created man and woman for different purposes, and to gainsay that was to defy the Almighty himself.

Whence sprung this desire for independence? For what says Ephesians?

'*Wives, submit yourselves unto your own husbands, as unto the Lord. For the husband is the head of the wife, even as Christ is the head of the church: and he is the saviour of the body. Therefore as the church is subject unto Christ, so let the wives be to their own husbands in every thing.*'

'Father, you're talking to yourself,' Sarah commented. 'Folk in bedlam do such.'

'I was talking to God,' replied William stoutly. 'And he hears all things.'

Sarah had a momentary comical image of an old man with a long beard being assailed on all sides like a golden eagle besieged by a flock of hoodie crows. All these voices; how can you tell one from the other?

Or another more disturbing image of poor Saint Sebastian, his naked body shot through with arrows to cause terrible suffering, miraculously healed but then clubbed to death for speaking against authority.

It would seem speaking out of turn against those in command was never a good idea, unless, perhaps, you were John Knox or arrow-proof.

Poor Saint Sebastian.

When a child, she had come upon a drawing in one of her mother's books and been transfixed by an agony that seemed immeasurable. A martyr Catholicism had made its own, and there was certainly no room for such in Old Greyfriars Kirk, which was to be their present destination.

This was the penance and price she paid for the allowance of the studio.

To be a dutiful daughter. Not one, for instance, that might paint the magpies of the Just Land should a certain elegant bawdy-hoose keeper give permission. The woman had an independence that seemed to transcend politics and religion.

'And what is your sermon tonight, Father?' she asked adopting a guise that she knew one day would be broken. By her own hand.

'Ephesians,' was the terse answer, but then William roused himself from deep reflection to expound a little further. 'You must have heard, of course, about poor Donald Dunwoody?'

An upright member of the congregation whose wife had not long ago run away with a Scandinavian sea-captain.

Sarah had never liked the man Dunwoody and it was a blessing that the couple had no children, but no doubt Martha Young and the other righteous harridans of the congregation would be dining out on the event.

Jenny Dunwoody had seemed a person who would not say boo to a goose, though Sarah might have noted a certain sensual quality to her singing voice and a catlike tread that whalebone might not completely confine.

And what if Sarah did the same? Ran away.

But not with a sailorboy.

Try the headmistress of St Leonard's school,

where young ladies were turned out neat as ninepins.

Or was it all in her imagination that Louisa Lumsden had looked at her with a mischievous glint in her eye at a previous meeting?

And how did Sarah herself feel about this? Confused, would be the answer.

For the next gathering would be at her own studio — would Miss Lumsden be the last to leave?

The cab drew up in front of Greyfriars Kirk and William grunted slightly as he levered himself out of the vehicle to offer up a hand.

He had once been a decent sportsman, a man with which to be reckoned on a rugby field, but now, given only to the odd game of golf, quite portly, his face ruddy with effort, the offered hand a bit puffy, and for a moment she was suddenly struck by a feeling of painful affection.

Every day she grew further away from this man — her father — the seed supplier to her mother's egg, the disseminator of Biblical wisdom who put a roof over her head, would keep her in whalebone and frowned upon change.

In Sarah or in anything.

Yet he was a kind, decent enough soul, mired in a Presbyterian peat bog.

'I am standing here, Sarah,' said William with some asperity. 'Time and tide waits for no man.'

She stifled a smile and took the proffered hand. Neither of them realised that tragedy was a different kind of arrow. One that seldom missed the mark.

18

A carrion crow sat on an oak,
Watching a tailor shape his cloak;
Wife, cried he, bring me my bow,
That I may shoot yon carrion crow.

While Hilton Abercrombie further stiffened indignantly on the cheese table and a dark night began to invade what little light remained in the sky, Jean Brash sat in her kitchen and tried to piece together what she and Hannah Semple had gleaned from investigations so far. Lean back. Take a deep breath.

Her instinct was that Jack Burns had nothing to do with the murder. He might harm in hot temper, but an action such as hoisting Abercrombie on to a complex sexual apparatus and leaving him in suspension there, was, in her surmise, not the man's style. His reaction to her insistent questioning after the girl had left was more of puzzlement than guilt.

Furthermore, Jack had blurted out that, in fact, he had felt like such an idiot the next day for such a loss of temper, even though well justified, that he had called upon the judge's house to express a somewhat stiff and formal apology.

No one had answered the door, and, Jean reflected, it had been a blessing that he did not glance up to the window before turning to go home.

143

That took care of that, then, it would seem.

As her mind drifted back to events of that night and the discovery of the body, she rediscovered something that had been all the time troubling her: why leave the body in such a parlous state, straddling the Berkley Horse — like some obscene joke at the perceived character of the judge?

And why — unless accidental — in the Just Land?

Was this by any chance aimed at her?

Again, Jean had a feeling that the past was poking through the present like a knife through a curtain to effect some stab in the back.

On to the present moment.

After their exchange, the old woman had announced that murder or no murder a body needed sustenance, and was now busy rustling up a fresh egg poached in liver gravy. While the shadowy liquid thickened, she had cut hunks of plain bread to go with the fare that followed — Brie and Roquefort — too smelly for Hannah but a delight for the mistress, who liked to plumb the olfactory depths of La Belle France.

The Orkney cheddar, which the old woman would have relished, had mysteriously disappeared, in point of fact shoved into a drawer in Lily and Maisie's room — the deaf and dumb girl thrown into fierce panic at the inspector's unexpected arrival earlier that day.

Only that very morning, but time being the unique subjective, it might be that an infinite eternity had passed.

Hannah, having dealt with the bread, was now

slicing at a cold but plump howtowdie chicken to augment the rest and had some curly kale boiling in fat stock.

While Jean pondered, a detail struck home as the old woman carved with fierce concentration.

'Is that yon same knife was stuck in Abercrombie's back?'

Hannah nodded. 'I washed it, mind you.'

'Glad to hear so.'

'Waste not, want not.'

The leg of the young chicken was resting on the cutting block — meek as the displayed Saviour.

So, Jack Burns discounted, from what Hannah had brought home, Jean could now see a plausible connection. Might it be that the death of the young boy, John Finch, linked all these men? But then how?

And why the murders?

Why now? What had happened at the workhouse?

Tom Drayton had said *a just punishment that became unjust*. What could that mean?

How to dig deeper? From the sound of it, there were no official reports on that death. The body of John Finch had simply disappeared. If only the judge would do the same. And now she had an attendant complication.

'D'you think McLevy believed you?'

Hannah split the breastbone with a savage cut as her memory went back to the inspector's stolid face, grey eyes like a hunting wolf, while she had spun a hasty tale of meeting Tam Drayton now and then on a New Year's Day to reminisce over old times.

Drayton had left hurriedly, clutching his bottle and muttering of a business appointment to keep. The inspector, of course, would be used to folk quitting company as soon as he arrived.

He had watched Drayton go with a benign air, commended Hannah on her charitable impulses towards the financially afflicted, offered to see her through the harbour and, that offer declined, sauntered out the door again with Mulholland loping after having not said one word.

Shug had watched them quit the place, one hand clutching hard at the purloined coin in his pocket.

'McLevy wouldnae trust his ain mother's milk,' said Hannah.

'What was he doing there anyhow?'

'He didnae say.'

In fact the inspector had found no further information on Alexander Moncrieff from yet another trawl round the lower depths of Leith, although a few times the name of Tam Drayton had been mentioned — the two men sometimes seen together. Moncrieff being notoriously tight had even been seen to buy the man a drink.

Again both McLevy and the constable had noted that even amongst the down and outs, the outcasts, folk spat on the ground as Moncrieff's name was brought to bear. Something about the man made their flesh crawl.

As if he were rotting inside and they feared contagion.

Not much, but since he and Mulholland had found themselves in the harbour vicinity, they

146

had decided to drop into Drayton's haunt, the Rusty Nail.

The inspector had let his quarry quit the place because he knew where the man lived — a house his parents had bought him as a parting gift. That is, Tam departed and they stayed at home to hopefully never see him again.

More would be extracted from the man without Hannah's presence. McLevy had also noted the bottle clutched under Drayton's arm and knew the only business conducted later would be between Tam's mouth and the bottle's contents.

After a bit of meaningless conversation, he had bade the old woman farewell but as he and Mulholland trod the wet cobblestones outside, the constable broke silence after much thought.

'Jean Brash,' he said. 'You're right. She's up to something.'

The inspector nodded agreement with that observation and his own perspicacity, then they disappeared into the gathering gloom leaving the constable's words hanging in the air like oyster catchers on the wing.

Skirly-wheeters, in local parlance. To the oyster it's all the same.

The drappit egg had meanwhile poached to a treat.

Jean broke the skin and the yellow yolk spread out over the gravy in a viscous stain that looked somewhat alarming but tasted like a blessing from heaven. She realised suddenly, as she dipped bread and crammed a far from delicate mouthful in where teeth and tongue meet with passion, that she was ravenously hungry, not having broken fast since a post-murder coffee.

Homicidal investigation demands energy and provokes hunger. No wonder McLevy was always on the scrounge.

Hannah seemed to be in the same frame and the next twenty minutes or so were spent in gluttonous silence as the chicken and curly kale galloped after the poached egg, all washed down with a slosh of claret — fine wine that possibly deserved a little more appreciation than that provided by the two diners.

The cheese came last. Hannah had found a scrap of crowdie that she spread on the crust while Jean took the Roquefort and Brie to task.

Replete — the animal at rest — they both leant back and while Jean wiped at her mouth with a hitherto unused napkin Hannah picked up the carving knife and hit idly upon the chicken bones as if tapping out a message.

'Whit's the next move?' she asked.

The food and wine had awakened a certain carnal impetus in the Mistress of the Just Land. For some reason the image of a near naked Jack Burns flashed into her mind, arrayed as Mercury with little wings on his hat and heels. The Greek costume he wore left a lot to be desired.

Or rather, a great deal to be desired.

But that was not the next move.

She rose from the table and walked into the main salon where the octopus was still busy hauling his prey to the depths of the foaming sea. Jean kept this painting because it reminded her of what happens when you take your eye off a beast that has more suction than might be at your command to resist.

As was the potential of this present case.

After Henry Preger's death she had taken over the Holy Land, sold it quick as being too low class, moved to a slightly better domicile known as the Happy Land — a domicile that had mysteriously burnt down yet had the advantage of being well insured thanks to the immaculate service provided to and from an esteemed and favourable client — and thence to the Just Land with the windfall money.

The best establishment in Edinburgh, undoubtedly in Scotland, possibly in Europe, although Francine of the *soigné chastisement* had sworn to Jean that one in the Rue Chabanais, which had opened recently, might run her close.

This was her kingdom. Her Ship of State. And it was in peril of going under — down to the depths. Never to rise again.

Hannah had followed Jean into the salon, which seemed oddly empty — untenanted of licentious activity. She saw her mistress as if for the first time, standing stock still in the middle of the room. A young wagtail no longer, she was in her prime. Ripe on the bough.

A tall, slim, red-haired beauty so lightly corseted as to be unencumbered by prevailing fashion, ensconced in a lavender-blue gown that had been carefully chosen before recently visiting a certain sculptor and which set off the emerald hue of her eyes.

Green eyes that delivered a cool, intelligent appraisal, in itself a challenge to any male worth his salt, while the hint of a smile was never far away from those lips.

Nature had arranged otherwise than for Jean to be flat-chested and had her flanks been visible, the curves with predatory elegance would have provided more than a little hint of a tigress in the jungle.

Most decidedly a carnivore.

'Let us reprise the situation,' said Jean Brash.

'I'll light the fire,' answered Hannah Semple.

'Do so.'

While the old woman set kindling aflame and placed logs so that the sparks flew up the chimney like shooting stars on an opposite trajectory, Jean observed herself being reflected in all the surrounding mirrors.

Each image with a different story to tell.

An abandoned child, a street nymph apprentice, thralldom to a violent and vicious man, possible purveyor of arsenic or even arson if you believed the rumours, a daft romantic when passion stuck its oar in, a hard-headed businesswoman who could measure a client's financial worth the instant he set foot in her establishment, a dead shot with a derringer: these were only a few of the many faces she wore.

Many masks, but behind them all, one commandment not in the ten:

Wait for your moment, then strike the blow. There will always be one moment — one chance to take — don't miss. One chance.

'To reprise,' said Jean. 'Hilton Abercrombie, a miserable swine but deserving of a justice he did not necessarily extend to others, is plunged in my house and then pinned up like a Christmas decoration.'

'He was stranglet first, mind you,' Hannah interjected as she stuck the iron poker into the heart of the fire to ginger up the logs.

'I was coming to that,' Jean replied. 'Hold your horses.'

One of her images shook its head — a reprise does not welcome interruptions.

'Another man, Alexander Moncrieff, a dirty, low, slavering parasite, is also choked out of life, then hung from on high. Was it to pretend suicide or to imitate an execution? A hangman? Both have a playing card stuck upon their person.'

'Ten and Jack o' Spades,' contributed Hannah, who enjoyed a good game of cards.

Another image pursed lips in disapproval as an opposite took up the tale.

'I find a list with both of their names on it plus some others, in Abercrombie's safe, along with an envelope of photographs that deserve to be burnt but best hold on to them in case of traceable evidence — all might be connected to a death in a home where they held sway as governors and that slavering Moncrieff had rule. The dead boy, John Finch. That much we know for sure.'

Hannah had stopped poking. The fire was fine.

'If ye can call anything from Tam Drayton a sure thing.'

The feeling that the man had been laughing up his sleeve as if he held something back still

151

worried the old woman, but there was enough damned complication as it was. Better keep this one to herself.

'It's all we've got for now,' said Jean. 'But we need to make a move. If I know McLevy, and I know him as well as anyone can, he's on the hunt. He may not know it yet but he can smell that corpse. Only a matter of time and time is in short supply.'

There was a tension building up in her, but to go with that, a feeling of outrage and indignation. The other side of fear.

'So whit do we do?'

Jean had a secret pocket fashioned into all her fashionable gowns — the folds of crinoline were perfect for a snug little nook where a derringer could hide.

In answer to Hannah's question and also a sudden blind impulse from her deepest self, Jean pulled out the gun, let out a howl close to a witch's eldritch shriek and shot the octopus right between the eyes.

The monster did not let go but Hannah Semple jumped out of her skin.

'Holy God! Whit for did you commit that Mistress?'

As a wisp of smoke curled up from the barrel of the derringer, Jean reminded herself to replace the bullet later and get the painting fixed.

The gun contained only two shots, dismissed by a certain police inspector as not nearly powerful enough for any charging foe, but Jean hated to spoil the clean lines of her close-fitting gowns with anything larger.

Fashion will out.

'It's a signal,' she replied.

'Whit the hell *kind* of signal?'

'It means I'm coming out fighting.'

While Hannah chewed that over, Jean noted with some satisfaction that she had hit exactly where aimed. A shot to the head will arrest anything but a hurtling rhino and there are few of that particular species to be found in Leith.

'Fighting how?' Hannah responded finally.

'Start with one of the names on that list. Find out what he can tell about Finch's death.'

'How do you do that?'

'Alone.'

'Eh?'

'You heard me.'

The look in her eye brooked no argumentation and it made sense. However and whatever manipulations the mistress used to tease out the truth, it might be easier without a witness.

But a damned sight more dangerous.

'Go for the weakest, then?'

'No. Not the weakest. I'll go for the man who thinks he's the strongest.'

Jean had a look in her eye that Hannah had rarely seen before. It was reflected in every mirror.

A tiger on the prowl.

19

Will you wake him?
No, not I.
For if I do,
He'll be sure to cry.

The Smiler felt his way along the catacomb wall with great caution. He had forgotten his fancy-dan gloves and bare hands and fingers registered the clammy, dank suction in the brick like a mould settling over his skin.

Under cover of darkness it had been easy to squeeze through the door, lift the hidden grill on ground level, but then to lower himself down into the depths — even though he'd done it the once before, although that was in daylight, such an action set up a pounding in his heart. Like entering another existence.

In this pitch black he might as well be sightless — a blind traveller with an unknown destination.

He had been relying on Jeb hearing his voice and supplying a light of sorts, however, he had called the name a few times and received no answer. The dwarf might well be out scavenging, despite having made arrangements to meet this night.

A foot slipped on the slimy muddy surface below to send some sticky liquid shooting up his nice clean socks into his nice clean shoes and he stifled a curse.

Like an eyeless monster in the dark, he stumbled onwards, driven by a fierce anger. That bastard Laidlaw was playing them for fools. He had stuffed his fat face, drunk his fill and then left the Bristol men hanging like paper dolls.

They had made their best offer but he had smirked in apparent regret and told them that it did not measure up. Laidlaw had so many mouths to feed, he informed them, like cuckoos in the nest. His eyes were hard as a mason's chisel.

Of course, the councillor could be bluffing and might be all sweetness and light tomorrow. But if not? The game would be up and gone.

As he looked at the man's greasy chops and waxed moustache, the porcine glint of greed in the beady little eyes, that was when Dirk had decided to kill two birds with the one stone.

With Laidlaw out of the picture and the man below him in their pocket, the way, after a small tincture of bureaucratic mourning, would be smooth and trouble-free. All it would take was a death.

And yet there was a questioning voice to that decision: how had it come to this?

The first murders had been at Jeb's urging, but now the taste for blood was Dirk's own. Part of him, alarmed at what was running in his veins, had toyed with the idea of closing the deal and leaving the city, leave Jeb to his own devices. But now it had all changed.

The deal could not yet be closed. He would have to stay and see it out.

The Smiler had come to an opening that

surely led to Jeb's hidey-hole — he could hear a whimpering, mewling sound that set his teeth on edge.

'Jeb?' he whispered. 'It's Dirk. Are you there?'

The mewling noise became louder and Dirk knocked against a waxy object set into a cut in the wall. His eyes were growing used to the gloom — a candle, it was a candle with a box of matches beside, no doubt kept there by the owner of this fine establishment.

He lit a match, then the candle and the pale glimmer revealed Jeb's lair with the man himself shrunk into the furthest corner. The dwarf held the limp form of a small animal in his hands, cradling the thing as if it were a sacred relic.

Dirk recognised this bundle as the white rat. And the mewling noise was Jeb crying — for certain the tears were rolling down his alabaster face.

Surely the crazy wee bastard was not in grief over a dead rodent?

'He wis poisoned,' Jeb muttered brokenly. 'Some dirty swine. Did for him. See!'

He held out the unmoving form, which lay draped over his hands like a French pancake.

'He made it back. Then he spat and coughed and jumped and jumped. Then — he went dead.'

Not unlike the judge was an errant thought that came into Dirk's mind. He found it hard to make response. How do you mourn a poisoned rat?

'That's bad luck,' he managed.

Jeb laid the dead body down carefully in a corner.

'I'll make a wee box for him. Bury him proper.'

'Did he have a name?' asked Dirk, feeling like a fool but better humour the runty maniac.

'Beastie,' Jeb answered. 'Jist Beastie.'

The dwarf's hand was palm up and the long cut, healed long ago but marked still, was visible on his white skin. Dirk had a brainwave and laid his own hand beside the other, scar for scar.

'Vengeance, eh? For everybody.'

Jeb's pale eyes raised up and he nodded slowly in shared memory.

★ ★ ★

They had found out the next day that Johnny Finch was dead. An accidental heart attack, a bolt from the blue, a blessing of the lord — certainly not the result of a vicious beating. The body removed before a soul could see it and then a solemn ceremony some time later when the boys were given tea and cakes and dressed up clean while the governors, who usually visited only once a year came out of turn and spoke solemnly to the assembled company. A memorial of lies.

The last one was a minister. To Dirk's eyes he looked uneasy as he intoned a prayer for the dead. It was never mentioned, and the boys did not dare ask, where Johnny was buried. In a scaffie cart, probably.

Then the governors left. The guilty bastards. A judge, a merchant, a man of God — and a dirty, fat, slobbery councillor. They departed but

Moncrieff stayed on, a sly, insidious smile on his face. All friends now. Dirk and his wee pal would get special privileges. All friends.

Dirk wasn't sure how this had come about but he took advantage, shameful advantage, sookin' up to Moncrieff as if the man were his best friend. However, that was not the case, Johnny had died under that scaly murderous eye.

But one thing Moncrieff had not known. The night Johnny died the two could not sleep and in the early morning Jeb produced a long nail that he'd scavenged from somewhere. It was cleaned and sharpened to an edge that would cut through glass — although glass was not what Jeb had in mind.

Dirk watched with bedevilled fascination as the point sliced across Jeb's palm to leave a thin trail of red that broadened into a dark stream. As if in a dream he held out his hand and Jeb cut across. He hardly felt pain but when Dirk stole a look down the same stream flowed. Jeb's fierce grip hooked into his palm and blood mixed as their hands touched.

Johnny was dead. No one gave a damn.

'One day,' said Jeb Summers. 'Vengeance.'

★   ★   ★

That blood had long dried, of course, but the line still held firm.

'They killed your wee beastie, jist lik' Johnny.'

To this statement of Dirk's that he couched for a moment in the rough tongue of Leith, Jeb nodded a solemn agreement. The Smiler felt a

158

spasmodic tremble right down to his groin.

Two birds. One stone.

Jeb produced the wire garrotte and passed it over to Dirk.

'Your turn,' said Jeb. 'This time.'

20

I went to the toad that lies under the wall,
I charmed him out and he came at my call.

For Barton Laidlaw this was the perfect end to a perfect day. He had so much enjoyed the sick look on the faces of the Bristol men. They had raised their offer, but not quite enough, he could surely squeeze a dribble or two more out of them tomorrow. To be truthful, there was indeed a Liverpool consortium but their bid was well below the Bristol tender.

Nothing pleased him more than clever manipulation and the rewards it brought.

Last night, for instance, at the Just Land, a quiet word with Judge Abercrombie as regards an upcoming case of embezzlement — a dear friend of Laidlaw's who would surely benefit from a light sentence. Of course, the judge would never be swayed from rectitude, but the merest hint of certain photographs had been enough.

Abercrombie's face had registered a cold dislike but he had not outright rejected this plea for clemency.

What a delight it was to know so many secrets. So many supplied by Alexander Moncrieff — a valuable and loyal servant; what a pity to hear of his bizarre and mysterious death, though the fellow had, to a certain extent, brought it upon himself.

Foolish man to lay hands upon that young girl. Laidlaw had recommended him for the position after the workhouse death, but Barton was not a governor at the new establishment and so could not once more protect him. Moncrieff had been lucky only to be dismissed and not prosecuted also, for fear of the scandal. Now he was gone.

However, no doubt someone would take his place. So sweep that aside!

For presently Laidlaw sat opposite one of the most attractive and beguiling women in the city who also seemed to be in need of his help.

How would she pay? Handsomely for sure. What a delight.

A note had been delivered to his door, eliciting a quick reply. What else might a gentleman do?

The note itself he stored carefully in a small drawer inside his ornate walnut desk to be transferred later to the safe for who knew when such, in future, might be useful? To that purpose as well, he marked the date upon it — his memory was excellent, but better safe than sorry.

Not long after his own missive had been sent, in immediate reply came a soft knock at the door. A cloaked and hooded figure entered, the hood was thrown back, disguise discarded and there was Jean Brash. In all her glory.

She sat nursing her pretty doeskin gloves that were now stained by uncouth raindrops, perhaps a little distraught, perhaps a little brittle of manner. Perhaps a mistaken conclusion or was something eating at her like a rat in the skull?

Barton had no interest at all in women, but power was quite another matter.

For instance, this particular female charged him a high amount for the occasional nights of 'entertainment' he laid on for important visiting dignitaries. Many's the time Barton had tried to negotiate more moderate contribution but been met with a blunt refusal; indeed, it was rather difficult to avoid the thought that Mistress Brash might not be overly fond of him.

Yet this might be about to change. Whatever he had to offer would cost. Perhaps in the form of a reduction in charges; perhaps in the form of no charge at all. With perhaps some champagne thrown in. Or quite a lot of the best quality.

What a delight.

A little small talk had been exchanged as regards the inclement weather for a heavy squall had made its bow, and now he waited like a spider in the web.

And it was an opulent web, for Laidlaw's house was surprisingly lush in curtains and hangings. He himself was arrayed in a brocaded dressing gown the like of which he saw no reason to change — certainly not apposite for council chambers but perfect for receiving a bawdy-hoose keeper.

As were the Turkish house slippers that ensconced his surprisingly dainty and well-tended feet.

From Jean's point of view, she had always detested Laidlaw. He was a slimy opportunist who controlled the city council like a puppet master and hid his venality behind a hearty and affable exterior.

That bleached-moon face and those waxed

whiskers always reminded her of a corrupt children's toy, the little eyes like two glass buttons in the doughy flesh.

'I need some information from you, Mister Laidlaw,' she commenced. '*Important* information.'

'I am yours to command, dear lady,' was the smooth reply as he wondered idly why she had refused the offer to remove her vivid lilac outdoor coat. It was liberally sprinkled with rain and she had obviously been walking a while before finding a cab, so why sit in the damp? Unless she did not intend to stay for an extensive period.

He would decide that, however — keep her dangling for as long as he pleased. And to that end he lit up a fine cigar and blew out a spiral of smoke from delicately pursed lips. Style maketh the man.

'Though, of course, information may come at a price,' he murmured. 'However I am sure we can utilise the maxim *fair exchange is no robbery.*'

He wheezed a little in laughter.

Jean's lips tightened. Normally a practice she tried to avoid because of the lines it might leave on the face, but in this case there was an inner distaste that could not be denied.

Barton blew a smoke ring with evidential pleasure — he had a blazing fire going in the hearth and the place was stifling hot. Laidlaw liked it that way.

'A boy died,' she said. 'His name was Finch. John Finch.'

163

Laidlaw stopped wheezing. Laughter frozen.

'I regret, Mistress Brash, that I cannot be of assistance, the name means nothing.'

'A Charity workhouse. In Leith. He died there. Four governors. You were one of them.'

'Ah. So long ago. I remember the workhouse, of course, a fine institution but, sadly, having served its purpose, it was closed and the unfortunates therein . . . transferred to a larger institution.'

'It was sold, was it not?'

'Was it?'

'At a good profit.'

'Really?'

'You should know; you owned it.'

For a moment there was a flicker of unease in his eyes. So Drayton's information to Hannah was, at least in this instance, correct.

'I have so many . . . business transactions,' Laidlaw murmured. 'And such fallible memory.'

Time to unsheathe the claws.

'John Finch. What happened?'

'As I have said, the name means naught to me.'

'You're a liar.'

It was as if Jean had slapped him straight across the face and she noted with some satisfaction that one of his podgy plump hands had clenched into a fist.

'That is an unfortunate remark, Mistress Brash.'

'It is, however, accurate. You're a liar.'

'I refute that accusation.'

'Refute and be damned. You're a liar.'

164

Laidlaw swelled up like a bullfrog, his face blotchy with outrage.

'I'm afraid I must ask you, madam, to leave this house on the instant!'

His words hung in the air and then disappeared like the previous smoke rings — his cigar no longer inhaled or desired, having died in the fat fingers.

'Leave this house!'

A repeated and thunderous command and yet the woman sat there.

Something in her stillness should have warned Laidlaw, who, though a far from admirable man, was not a stupid one.

'John Finch,' she repeated. 'What happened?'

Laidlaw pulled himself out of his armchair and thought to tower over the seated figure in a menacing fashion, but this threat was ignored save for her steady scrutiny of his rage-flushed face.

She then said two words that punctured him like a child's balloon.

'Betty Driver.'

* * *

The door crashed open and the three men in the room were startled into motion. Two younger specimens, diving for their clothes, the third older and flabbier, flailing around to somewhat pathetically try covering his groin area as if that would somehow render him invisible.

The two burly men who had kicked through the portal were unimpressed. Glasgow police

165

often are. The larger man, a Highlander, Campbell by name and clan, shook his head at the sight as if they had disturbed a rock and the creepy-crawlies underneath had displayed their awful scuttling world for all to see. He then turned and left to join what seemed a continuing fracas in other places as high-pitched voices pitched even higher, fuelled by outrage and indignation.

The remaining man — a sergeant, Duncan Adams — looked at the quivering mollusc on the bed.

'This is going tae cost ye,' he announced.

★ ★ ★

Jean's voice cut into a most unwelcome memory.

'Betty keeps a Molly House at the top of Hope Street in our rival city of the west. But she's a forgetful wee soul and missed her payments to certain members of the constabulary. It goes on everywhere, of course, but we're more sleekit on the east coast.

'Anyway, she forgot. So she was raided to be taught a lesson. And so were you. Taught a lesson.'

Laidlaw was still standing, but all the strings that held him together had been cut.

'You bribed your way out of it but had to sign a confession. The sergeant concerned fell on hard times. He sold the confession back to Betty.'

In fact Laidlaw had never returned to the place or the city, hoping that it would all be

166

forgotten. He had lived in abject fear for a while, but then, as time went by and no ugly repercussions sounded in his ears, thought himself to be in the clear.

But no man is ever in the clear.

Jean continued, speaking in a quiet, confidential tone that made the words a deal more deadly.

'Betty and I meet every so often, mostly my treat . . . she prefers the cake shops in Princes Street. Just a chance to catch up and share high tea. Passed the confession on to me. Never liked you; always trying to get something for nothing, she said. I couldn't agree more.'

In fact Jean was bluffing like the high-class poker player she could have been, had Mistress Brash the notion taken.

Betty had indeed told her about the event and the confession, but Sergeant Duncan Adams had been thrown out of the force for bribery and corruption, and disappeared from sight — the confession long ago destroyed, no doubt.

Barton Laidlaw, however, didn't know such and Jean was gambling that because she had the other facts on hand, he would crumple like a soggy sugar biscuit.

If he asked to see the paper, she would simply reply that she was not a blind fool and the confession was in the safe keeping of her lawyers — it would see the light of day if and when it suited.

But he didn't even ask. He just stood there. Stricken.

'Sit back down,' she commanded.

167

Barton did so. Like a jellyfish.

Jean took the derringer out and held it in her lap, just for good measure.

While he quivered, she was adamantine. She pointed with the gun to the floor in front of her and he slid off the chair to land on his knees, at a spot beside the still blazing fire.

'Now my good man,' said Jean, trying to suppress an unwarranted giggle that threatened to undo the deadly seriousness of the situation. 'You will tell me everything that happened with John Finch and if I smell or sense that you are in any way lying, that confession will wing its way to the newspapers and you will be torn to pieces.'

The bluff, for sure, was not called for. Who is to say that we, all of us, do not live in fear of the awful day when the truth about ourselves is finally uncovered and we are revealed in our dreadful naked lack of splendour — not unlike a plucked howtowdie chicken?

Barton Laidlaw gazed into the unwavering barrel of the derringer and his waxed moustache began to droop at both ends.

Melting in the heat.

21

As I went over the water,
The water went over me.
I saw two little blackbirds
Sitting on a tree.
One called me a rascal,
And one called me a thief,
I took up my little black stick
And knocked out all their teeth.

The rain was still sweeping across the streets, driven by gusts of wind that signalled a hard year ahead.

The Smiler cursed silently to himself, but Jeb Summers seemed impervious.

As the drops ran over the other's face, Dirk was weirdly reminded of Finch's spittle sliding down and wee runtie Jeb laughing fit to burst.

Things were not going to plan.

They had been about to effect entrance to Laidlaw's big house in Warriston Crescent — a row of fine, secluded houses that curved down towards the Water of Leith — when a hansom-cab pulled up, a muffled female figure had descended, tugged the bell rope and then been admitted inside.

Now they were stuck until the bloody woman came out again and the rain was hard and slanty, in stair-rods from the east, straight into their faces where they crouched by some iron railings

169

at the side of a garden.

The hour was late. Anyone with any sense had quit the streets and only potential murderers kept vigil.

Dirk's nerves were shot. He had been ready to do the deed in the heat of a moment, but now it was cold and wet — hot deeds don't enjoy the wet and cold.

They had waited a fair time, give it another few minutes and he was off — it was a fault of his — he could not endure. Not be still. He had to be on the move.

Jeb just sat there like a garden ornament.

'It's not going to work,' Dirk muttered. 'That bitch could be his mistress. He could be on the bones right now. She might stay till morning. Banging the drum.'

'Wait!'

As Dirk shifted restively, Jeb had spotted the door opening. Sure enough, out she came. For a moment the woman drew back the hood and her face was revealed.

Jean Brash.

They were both taken very much aback.

'Whit's *she* doin' here?'

Jeb's hissed comment received no immediate answer but Dirk felt uneasy. He had waited to hear news of the judge's body being discovered but nothing had transpired. Had the whores dumped the corpse? That would make sense but what didn't was her turning up in this time and place. Although Dirk had gloried in the fact that she had not recognised him at the Just Land, he was still nervous Jean might aim a

170

finger in his direction.

Out of the blue.

Of course, it could just be coincidence, but he worried that when lines cross, accidentally or not, the point of contact could be explosive and dangerous.

As if to illustrate, the woman did something that put the fear of God into him. She threw back her head and let out a howl that echoed through the air before being doused by the rain.

Like an animal. A hunting animal.

He crouched down behind Jeb and they watched as the figure stayed still for a moment as if listening to the echoes then pulled the hood over her face again and headed off at a brisk pace, almost at a run, boots splashing through the puddles, no doubt heading for Broughton Road where she might more easily search out another cab. Or a throat to cut.

Jeb frowned — an indication of thought above his usual feral instincts.

'Whit the hell wis that for?'

'I don't know.'

But the sound had troubled the Smiler: animals that hunt usually have a prey in mind. Be that as it may, the rain was still lashing down.

The dwarf grinned. The coast was clear.

'Your turn now,' said Jeb Summers.

Inside the house, Barton Laidlaw, hands shaking, lifted up a large glass of brandy and poured it down. The fiery liquid burnt a path through his gullet and hit the stomach like a fireball.

He gasped and tried to shut out the memory

of what had just happened, yet the random images and words haunted him, spinning round his mind without mercy.

His craven acquiescence to Jean Brash — he had, at her feet, grovelled like a terrified dog afraid of a beating, and told everything.

Everything he knew. All he *could* tell, the words spilling out like so many maggots from a corpse at the wayside.

He had seen a horse once, dead in a ditch and the white fibrous worms already at their work: a seething mass swarming over the flesh as if they had sprouted from the intestines. Spilling out.

Another hard slam of spirit went down and the habit of a lifetime took over.

He was still alive, he could still find room to lie low and survive.

Mendacity never fails.

Avoid the Just Land, avoid public performance, take a back seat, play the humble councillor. True, he would always be her creature, but what harm could she inflict if he kept out of her way and caused no offence? And if she tried to corrupt him with threat, that was fine.

He was used to corruption; he would do as she asked. Corruption would be easy.

Yet the bleak contempt in her eyes was hard to forget, as was the way she had drawn in her skirts when standing up as if to avoid contamination. He had still been crouching on the floor, not daring to raise his eyes as he heard her voice.

'Have you told *everything*?'

He had produced a gurgling, cowed noise like a good, obedient cur.

Then she issued a last demand. It shook him to the core but he had no option but to do as commanded. At least he could get off his knees to fulfil and provide. And after that he had nothing left to give.

She had left, and he had gone for the brandy. One more drink. Just for luck. He was still alive!

A bang of the doorknocker startled him.

Had the woman come back to torment him? How unfair. That would not be a delight. His wits were scattered. So. He crossed to the curtains and peeked out into the street. Hard to see in the pouring rain. Yes. It was one of the Bristol men.

Laidlaw cheered up. The fellow must have come with a better offer. This was good. A last killing, a triumph. A deal of money. Then perhaps he could sell the house, leave — another country, another land — the New World.

Or even Paris. The French are free and easy. Careful though, careful; let not the brandy make a fool out of you.

Laidlaw looked at his image in a mirror, tweaked his moustache back to a nice sharp point. Himself again.

He went to the front door and opened it.

The man stood there with something at his back. A dog or creature of some kind.

'I've come to pay,' he said. 'A reckoning.'

Barton Laidlaw smiled in triumph.

He was still alive!

22

Let's go to the wood, says this pig,
What to do there? says that pig.
To look for my mother, says this pig,
What to do with her? says that pig.
Kiss her to death, says this pig.

Another knock upon another door and Jack Burns frowned to be disturbed at this late hour. It was near eleven, and he had been putting together a rough papier mâché structure on the Pallas Athena theme, using outlines from his sketches of Sarah Baines.

Some of the curvaceous linear swoops he would have to add from imagination, especially the breasts, the reality being pert enough but not remotely up to Olympian standards.

The structure, once smoothed and sanded, would act as a guideline of sorts when the block was eventually put in place for him to begin carving in stone.

Not life size — that he could not afford — but he had in mind something of, say, two to three feet, on a plinth, reclining — almost as if the goddess was coming out of the rock itself.

A revelation. A new order emerging.

Jack's body ached from the amount of energy expended these many hours, and therefore he had not welcomed the knocking.

That is, until he opened the door to find

himself facing a verdant creature, sleek lilac coat glistening with water like a mythical sea creature, the hood thrown back, fiery red hair and eyes glittering like a serpent from the depths.

Somewhat short of breath, however, for she had run all the way from Warriston Crescent, happily for the most part downhill, to get here — howling like a moonstruck wolf at various times.

The creature walked past Jack without a word and stopped before the papier mâché persona.

'Your goddess looks a bit the worse for wear,' said Jean Brash. 'But I'm glad the fire still holds true.'

Indeed, Jack had banked up the embers not long ago but a lack of warmth was the last thing on his mind. He felt as if he were standing before another elemental being that might wreak havoc at any moment.

As regards Jean, what Laidlaw confessed had sent her blood pounding and senses racing. She was on the chase.

But who was the predator and who the prey? That can change in an instant as any mantis male can tell you.

She had once pursued a brief affair with an insectologist from Italy and the man, though no great shakes as a lover (Italian men being over-occupied with their mothers) was a treasure trove of fascinating facts as regards the sexual lore of nature's wee beasties.

The female mantis often indulges in post-coital cannibalism with a far from willing mate, who, as it were, has got in the wrong position at the wrong time.

He represents, for the recently conjoined female, the nearest source of provender. She being hungry for more of the same, whereas the male is looking for a nice long rest.

Which is what he gets as she eats him alive.

Having told her of this, the insectologist became rather disturbed at a certain gleam in Jean's eye. Perhaps he sensed that, to paraphrase the immortal Bard of Ayrshire, like King David of old with the daughters of Jerusalem, *he raised their blood up intae flames he couldna' drown for a' that.*

So it is never certain — when you are on the hunt — if somebody might be at the same time hunting you. Leap forward mouth agape, but keep a weather eye open behind.

'Might I offer you a hot . . . morsel of drink?' asked Jack Burns, a little nonplussed that, having burst into his studio, the woman had fallen silent as the grave.

'How did you describe that goddess?'

She had turned and smiled while delivering the question and at the same time slipping off the coat to drape it over the papier mâché effigy.

A poor imitation of the real thing.

Jean wore a simple white yet elegantly shaped blouse with a high-waisted skirt, and as far as Jack could discern, a complete absence of whalebone.

A woman unconfined.

Gardyloo!

The toe of her right boot tapped impatiently

176

on the wooden floor, obviously waiting for an answer.

'I believe I may have said,' he responded carefully, for this was no moment to get things wrong, 'lean-flanked and fertile-breasted.'

'In that case I think I may just qualify, but now I remember it was the virginal part that created a difficulty.'

'I'm prepared to overlook that,' he managed while the fire shot a little spark heavenwards. She laughed suddenly. Full-throated. Vibrant.

'Are you now?'

From what she could see, he had a hard, muscular body, the aforenoted strong, gripping hands, and, though needing a shave, a strong enough jawline.

'I don't like men with fallible chins,' she murmured. 'It betokens a lack of substance and stamina.'

Jack rubbed at his jaw.

'I'm sure I could last the course,' he remarked boldly, ignoring a slight tic that had appeared at the corner of his left eye.

'That's in the lap of the gods, is it not?' was her reply. 'In the lap of the gods. As are we all.'

This was foolish prattle and Jean knew it, but she had a sensual current running like a high tide and a girl has to have fun sometime, even when investigating murder.

She wondered if McLevy ever felt similar urges when urgent on the case. Possibly not. Though that again might explain the sugar biscuits and a few wee collisions between them.

Time to make a move before she lost the

notion and common sense made an uninvited intervention.

She looked towards the bed, which was crumpled and crammed into a corner of the room. A mattress on the floor — *paillasse* the French would call it.

Jack winced at the sight, the tic beating a little more insistently.

'I'm afraid I lead . . . a very simple life.'

'Well,' said the Mistress of the Just Land. 'Let's see if we can complicate it up a wee bit.'

He came towards her a mite awkwardly and Jean thought it best to meet him halfway.

'By the by,' she whispered, for now they were at close quarters like two ships about to grapple. 'Where's your cat?'

'He — he goes out at night.'

'What's his name?'

'Horace.'

'Like the Latin poet?'

'I expect so.'

She roared again with that full-throated laughter and then slipped into his arms while the papier mâché goddess, now under modest cover, did not move a muscle.

Out in the darkness, Horace, who was not neutral and certainly would not have welcomed such, arched his back and walked stiff-legged across the high roof slates as he displayed his manly charms to a black cat named Bathsheba who called in now and again to James McLevy's attic room and was often treated to a saucer of milk.

A feline seductress, who, like her namesake,

178

spent a lot of life on the tiles.

Mark you, the original Bathsheba could well plead innocence of the riveting effect her naked body had on the aforementioned King David. However, bathing nude in the open air on a rooftop with overhanging voyeuristic royalty, might well have attendant consequences.

From a Biblical roof to the slippery slates of Leith, the art of enchantment knows no bounds.

Female cats are in the main wary of masculine insertion from their opposites, due to the barbs that cut in both directions.

This does not apply to bawdy-hoose keepers.

23

Four and twenty tailors
Went to kill a snail,
The best man among them
Durst not touch her tail.

In the time that followed events of the night before a few things happened, all of them connected in one way or another to a kind of awakening.

Jack Burns reached out in his sleep and found an empty space where the goddess had been. Not only that but Horace the cat was sitting on his chest and yowling to be fed, having earned his corn the previous night.

Like his master.

The sculptor sat up with a start, shoving Horace to the floor, and while the cat stalked indignantly towards its empty tin bowl, Jack looked around his studio.

Empty.

The papier mâché figure, however, seemed to have a faintly enigmatic smile upon her face; or was that just artistic imagination?

★ ★ ★

Mary Pettigrew screamed loud enough to call the dead from their tombs in the nearby

Warriston cemetery. She had cleaned for Barton Laidlaw these many years, never been paid a decent wage or given any kind of festive gift, but needed the miserable swine's pittance to keep a large family in some kind of bearable circumstance.

Her husband worked as a cobbler, an honest man nowadays from what was once a life of crime, but he just needed to look at her sideways and Mary found herself with another Pettigrew on the doorstep. If Donnie would just stick to the last, life would be a deal simpler, heel and sole.

She had found the street door slightly open on her morning arrival, which was odd but not near the heights of a further peculiarity upon entrance, when she discovered her employer's velvet Turkish slippers with the gormless, in Mary's opinion, turned-up toes undulating before her eyes.

The dance of the Far Eastern slippers had been initiated by the draught from her opening of the front portal.

The rest of Barton's body dangled above, a rope round its fat neck. It was hanging from an iron bolt in the shape of a spear that protruded from a shield high upon the wall — the shield bore the badge and motto of the Scott clan to which the Laidlaws were affiliated, and the motto on the crest was *AMO*: 'I love'.

Adding insult to injury, under further breeze and resultant movement, the velvet slipper slowly detached itself and slid gently off to land on the carpet below like a nesting bird, leaving a bare foot behind with — to Mary's incremental horror — painted toenails.

Another, even louder, scream winged its way across the turgid air of Warriston Crescent to disturb the somnolent ducks on the nearby Water of Leith.

★ ★ ★

And it was yet only the second day of a New Year.

More bells ringing unto the Lord.

The Smiler woke in his hotel bed and felt strangely unmoved by the transactions of the night before, as if he had become, in sleep, hardened to mortal guilt; as if his soul had been pickled overnight.

His mind, however, was clear — a later morning meeting with the relevant council members (if Laidlaw was not there, and he most certainly would fail to be so, then his deputy was on hand) tie up the deal as far as possible and take the man aside to oil the wheels of decision-making.

He and his business partner would operate full tilt in the absence of Barton Laidlaw — one in knowledge, one in hope. Full tilt. All guns blazing.

Yes, it would entirely fall into place. And if news of the death by any chance arrived early, then throw up hands in horror but still take the deputy aside.

The man hated his superior in any case.

It would all fall into place. Dirk's toes twitched and he felt that thrill straight down to his groin. What he would not give for a magpie now!

He heard the clink of a tea tray. Room service. It would be porridge and fresh rolls.

Dirk was ravenous. The smell of fried ham was wafting up the corridor. He had ordered that dish as well and if there was black pudding on hand, so much the better. And eggs. Poached. He loved poached eggs. Two on the plate.

For a moment he entertained the disconcerting image of Laidlaw's bulging optics just after his rancid soul had departed to an unknown destination — sent on its way through an inexpert hauling on Jeb's thick wire by the Smiler, who had the man pinned to the floor, knee in the middle of the back, face down while the assassin heaved up.

When the struggles ceased, they turned the body over and before them were the poached-egg eyes.

Jeb had giggled and shaken his head in mock reproof at the untidy execution of his craft.

A sharp sound disturbed this pleasant dream. Retribution?

Knock, knock. Ah, yes. Room service had finally arrived and Dirk could smell the ham through the door.

He was already fully dressed and in celebration shot out his shirt cuffs, one of which was lacking a small gemstone but that fact had not yet come to his attention.

He had also ordered a box of cigars to be sent

up. After the meal he would smoke his fill.

This was the life.

★　★　★

Jeb Summers had risen early. He slept little.

Last night he had scratched another drawing on the wall. A hanging man with turned-up toes. It pleased him well enough but his albino face was sombre.

A burial to take place. The white rat carefully wrapped in a fine piece of silk brocade lining that he had ripped from the inside of Laidlaw's dressing gown.

Dirk Martins had winced at such desecration but considering the Smiler had just killed a man, he could hardly take much of the high ground.

And he'd made a terrible mess of what should have been, when all was said and done, a simple strangulation.

The dwarf looked down at the tidy, dignified package he'd made to hold his best friend. Death without dignity is a terrible thing. Jeb had already dug a little grave in the corner of the cave, with a rough cross to add once the hole was filled in once more.

His eyes filled again with tears as he laid the rat down tenderly and then began to scrape the earth over.

Two more to go. Tobacco and the holy man.

God rest the wee beastie.

★　★　★

Tam Drayton was never sure of the difference between being awake and its opposite. Or rather, his sleep was so much like a fever of images sprouting other gargoyle offshoots, that he could hardly tell one state from the other.

Especially after his little session with McLevy — there was something about the inspector's grey eyes which unnerved him. Tam had kept carefully to the story concerning the first part of what Hannah Semple had asked and how he had responded to her.

Which was that she'd been curious about the death of Moncrieff for some reason and wanted to know the history of the man. Tam made no mention of the list. Should McLevy follow it up, he could rely on the old woman providing little more than a bare minimum.

The inspector had been more than curious about Jean Brash's part in all this and here Tam could, for once, risk veracity. From what Hannah said, the Mistress of the Just Land had a finger in the pie, but he knew no more than that.

The ways of that woman were dark and mysterious, as the inspector and the whole of Leith well knew.

Luckily Tam had been drinking hard — he could slur the words. Drink is a great refuge and so is letting a snotter escape from one of your nasal passages to then give it a slovenly wipe with a grubby handkerchief. Constable Mulholland had sniffed in distaste but McLevy did not even blink.

They finally left his house — a house near the Kirkgate that his dear mamma and papa had bought to get rid of him, his presence in the family home being no longer parentally cherished.

Tam was glad to see the police go out into the night. He had pulled out his one fine possession, a slim, curved Meerschaum pipe, the bowl of which he had filled with best hashish flakes, fired himself into oblivion and then plunged into a jagged sleep from which he had just this moment awoken.

Of course, there was so much more he knew about certain aspects of all this — so much that he kept for his own use — and had he realised that McLevy was following like a wolf on the trail, he would have told Hannah Semple nothing at all.

It had amused him to spin a tale to her. But he feared that might have been a foolish act. Too late now. He had a busy day ahead. A talented day. Creative.

The whisky bottle was near empty and he neatly emptied the dregs into a chipped eggcup before throwing it back in one gulp.

Never do, to drink from the neck.

A gentleman never performs so.

★ ★ ★

Sarah Baines had slept like a child. Her room was pristine and well kept — not a hair out of place — and she maintained it deliberately so. No one on looking in could guess the ferment in her blood.

Today was the meeting. At her studio. Miss

186

Louisa Lumsden would address them and put fire in Sarah's belly. A sermon of sorts.

Her father believed Sarah to be a virgin and — sadly — he was correct.

How would Miss Lumsden look, naked on a chaise longue, eating a bunch of grapes?

A perfect portrait.

Pallas Athena be damned.

★　★　★

William Baines and Gavin Young awoke in their respective resting places, one clutching his Bible, the other in the mountainous shadow of his wife.

They had both been to church and heard Baines's discourse upon a new year of uxorial obedience — water off a duck's back as far as Martha was concerned, but all congregational eyes had turned to the empty pew seat beside Donald Dunwoody.

Death also leaves a space that cannot be filled.

★　★　★

James McLevy hardly ever slept a wink due to the amount of ingested coffee. Of poor quality and badly made by himself as a rule, unless he might scrounge some brew from a certain bawdy-hoose keeper with impeccable taste in fine grinding.

Hers was from the Lebanon, his from the marketplace — poor quality but drunk in copious quantities while poring over various forensic papers upon the advances of science against the citadels of crime.

For light relief he also perused the novels of Edgar Allen Poe, not in themselves a subject matter guaranteed to provide a peaceful slumber: 'The Masque of the Red Death' is no lullaby.

★ ★ ★

Mulholland on the other hand slept soundly as a winter bee.

★ ★ ★

When the news came into the station of a latest calamity in the parish, their lieutenant Robert Roach near had a blue fit.

A kind of awakening surely.

★ ★ ★

In bed, Jean Brash stretched like a tigress, silk bedclothes slithering as she moved — a mind already alive with possible lines of investigation and a faint but voluptuous ripple in her body a reminder that she had not been wrong about the strength in a certain sculptor's hands.

Indeed, it had not been an empty assertion from the same artist that he could last the course.

She could hear Hannah crashing around in the kitchen — the old woman had not been impressed by her mistress's arrival back in the small hours of the early morning and a lack of

188

provided explanation — but all work and no play can make dullards of us all.

Jean let out a short yip to exemplify that, and then jumped out of bed, a woman refreshed.

★ ★ ★

All had slept, all awoke. Save for three that would never rise again — with two more to follow.

24

There was a rat, for want of stairs,
Went down a rope to say his prayers.

Robert Roach's countenance would in no way ever put anyone in mind of a cheerful Man in the Moon. The lieutenant had a long and doleful mien, not improved by what was dangling above him like a melting icicle.

Witness one defunct councillor with bizarre toenails, a ripped dressing gown and protruding tongue.

McLevy, who was balanced precariously on a small stepladder, would rather his superior had not come to the scene at all, but was left with little option when a near hysterical Mary Pettigrew had been ushered into the station. Thank God the dead man wasn't a member of a Masonic lodge or life would not have been worth the living.

Mind you, as far as Barton Laidlaw was concerned, it was not worth living in any case. Death is seldom such.

The inspector glanced across at Mulholland, who, due to his superior height, was able to merely stand upon a small stool in order to view the corpse in situ.

The rope hanging from the spear that also served to suspend the dangling man had a familiar look and texture.

'A pulley rope,' said Mulholland out of the blue. 'It has that appearance.'

They had both attended a past suicide that used such a mode of suspension: it had spelt the end of a particular romantic attachment for Mulholland, so tended to stick in his mind.

McLevy nodded and called down to one of the constables, Ballantyne, who could be trusted only to do very small domestic errands.

'Away intae the kitchen, Ballantyne, and see if one of the pulleys is by any chance lacking a length of rope.'

The constable nodded and marched off like a man with a mission. The lieutenant was less easily impressed.

'Is that your primary conclusion, then, Inspector: a pulley rope?'

'Well, it might mean that whoever killed the councillor didnae come with a total complete plan. Just used what was there. Near tae hand like.'

Though McLevy had spelled this out in laborious detail to his lieutenant, there was something else he did not mention.

To wit, something grotesque and evidential of a black twisted humour. Hoist by your own petard is one thing; hung from a clan motto by your own kitchen pulley rope is quite another.

Ballantyne returned to confirm this, his bright blue eyes narrowed to indicate investigative scrutiny.

'One o' the wooden frames is hangin' a' slanty,' he announced, as if that solved the whole case.

'You discount suicide, then?' asked Roach, peering upwards at the stocky blunt figure that still had its low-brimmed bowler jammed upon the head.

'Tell ye in a minute,' replied the inspector.

He signalled to Mulholland, who put his long arms round the moribund sagging flesh and hoisted the man up enough to take pressure off the rope so that McLevy could prise it loose a little from the folds of the neck.

Sure enough there was the telltale thin embedded imprint of the garrotte, but it was less of a straight line this time, hooked up hard at the ends, the skin scraped raw. Perhaps the man had struggled more? Anyhow. Murder.

Mulholland had been craning to see and came to the same conclusion.

'Gettin' to be an epidemic,' he muttered.

'Definitely not suicide, sir,' McLevy called. 'And now, if you'd just stand aside a wee touch, we'll lower the corpus unto what I take tae be his Persian carpet.'

Roach stood hastily away in case the body took a flier towards him. The rope knot was slid from the point of the spear and the hefty lump of what was once a prime manipulator of civic manifestations made slow descent towards the waiting hands of Leith constabulary, thence to be laid upon the carpet.

McLevy and Mulholland both descended to join their lieutenant; the inspector waved away the curious constables and the three main providers of justice in Leith — discounting the unauthorised female version who was most

192

definitely on the case as she pranced around her boudoir higher up the hill — gazed solemnly downwards.

Barton Laidlaw was on his back and looking not unlike a toad fished out of the pond.

Roach — who was somewhat squeamish about visceral images of death and besides had been provided kippers for breakfast, which tended, though enjoyable enough, to repeat upon him afterwards — stifled a delicate belch and pointed at the spread-eagled dressing gown.

'A large piece of the lining has been ripped away. I wonder why this is so?'

'Mystery upon mystery,' muttered McLevy, who was itching to get burrowed into the corpse but constrained by the presence of his erstwhile superior.

'Mystery's a terrible thing,' Mulholland contributed, also hoping his lieutenant would clear off and leave them to it.

He and McLevy had their own secret ways, often unsaid, sometimes muttered under the breath but more than usually irreverent, and the presence of, as the Scots would have it, a *high heid yin* put a damper on their due anarchic process.

Roach sensed this unspoken desire to see him quit the murder scene and the nostrils flared in his long and long-suffering face. Had he not been so many times held back by his official duties of administration, the lieutenant would be out in the field demonstrating his own abilities.

Which were, in his opinion, considerable.

'This had better be solved, Inspector. And solved at speed.'

'That would be my intention.'

'Certain resemblances between this and the previous suspended other,' chipped in Mulholland helpfully.

'Such as?'

'Hangin' up high, strangled beforehand. Peas in a pod, sir.'

'With one *important* difference, Constable!'

'And whit is that, Lieutenant?' asked McLevy, knowing full well the potential contents of the answer.

'Alexander Moncrieff was a low type of the worst sort. Lucky to escape jail.'

'And?'

'Barton Laidlaw is a respectable man!'

Roach looked at the two blank faces before him and realised he would have to elaborate upon this theme.

'We cannot have . . . decent members of the community murdered in their own domiciles. The man was a pillar of our society!'

'Well, he's dead now,' replied McLevy rubbing his hands together as a signal he was about to get to work on the recumbent pillar.

'Respected!'

Roach, who often found dealing with his inspector not unlike being stuck with an unplayable lie in the cavernous fifteenth bunker of Leith Links Golf Course, near spat the word into the inspector's face.

'In some quarters,' was the cryptic response.

'What?'

McLevy glanced round the room at the flapping ears of his constables and spoke somewhat privately.

'There are rumours, sir.'

'Rumours?'

Roach looked towards Mulholland, who nodded in earnest agreement as his inspector exemplified.

'Corruption in high places, and even a wee hint' — here McLevy looked meaningfully at the toenails — 'of the odd sojourn in the lower depths.'

The lieutenant had heard these whispers himself but dismissed the suggestion out of hand despite finding the afore-indicated toenails hard to ignore.

To be truthful, he was not at all a stupid man, but he was aware of the pressure from on high that would erupt as regards this blatant murderous act, and most of it would descend on him. A man in the middle always gets the squeeze.

'There is aye tittle-tattle and scurrilous innuendo about those who hold power. Mere tittle-tattle.'

This had been exchanged quietly enough but Roach then strode to the door, turned, and made his next statement more declamatory.

'I am now going to report this dreadful event to Chief Constable Craddock. He will want to know what you plan to do to solve this heinous crime. This is a blot on the proud record of our station.'

McLevy was tempted to reply that were it not

for his success in solving the various crimes and murders in the parish of Leith, there would be no proud record worth a straw to consider or defend — but his attention had been caught by a scuffed far area of the carpet and so he settled for a noncommittal grunt.

Roach raised his voice louder as if the whole of Leith or perhaps even the Almighty himself were listening from afar.

'By the time I see you again, Inspector, I will want to know that the perpetrators of this crime are either in the cells or on their way towards the same. No excuses will be accepted for such lack of achievement. We all tremble upon the edge of disgrace!'

With that magisterial and dramatic pronouncement, the lieutenant turned sharply on his heel and left.

Silence.

Mulholland could see a sulphurous yellow glint in his inspector's grey eyes as he, for the moment, ignored the corpse and walked over to the scuffed area of carpet. The constable followed and they both knelt down.

The pile of the material had been scraped and gouged — a pity for it was a nice weave.

'Check the fingernails,' muttered McLevy as he scanned the surrounding area, bending close to the fabric to see if there was any criminal bequest to hand.

There was nothing except . . . his eyes squinted at what seemed to glint somewhere in the depths of the pile.

'Ballantyne!'

196

In answer the young constable came in eager response and knelt beside his inspector.

'Your eyes are the best part of ye,' muttered the inspector. 'Whit's that there?'

Ballantyne followed the pointing finger and fished out a long, thin metal pin that his mother had gifted him — she was a nurse and forever passing on unwanted or discarded pieces of hospital apparatus to her son.

He fished in the deep pile and carefully scraped out the glittering object before passing it gingerly on to the outstretched palm of his inspector.

McLevy peered close as Mulholland called over.

'No denyin' you, sir. Scraping of carpet under the nails. He'd be strangled where you kneel and then strung up after. Same modus operandi.'

Ballantyne thought to ask what that might mean but was glorying in the envious glances being cast his way by the other constables and so nodded wisely as he and the inspector both rose from the corpse.

'I wouldnae conclude exact the same,' replied McLevy. 'This is more . . . savage . . . careless.'

'Careless?'

In answer to Mulholland, the inspector held out his hand, palm upwards.

'Whit do ye think tae this?'

Mulholland crossed back and peered closely at the tiny fragment glittering against the pale skin of the inspector's dainty little paw. It forever surprised the constable that these same small hands could dish out such violence on a terrifying scale, but nature holds a wealth of contradictions.

He poked at the fragment as if it were a piece of honeycomb and himself a worker bee.

'A paste . . . like a little gem . . . off a brooch or something. Women's jewellery, maybe? Hard to tell.'

'Uhuh,' agreed McLevy dryly. 'Hard tae tell but . . . near tae where murder took place.'

He placed the fragment carefully into a small envelope, licked and sealed it, then stowed the paper away in his inside pocket. The inspector then fell silent.

Mulholland was fine with silence but Ballantyne found it hard to bear. After all, he was on the case with them. A trusty companion.

'Whit do we do now, sir?'

'We obey the orders of our bounden superior,' muttered McLevy.

Mulholland could sense the sulphur still burning. That pronouncement of Roach's had bitten deep and McLevy would not appreciate being shown up before his own men.

'Ah sure, the lieutenant's going to have it in the neck from the chief constable. He'd just be passing it on before he receives the same.'

This piece of Irish logic cut no ice.

'Well, whit are ye all standing around like a pile of knotless threids for, eh?'

McLevy's sudden bellow stiffened the sinews and backs of the constables. That was more like it.

'This is bound tae be a nosy street. Posh folk wi' bugger all else tae do but spy on their neighbours. Two of you each to a house, cover it up and down. Bang the door till they answer. Whit did they see last night? Anything at all? On your way!'

Another roar sent them scattering like a flock of seagulls after a herring boat.

This just left Ballantyne.

'Whit is it ye have in mind for me, sir?'

McLevy blinked as if seeing the boy for the first time. How this gormless specimen had ever got into the station was a mystery to one and all, but somehow he had arrived and his very lack of guile, all round treachery and further lack of a devious, pitiless nature — necessary possessions for any self-respecting member of the force — had circumvented the inspector's usual dismissal of those lacking the steel for ruthless investigation.

For what is a policeman but a hangman in disguise?

Yet Ballantyne was a special case in that the boy had a livid red birthmark running down part of his face and neck. He had been mercilessly teased by the other young constables until McLevy took a hand, or perhaps more of a boot, since he gave one of the tormentors such a hefty kick in the backside that he was near lifted into space.

Ye pick on this boy, ye pick a fight wi' me.

That took care of that. But now he was stuck with the creature.

'You, Constable, can carry the messages.'

'Messages?'

'From the constables back tae us. And frae us

199

tae the constables. Like Mercury.'

'Mercury?'

McLevy nodded gravely. 'Mercury carried the messages from humanity up tae the gods. And back.'

'And which one are we, sir?'

Mulholland stifled an urge to snicker — you could never tell with Ballantyne whether there was a sneaky jab behind his words or whether he possessed a deeper and wiser unconscious than he or anyone else had realised.

McLevy did not rise to the bait, unconscious or otherwise.

'Away tae the door, Constable. And wait there. For the messages.'

Off trotted Ballantyne and then there were two.

'Now we begin,' Mulholland remarked quietly.

'Indeed we do,' was the grim reply. 'Start wi' the corpse and then search this room, top tae bottom.'

Both men knelt down and began slowly and fastidiously going through the pockets of the dead man. The first thing they found, tucked into the side pocket of the fancy dressing gown, was a playing card.

The Queen of Spades.

25

Hark, hark,
The dogs do bark.
The beggars are coming to town.

Lily Baxter and Maisie Powers huddled together at the side of the street while a scene out of hell took place before them.

They had decided to escape the madhouse that was the Powers family residence — a fancy name for three rooms in a tenement near Water Lane that housed the entire brawling broody gathering — augmented by the new baby, Winifred Margaret, named after her diminutive grandmother who ruled the tribe with a rod of iron.

The baby's mother, Jessie, Maisie's younger sister, newly returned from the Perth Penitentiary, had been making up for lost time by flaming the candle at both ends while at the same time dancing the buckles off her shoes, and so the two visitors had been landed with looking after the poor wee mite.

A far cry from a bawdy-hoose pursuit of leathering the wilting backsides of the rich and powerful.

'Once Jessie settles herself,' said the indulgent elder Winifred, whose one soft spot was for the best shoplifter in the clan, whose unfortunate discovery and arrest was due to the fact that

201

pregnancy gave her less room to stash the lift, 'she'll be a born mother.'

Be such as it may, but until that happy day, the two of them had fed, bathed, wiped and swiped with little respite and no lovemaking since privacy was at a premium — and while Maisie would cheerfully have pulled a blanket over them to fiddle while the coal fire burned, Lily was only too conscious that eyes of all ages were everywhere.

And nothing intrigues the odd sibling more than movement under a blanket.

Going back to Jean Brash in the Just Land did not offer much of an option, given the proximity of a dead judge, so they resolved to make the best of it and had sneaked out to wander the ways of Leith on the second day of a cold damp new year, only to come upon a brutality that seared the soul.

Salamander Street.

They had turned a corner into the place and noticed folk lining the thoroughfare on both sides.

Their faces were lit with a strange excitement and children had been hoisted high on their fathers' shoulders. Signs of some celebration or carnival on the way, perhaps? But it was a parade of death that approached the waiting throng.

At first only the sound was heard — not by Lily, of course, but she saw Maisie flinch and signalled in their language *What is it?* Then the deaf and dumb girl felt the ground shake underfoot and looked up to see a stampeding drove of terrified cattle bullocking their way over the cobblestones.

Dark-clad men behind were herding the beasts towards the top of the street where a tall black building waited, the large gates heaved apart like an open mouth.

The slaughterhouse of Salamander Street.

The fear-crazed animals either sensed their fate or were simply unhinged by the unfamiliar smells, sights and sounds, while the onlookers shouted encouragement at the men who jabbed and bawled to urge the herd onwards.

Maisie could hear it all like a hellish cacophony and would have wished most devoutly for the gift of deafness, but then her sight would have become as sharp as Lily's, to see the sweat-lashed foaming flanks of the cattle and their rolling, frightened eyes. The human beings in attendance were even worse to behold, but for a very different reason.

Not the cowherds; they were just blind harriers, muffled and swathed like medieval collectors of the plague dead. No, worse to behold were the onlookers that somehow found enjoyment in the cruelty, lips moist, eyes snapping, the hoisted children mouth open, stunned at what they saw below.

Is it always so that every suffering soul, whether hung on a cross or prodded down a street to their death, has an audience caught between horror and delight?

Then the legs buckled and broke under one of the cows. It fell to the ground and no amount of blows or shouts could get the poor beast to budge. The men moved on — they would pick it up later — and the crowd followed, leaving the animal behind to bawl in agony, unable to move, only to feel a dreadful, unending pain.

For a moment the scene froze for Lily — only the beast seemed alive in its anguish — and then a tiny figure darted out from a side alley, dressed in a rough covering with a hood that hid the face.

The figure straddled the cow, slipped something round its neck and pulled its head back with a strength out of proportion to the slight, dwarfish frame.

It seemed to take only seconds; a moment of time, and then the poor beast was put out of its misery, the tongue flopping grotesquely out of the mouth as if waving a last farewell.

The figure slipped back into the alley to disappear, but just before it did so, the hood fell backwards — all this was directly opposite to where Lily stood, separated from the crowd and Maisie, who had been wrenched away by a press of bodies — for an instant the man looked back and Lily flinched as if she had been hammered in the face.

Though the crouching homunculus had done a kind deed there was no humanity in the visage — its was a malign and savage stare, the hair and face pure white, the eyes not like the black holes she remembered from the time before but pale and milky in the light of day.

Then it was gone.

But the stamp of evil remained. Like a stench. And she knew — unmistakably — it was the same apparition she had seen in the garden of the Just Land.

From the window, the night the judge had been murdered.

It had not been a dream.

The nightmare was real.

26

There was a man who had no eyes,
He went abroad to view the skies.

Jean had decided not to put on a face this morning. Not that she ever did much anyway. No real need. As of yet, madame.

Though she had noticed at the corners of her mouth some unwanted lines curving upwards. Possibly from too much smiling at concupiscent clientele.

Let other women cover their countenances with pearl powder to give themselves the pale skin of a privileged class, beeswax to shine their lips, rub beet juice into cheeks and drop belladonna into their pupils — this day Jean would be plain and wholesome save perhaps for a little eye paint and some lightly coloured lip balm to keep the withering east wind at bay.

However, nothing clears the complexion like a hectic tangle of limbs in the night-time.

Pop goes the weasel.

She had thrown on an old and favourite flannel dressing gown and bounced into the kitchen where a tight-lipped Hannah Semple hunched over a bowl of mealy brose. Jean had then helped herself to a mug of coffee from the enamel pot that rested atop of the warm stove and decided to raid the sweetie tin.

206

A craving for luscious titbits. An awakened appetite.

She sat at the table with a heaped plate of sugar biscuits in tribute to Inspector James McLevy and munched her way cheerily through the lot.

'How's the judge?' she enquired.

'Stiffer by the day. Lik' a coffin lid.'

As well as an unedifying and unsettling visit earlier this morning — to the cellar cheese room where Abercrombie lay under a death sentence he had most certainly not authorised — Hannah had found herself a trifle in the huff.

Her mistress had returned late as hell the previous night with no explanation but somewhat smudged and rough at the edges, before going at once up to bed whistling a tune through her teeth that, unless Hannah was mistaken, sounded like a jaunty version of 'Cock up your Beaver' by Scotland's premier poet.

However, as the last sugar biscuit bit the dust, Hannah resolved to cast all this aside. It was the second day of January and they had more to worry about than being either in the huff or rough at the edges.

To hell with the inconsequentials of life.

Besides, she knew her mistress and had a damned good idea what may have transpired. And who was transpiring.

She had seen such a glint in Jean's eye before. That sculptor laddie no doubt possessed a decent girth and nature abhors a vacuum.

'Well. Now your appetite is stappit,' she remarked wryly, 'whit's the story, Mistress?'

207

Jean wiped the biscuit crumbs delicately from her recently protected lips and related what she had found from the craven outpourings of one Barton Laidlaw.

John Finch, it would seem, had died as a result of administered beating by Alexander Moncrieff, although according to Laidlaw the man swore blind that the boy was still defiant and conscious when left alone in the room.

In fact, from what Moncrieff told Laidlaw, he was still cursing at his persecutor through blood and tears even though badly weakened by the beating, and slumped over the Pole of Correction. Of course, the man would perjure himself stone blind but Moncrieff had been curiously adamant upon that point.

What, however, could not be argued was that by the next morning — when the master returned to his room — the boy was dead.

A weak heart, perhaps, who knows?

But dead in any case.

The governors had consulted and then colluded for their various reasons in a cover up. When pressed harder and unmercifully held to strict account by Jean, Laidlaw confessed that Moncrieff had supplied some of these august and respectable men with certain 'photographs'.

Jean had been ahead of him there and further increased the panic in his eyes — she knew the content of these vile images and the perversion it signalled. Who amongst them were the recipients?

Barton swore not him and she could believe it

— his deviance lay in other parts. But who amongst the rest?

The judge for sure and Young the tobacconist — Moncrieff had boasted to his erstwhile landlord about that — but not, as far as Laidlaw could tell, Baines. The reverend would go along with the decision, however, because the other three did; there was safety in numbers and the minister lacked the nerve to oppose Abercrombie in particular.

Laidlaw himself had led the acquiescence because Moncrieff — a former tenant — was his own appointment and had to be protected. Much good it did the fool later on.

Barton did not know the source of the photographs; that was Moncrieff's precious secret, though the man implied that they were from near at hand.

Home-grown.

Jean had sensed the councillor was still concealing something, put the gun aside and with her two hands grabbed him up by the collar so that she could stare into his piggy little eyes.

What else? Or you'll be reading the paper tomorrow and wishing to die.

The pig squealed.

Two other boys. Friends of John Finch, better known amongst the other inmates as Johnny.

The corpse had been taken away to an unknown grave but the boys remained. A dangerous proposition.

They may know something; they may have seen something. Let them crow on the dunghill for a time, then get rid of them as well. One to be adopted — taken off to England, no records kept, and disappeared from sight; the other allowed to 'escape' — back to the streets where he belonged. He had also vanished out of sight like a rodent down the drain. Neither ever seen again.

Their names?

When Laidlaw spewed them up, she had thrown him back down to grovel on the floor.

These names were known to Jean. She remembered them from childhood and could summon up faces from a moment recalled — a moment of being cornered by both little hunker-sliders in one of the wynds. A long time ago.

She had kept them at bay for a time by dint of being a Queen Bee, but finally they had summoned up the nerve.

One with a mop of blond hair, the other white as a dead rat. Thought her ripe for the plunder they had in mind. Insidious and slimy.

She kicked one of the pair full in the cleavings — an easy enough stretch — and the other had roared with laughter to see his companion writhing on the ground but it was nervous laughter lest he be next in line.

The Smiler was Dirk Martins. The retching dwarf was Jeb Summers.

End of the story so far.

What Jean did not mention to Hannah in the kitchen, because she aye kept something back for herself, was a last request she had made to Barton Laidlaw — a request the man had dared not refuse. That would be Jean's little secret, until she decided to reveal it.

In life it is always best to keep something up the sleeve. A dirty game might need a hole card.

Hannah Semple sniffed. By now she had also acquired a mug of coffee and slugged back half the contents.

'And where does all that get ye?'

It would have been tempting to think that what Laidlaw had told her might have lost its edge in the cold light of day, but Jean had now developed a keen hunger for this investigation. It was more than a matter of defending her way of life, the Just Land — her *Pleasure Dome of Depravity* as McLevy liked to call it, the big baw-faced balloon thinking he was the only one in the world who ever read Samuel Taylor Coleridge.

No, it was now more than that.

And as regards Coleridge and the like? As soon as Jean was able, she had expanded her ability to read and delved into literature like a heron in the pond. Besides the male poets, Christina Rossetti and Elizabeth Barrett Browning both spoke to her in a familiar tongue, and when she came upon Jane Eyre, she near howled aloud in triumph. Another angry, passionate and defiant child, another orphan in the storm who would never apologise for the wildness in her soul.

Her intelligence had a hunger for that written word and the power of that story, and now she had a second hunger, with an instinct alongside.

Perhaps it had lain dormant inside the complex skein of emotions that made up her total force for survival.

But Jean *knew* — knew as sure as she had howled outside Barton Laidlaw's door — she was on the trail! And she was born to be so. A hunter.

To hell with Pallas Athena; she'd follow a different goddess, Artemis, and make a killing.

Hannah, mistaking Jean's silence for being a trifle discomfited, repeated the previous question.

'*Where does it get ye?*'

'I now have two suspects,' answered Jean quietly.

'Jist a wee notion. Nothing proved.'

'More than I had before.'

'They might have damn all tae do with it.'

'I have an instinct that is not the position.'

She had an expression on her face Hannah had never seen before — it was almost peaceful, as if the mistress had come upon some kind of balance.

But balance is a precarious beast.

'Even if ye're right, ye could wait a long time afore these murderous bastards show their hand. And time is what we havenae got — even wi' the cheese in the air, that judge is beginning tae hum.'

There was some truth in that remark. And then, as if in answer to an unspoken question in Jean's mind — how was she to flush out these killers? — there came a sharp knock at the front door.

Hannah patted a cut-throat razor to make sure it was well concealed yet readily available behind her apron, and marched off to answer the summons.

She returned with Maisie Powers and Lily Baxter — they had yet another tale to tell.

Meanwhile, in the back garden, it was not yet cold enough to form ice on the still waters of the ornamental pond where the sluggish forms of Jean's exotic fish moved slowly and kept low-lying, no doubt dreaming of warmer climes.

A ginger tomcat, who might have answered to the name of Horace were it called aloud, had leapt up on to the top of the garden wall to eye the scene below and reflect that had he only been born amphibian, life would have been much more rewarding. No point in trying the peacocks — they were safe behind bars.

He had been introduced to this pond by Bathsheba and it was a matter of male pride to succeed where the female had so far failed.

Thus it proceeds between polarities.

And so he pondered his next move.

Back to the other story.

Of no interest at all to Horace.

Maisie had a determined, almost defiant set to her face as she finished relating the events of Salamander Street and those from two nights before seen from the window — she had wrung it gesture by gesture out of a shaken, tearful Lily in the aftermath of the witnessed brutality.

She knew fine well that it might signal the end for the deaf and dumb girl in the bawdy-hoose, and her own finale as well, because she would never leave her love — but to hell with it.

'I thought ye should know the truth, Mistress,'

she avowed. 'You've been fair and you've been kind. We owe you that much, don't we, Lily?'

The girl nodded. She had watched Maisie's mouth, a mouth she had kissed so often with a darting tongue that Maisie had more than once admiringly described as *lik' a nine-eyed eel*, but now it was Maisie's tongue that told a story of Lily's own fear and lack of candour — a terrible fear that had its roots in neglect and pain.

The deaf and dumb girl had been abandoned early and made her living working for a vicious woman who ran a gang of female pocket delvers: Mother Heggarty, a brutal, heavy-handed monster who kept Lily in a state of terror — a terror that even now invaded her dreams and had never let her be.

But that life was all she had possessed.

One day in the streets, she went to dip a tall fancy female's purse, but as her fingers went in, another hand seized them.

She looked up into a cool, dispassionate face.

'Not bad,' said the woman. 'But I believe I could better you.'

Lily signed abject contrition, tears of shame in her eyes — and also signed she could not speak or hear.

'Dear me,' said the woman, mouthing the words slowly to make sure Lily could understand. 'You're in a dreadful taking. Like Wattie to the worm.'

Then Jean Brash laughed, hooked her arm through Lily's and took her back to the Just Land. She never worked as a magpie, the mistress saw to that — just filled the champagne

214

glasses, made the beds, helped out with domestic chores and kept out of Hannah's way.

But one day she met Francine, fell deeply in love and helped out in quite another fashion.

Francine left her, broke her heart — the French are notorious for breaking hearts — but then she met Maisie. And was finally truly happy.

Though now?

Lily forced herself to look Jean Brash straight in the eye and nodded acceptance of all that had been said. Hannah Semple she did not dare to face; the keeper of the keys would surely never forgive or forget — Lily would be banished forever.

She signed to Maisie, who nodded sombrely.

'Lily will leave as soon as you say the word, Mistress. And so will I.'

The other girl's eyes flashed at the thought her love would suffer because of her actions, and fingers flew as Maisie replied in kind.

For a moment, despite the gravity of what had passed, it was a comical sight to see a furious digital wrangle that ended with Maisie slamming her hand flat on the table so that the enamel mugs near slopped out their coffee while Lily glared and clenched a fist in response.

Then there was silence and they both turned to look back at Jean, who had listened, betraying nothing in reaction.

But there was no hint of remonstrance or blame, and then slowly a smile spread across her face as she glanced over at Hannah Semple.

'Ye hae the luck o' the devil,' muttered the old woman.

'Not at all,' was the response. 'The pure at heart deserve all good fortune.'

Hannah grunted sceptically.

She then at first glared towards the visitors, but then, to their astonishment, followed the basilisk stare by closing one eye in a wink. After that, of course, a tirade.

'You twa are mair trouble than a cage full o' monkeys — and you — Lily Baxter — do something like this one more time and I'll boot your arse out of this place all by myself!'

'Hannah is right, Lily,' Jean added quietly. 'If you have troubles, you tell me. This is your last chance.'

While the two girls sat holding their breath and not daring to move or express joy in case it provoked the opposite, Jean and Hannah put their heads together.

'Jeb Summers,' murmured Jean. 'It has to be.'

'It would seem so.'

'I'll pass word to my people on the streets. We know the area — you can't mistake the man. We'll find him.'

'Ye still have no proof.'

'True enough. But we're getting closer.'

Jean's green eyes narrowed thoughtfully.

'McLevy thought two men took a hand in Moncrieff being strangled and hauled up. I wonder if Dirk Martins is in this as well.'

'He left the city, ye were told.'

'You can always come back.'

Yet there was something that had not quite surfaced but was now nagging at her from the murder night. A moment that had passed her by . . . What was it?

A face? A look in the eye?

As if someone had put one over on her. Also as if something in herself had registered a moment, a sliver of recognition, but it was yet buried too deep to surface.

Well. Back to Jeb Summers.

'Find one, find all,' she murmured while Lily and Maisie linked hands under the table and wondered if they dared ask if it was possible to stay here at the Just Land until the other magpies came back and the place opened up again for business.

Even with a dead judge on hand — and they assumed him still to be in that position, like a lump of cheese — it would be more restful than an unstoppable at both ends infant.

It is a strange fact that the more bizarre the event, the more ordinary it seems as time goes by.

Jean began scribbling out some notes to be passed to those of her people that could read; the rest would be word of mouth. Maisie and Lily could help Hannah deliver them throughout Leith.

Once more on the trail. Hunger and intuition. On the prowl with a killer in mind. No mercy.

Outside in the garden, Horace plunged a predatory paw into the cold surface of the pool.

However, the cat had not allowed for refraction of water, and his claws emerged with nothing more than a clump of hitherto floating pond weed.

The fish disappeared down into the depths and one of the peacocks in its cage sent up a mocking screech.

Even the best investigator sometimes comes up short.

27

There was a crooked man,
and he walked a crooked mile,
He found a crooked sixpence against
a crooked stile;
He bought a crooked cat which caught
a crooked mouse,
And they all lived together in a little
crooked house.

The Smiler struggled to keep his face straight as he walked along the hotel corridor towards his room. True enough, news of Laidlaw's death had more than disturbed the atmosphere, but both he and his partner had sensed a measure of relief as well.

All expressed outrage that their poor colleague had been . . . Well, the facts were not *completely* known, but suffice it to say murdered with a hint of attendant unusual circumstances — such news coming from Chief Constable Craddock's office and spreading through the fields of civic commerce like wildfire in bone dry heather.

Yet there were a few glances exchanged in the council chamber room where portraits of previous God-fearing incumbents stared out — no doubt with equally God-fearing and unvarnished toenails.

Rumours had followed Laidlaw around like

penny dogs sniffing at their master's heel. Tales of strange bedfellows and quayside frolics inside taverns that were dens of more than the usual iniquities.

His deputy, Forbes Crichton, a sallow, pockmarked specimen with an Adam's apple that seemed to have a life of its own, a man described by Laidlaw himself as *born to play second fiddle*, suddenly found himself leader of the orchestra, and as he pondered this fact in a corner, he looked up to see two Bristol men fill the frame.

Both Samuel Deacon and Joseph Tucker were stern-faced, yet might there be a certain assiduous gleam in their eyes?

Tucker towered over the other two — a leonine figure, his thick hair like a golden harvest — Deacon was bald as a badger's backside, the same height as Crichton but bolting to fat at considerable speed.

Crichton was not held to be a clever creature; in fact it was thought by many that Laidlaw had kept him in office for the simple reason that he could trust the man not to possess intelligence enough for betrayal. He had been used as a doormat by many. Now it was his turn to wipe the feet.

Tucker took the lead as usual, concealing his usually gleaming teeth behind a set solemn mouth.

'A sad business,' he murmured.

'A great loss.'

Neither man added any more and Deacon merely bobbed his bald head enthusiastically as if they had delivered an aria of verbal mourning.

'Nevertheless' — now Tucker shot a quick look around to make sure no eavesdropper was lurking — 'it is important that the work dear Mister Laidlaw commenced with us does not wither on the vine.'

'Indeed.'

Deacon put in an eager contribution.

'I'm sure he would be anxious that we proceed with a heavy heart but in resolute Christian strength of mind.'

To this possibly well-meant but vacuous assertion, the other two nodded, and while Crichton moved back a little into the corner, Tucker shifting so that they were imperceptibly closer, Deacon wheeled to face outwards so that the other two were shielded from view. They also serve who only stand and provide cover.

'I am assuming,' said Tucker softly, 'that what we previously discussed with your good self before Mister Laidlaw — came upon the scene, will still be — how can I express myself — applicatory?'

Deacon could not see the faces but most certainly could divine the silence. No doubt his partner would be poised and deferential; the man was a born actor. He could tell almost any lie with truthful intent.

Crichton's voice was almost at a whisper but enough that the words were unmistakable.

'Applicatory. Is indeed the word.'

Tucker tried not to appear too roused. Too *priapic* in response. Don't dismay the horses.

'Might we — meet tomorrow, say?'

For a moment the Bristol man worried he could have been a little over-importunate, but Crichton sniffed in what Joseph Tucker took to be positive response. And so the dance of corruptibility continued.

'There is a business suite in our hotel. Would that suit you, sir?'

Another sniff.

'Shall we say the same time as today? Eleven of the morning?'

Forbes Crichton nodded briskly and then moved back out into the murmuring throng.

'If you will excuse me, gentlemen.'

Tucker joined Deacon and they watched with a certain suppressed glee as their quarry took his place amongst his fellows. No longer a second-class scraper on the strings.

In the hotel corridor, Dirk could restrain himself no longer and broke into stifled laughter that threatened to become a loud guffaw but no — no — keep muted the celebration lest it be noticed that a man who should be mourning the loss of a dear colleague of commerciality was dancing a sailor's hornpipe, he being a Bristol boy.

Wait until safe and sound behind four walls.

Yet when at the door of his room, he frowned. Cigar smoke. Fresh. He could smell it through the door — the Smiler always had a keen sense of smell and this was unmistakable.

Was it Laidlaw's ghostly presence — waiting with the rope still round the neck, eyes bulging, moustache waxed and pointing in accusation?

With a disjointed feeling of trepidation, Dirk

put key to lock, turned it, and entered the room.

It was dark — the curtains had been drawn to keep the pallid light of a dreich Edinburgh morning at bay.

A figure on the bed. Smoking. Dirk could see the light of a cigar as it was puffed. And puffed again, the smoke forming in the air like a phantom.

For some reason he had choked up, unable to form words. Was it guilt; the guilt he had pushed down, kept away? Or was it a dread; a terrible dread of being found out, the evil dirty secrets displayed before him like a hauled-out intestinal tract?

The panic almost caused him to turn and run out of the room once more, but instead he rushed to the window and pulled back the curtains.

There on the bed, grinning like a gravedigger — tapping dainty on the cigar with one long nail so that the ashes fell neatly into a nearby receptacle — was none other than Jeb Summers.

Dirk's heart rattled against his ribcasing like a beast in a cage.

'What — what in Christ's name are you doing in here?'

'Smokin',' was the calm reply.

'How — how did you get in?'

Jeb waggled his free hand, the nails curved like so many lockpicks.

'Easy.'

In fact he had climbed up the laundry chute of the hotel, undone the lock of the door, which was child's play, and sneaked inside. It smelled

223

nice. Nicer than his cave, although Jeb preferred the fetid, musty, dead-animal odour in which he lived — this just made a wee change.

There was a sewer drain near to the building. He had come up through that, into the cellars where the chute disgorged its contents, then found the right level and, as he said, easy.

The Smiler had boasted to him about his fancy hotel, the name, the place, even the room number. First floor. Grand suite.

Jeb took another puff of the cigar — the box had been lying open, and they were blood brothers, were they not?

Besides, he had earned it from his good deed.

That poor beast had no right to be left in such a broken pile of bones, folk were evil bastards to fellow creatures. Church on Sunday, cut a throat on Monday.

The thunder of hooves had disturbed him from the cave and on witnessing the carnage, it was the least he could do. For once he took no pleasure in the garrotting, but when he looked back, he saw a small female gazing back from the edge of the crowd. He had a half-caught memory of that face and by the looks of it she had a nice neck.

Perhaps one day he would do her a favour?

While Jeb smiled at that notion, Dirk was trying to hold himself together; if this scabby-heided dwarf was found on the premises, the game was well and truly up. He had to get the man out of here. Softly does it.

'Right. Clever. Whit can I do for you, my freen?'

His shift into the local tongue elicited a sly smile from the albino.

'It must have slipped your mind, then, Dirkie.'

'Eh?'

'This night. We finish it. Two more.'

Once more he held up his hand, palm towards the Smiler with the scar showing like a line of death.

As they had split up the previous night after the murder of Barton Laidlaw, Jeb had called softly that the blood oath still held true and Dirk, his own blood racing with the moment of killing, had nodded accordance.

But now things had changed. Now the death of Laidlaw had accomplished the aim of winning the contract and there was much to be lost by killing further.

If anything went wrong and they were caught, or, say, Jeb was apprehended and spilt his guts, or even if they managed to succeed — two more murders and the panic it might engender could put everything into question.

'Surely it would be better to wait, Jeb?'

'Why so?'

'Till things . . . quieten down. Then when they rest, they least expect, we can strike!'

The killing of last night, the blood bond, everything had vanished, as if he had become this morning another person — his true self. Or was that 'himself' and what he was now, facing Jeb, the false version?

Who was the real man? How many took their turn? Stepped up to play a part?

No. No. Last night was a dream, as if the child

had grown an adult body and ripped life apart. No. *Now* was real.

But what of Jeb? He was still the same. Unchanged. Ready to kill again.

All Dirk wanted to do now was tie up the deal. And then leave Edinburgh. Leave the dwarf to fester in his underground kingdom — promise to return at a later, safer date but in fact never visit the city again, or if he did so, never go near Salamander Street.

He had done enough. Surely? Paid his dues.

Nothing of this showed in the face. No. Just radiate an earnest sincerity and trust that he had lied well enough. That was his talent. Maybe a proverb would do the trick?

'All things come to he who waits, Jeb.'

Jeb squashed the cigar butt carefully into the ashtray and spoke one word.

'No.'

Then he giggled, slid off the bed and walked to the door.

'Tonight we finish it. First the wee tobacco man and then the man o' God. I'll do it. You make too much mess.'

Dirk kept the panic from showing in his face.

'This night I have much to accomplish, Jeb; business affairs that must be attended, meetings of great importance. Surely we can hold fire?'

For a moment an ugly expression showed in the white countenance before the dwarf pulled the hood up and over so that his face was hidden in shadow.

'This night you will come to me when the clock strikes seven. Johnny Finch must be

226

avenged. Your word was given. Tonight we finish it.'

Dirk said nothing.

'Or I'll come calling,' announced Jeb with a wicked gleeful glint in the one eye that could be seen in the recesses of the material. 'Tae smoke ye out.'

The Smiler nodded slowly. Jeb slid out of the door and was gone.

No way out. No way back.

Endgame. The Grand Finale.

Judgement Day.

28

Eeper Weeper, chimney sweeper,
Had a wife but couldn't keep her.
Had another, didn't love her,
Up the chimney he did shove her.

The east wind whipped through the streets of Leith in the pale daylight, unwelcome in many quarters, cutting into folk like a knife whether desired or otherwise.

McLevy and Mulholland were well enough protected while their constables shivered unsuccessfully up and down the length of Warriston Crescent, but so far their search had yielded nothing other than the small piece of jewellery stone spotted by the eagle-eyed, dauntless and growing grumpier by the minute inspector.

The killers had left no other traces either in the carpet or anywhere else — clean as a whistle — so other than causing death by strangulation and thieving a pulley rope from the kitchen, they had been model tenants.

There was something about the murder room that irritated the inspector. It was full of knicky-knacks and wee fragile boxes full of flaky Eastern-scented incense and fragments of pot pourri, all of which had to be opened and poked through with stubby fingers God had not intended for the sifting thereof.

How a body could exist in these surroundings

without knocking over something, was beyond him.

Mulholland's long fingers were better suited for the task but he was faring no better as regards results when Ballantyne hailed them from the front door with a wispy little old lady in tow.

The other two shot out to meet them in the hall — it would not do for what seemed at least an octogenarian to observe dead bodies with painted toenails.

'This is Mistress McGruder,' Ballantyne announced triumphantly. 'She has a tale tae tell, sir.'

'You're supposed to be at the door for messages,' muttered the inspector.

The old biddy's head nodded and bobbed incessantly and it was obvious to a trained observer such as he that the woman was more than a bit bereft in wits.

'I *was* at my post, sir,' replied Ballantyne. 'But it was freezing cold and I tried jumping up and down tae keep warm, and then this nice lady brought me a cup o' tea.'

Sure enough he was clutching a delicate bone-china cup and saucer in his bony hands like a knight of old with the Holy Grail.

'The least I could do,' chimed the new visitor scowling at the inspector. 'Ye should be ashamed putting a poor laddie wi' a face like that out into the cauld bitter wind.'

'Mistress McGruder lives opposite,' Ballantyne said blithely, ignoring reference to his mark of birth. 'And she has come tae bear witness, sir.'

'Was your door not knocked upon, ma'am?'

'Aye,' she replied to Mulholland's solicitous interjection. 'But I didnae like the look o' them so I never opened the thing.'

So much for the charms of Leith constabulary save Ballantyne, and McLevy sighed. This could take forever and he did not have the time.

No one ever has the time. Until it runs out: then you have all the time in the world. Yourself and the worms.

'Whit's the story, then?'

Ballantyne nodded encouragingly at Mistress McGruder, who had never stopped the motion.

She launched forth.

It turned out that the previous night, the old lady had been woken from righteous sleep by a howling wolf and darted to the window to see the cause.

Standing below, outside Barton Laidlaw's domicile, oblivious to the pouring rain, was the figure of a woman, and while the neighbour watched, this lycanthrope threw back once more her head and let rip. Then she went skipping off through the puddles and the awoken witness went back to her bed.

A little fearful in the night.

Thus, of course, missing the other two callers.

To the police this had all the hallmarks of some kind of demented dream and so Mulholland tried a gentle inquisition of sorts.

Perhaps the woman thought she was still dreaming — existence is a perilous fancy at best.

'Would you be able to describe the . . . apparition?'

'Lik' a witch.'

'With a broom?' asked McLevy sceptically.

'Not that I could see,' was the prim reply. 'But she threw back the hood. White face. Dirty hair.'

'Dirty?'

'Like the devil's tongue.'

Ballantyne joined the fray.

'I saw that in a book the once. It reached right down tae the ground. Black as pitch.'

'Dirty,' reproved McGruder.

This was getting nowhere.

'In the main,' the inspector asserted, 'the devil's tongue is red.'

'Dirty.'

In fact, Jean Brash's hair had been plastered against her head and face by the rain and may well have appeared a darker hue than usual, so both descriptions may have been applicable. However, the inspector was speaking from ignorance of what had actually happened, and the old biddy from a total prejudice against howling females in the darkest night — especially the kind that skip over puddles.

The old woman was, of course, nosy as hell about why the police were spreading like a plague all over the neighbourhood, but they fobbed her off with a generalised tale of burglary and criminal activity, which McLevy had primed all the constables to relate if asked.

'Burglars are low types,' McGruder said. 'I would have them shot. Like a dirty dog. Through the lughole.'

Mulholland tried to bring some sense into the exchange with another gentle question or two.

231

'What colour would the coat be, ma'am?'

'It wasnae dirty.'

'And would you, ma'am, recognise this woman if you saw her again?'

Mistress McGruder nodded vigorously and smiled.

'No,' she said.

This contradictory observer was packed off with the promise that someone would come to take her statement, Ballantyne sternly admonished to hold position at the front after escorting the witness back across the street, and off they tootled happily enough.

McLevy and Mulholland returned to the murder room — Barton Laidlaw had not yet made a run for it, so the inspector might look down upon him thoughtfully.

'Two men dead. Same style, a playing card, spades for death, I would imagine, hung up like a decoration. Has tae be a connection atween them, eh?'

'You're not wrong there,' replied Mulholland.

There must be a place these two lives intersected, the inspector mused, and it would be somewhere in the past. The past aye twists the present into strange and misbegotten shapes.

Both men unsavoury specimens at different ends of the social scale; yet they must meet somewhere.

A rattle of hooves sounded in the street and Ballantyne poked his head back in from the hall.

'The cairry wagon's arrived, sir. Shall we load up the corpus?'

'They can wait their hurry,' muttered the

inspector and Ballantyne disappeared again.

The police surgeon who would examine the body might find something useful, but he had been little help as regards Moncrieff, save for remarking on the neatness of the killing — a fact McLevy could have already told him.

'There has to be a connection. And we'll find it.'

Mulholland saw no reason to disagree with such, and both men's attention then turned to the walnut desk of Barton Laidlaw. The owner being defunct, there could be no objections raised about the prospect of rifling it from top to bottom. Not unlike a burglar.

And inside a small drawer of that desk, Jean Brash's note dated by Barton Laidlaw's own hand, lay waiting like an unexploded bomb.

Tick-tock.

★ ★ ★

A woman sat in front of Sarah Baines and, to be honest, the girl noted a face resembling the wreck of what might once have been a striking countenance — the eyes set so deep into the fissures of sockets that they looked out as something lost and doomed at the bottom of a pit.

At one time this face may have been bold and full of challenge, but the life led had worn it out, bled the sap till what remained looked like a desert bird.

Yet there was a fascination in those lines of dissolution, the marks scored deep, the downward cut of the mouth. A hangdog mortification.

Sarah had found the woman standing at the entrance to one of the wynds, swaying to and fro in the cold wind, and it had not taken much to persuade her to come into the relative warmth of the poky wee studio; that plus the promise of a few coins no doubt to be spent afterwards on the demon drink, for the woman still had a sour, fetid smell from last night's raw alcohol consumption.

Spiel the wa' whisky, no doubt. A brew that in local legend would have you climbing walls from the first dram.

Now she sat like a patient dumb animal, like a rock the seas washed over, perfectly happy to wish for little more than the absence of suffering. That would be in store later on.

The young woman's eyes registered some of such but not all, for she had not the life experience to understand this kind of suffering, only to observe from a distance and experience a vague indiscriminate compassion.

Thus it is to be young and tender before the heavy dunts of life bring a harsh message that you yourself are also dependent upon the kindness of strangers and that anguish is also indiscriminate.

And so her hand was firm enough as Sarah made the first clear stroke to chart an outline that would soon be filled with broken veins and ruined roads. But despite her concentration, another face kept swimming in the young woman's mind.

Louisa Lumsden. Light hazel eyes, not veined, not bloodshot, full of fire — rumours were rife that she already had formed a lesbian attachment to one of the teachers at her school in St Andrews. The woman had left, singed by the heat.

The headmistress stayed on. Unrepentant, it would seem, but valued highly by the school governors, or perhaps they just did not have the nerve to dismiss such a firebrand.

Later that evening, Sarah might find out if love and desire could be more than just a figment of the imagination. More than just a catch in the throat.

The broken woman had no such concerns.

Once in her prime she had looked down at a red-haired girl who crouched down on the cobblestones in the driving rain and announced herself as a Queen Bee.

Time is the real killer.

Deadly earnest.

The woman knew this in her bones, even if a vestige of bleak humour still clung to her shipwrecked form. She had been given a tin mug of tea and poked a pinkie daintily in the air as she gulped it down — just tae let this wee girl know that her drawers had been now and again rifled by men with manners and deportment.

A long time since.

The woman's name was Nan Dunlop.

A plaything for pain.

★ ★ ★

A strong bluster of wind through a partly open window had sent the papers for next Sunday's sermon scattering along the floor, where the errant flock danced skittishly out of reach as the Reverend William Baines tried to gather them together from a well-polished floor.

He had slept badly due to the event of an unappetising and disconcerting dream.

★ ★ ★

He had been preaching to the church congregation when it had been brought to his dismayed notice that the minister was, in fact, naked from the waist downwards.

Since the pulpit covered this flagrant display of private parts overhung somewhat by a rounded, remarkably cheerful belly, our William was for the moment protected. Nevertheless, the problem remained.

Nakedness. Flagrant. Rounded or otherwise.

And what to do about it?

For some reason also the congregation was entirely female. Martha Young and her coven sat directly front to the left, and it seemed to Baines that they were licking their lips in prurient anticipation: despite her weighty respectability, he had never warmed to the woman, though would never let this affect behaviour or judgement.

A French pastry was crammed into Martha's large, greedy mouth, sticking out in the most obscene fashion before being slowly sucked inside. Behind her ranged the matriarchy of Greyfriars Kirk, solemn-faced and unmoving like a herd of cows in the field.

For them to see him naked as a nail!

The other side of the church was filled with young women he had never seen before. Pretty, vivacious, chattering like skylarks; they were paying absolutely no attention to his solemn words; yet, wait, was he speaking at all?

The sermon had been on the subject of Adam and Eve thence original sin. But he had lost the thread. He was silent, the matriarchy was silent, the Son of God was silent, only the young women chattered on.

And he now noticed a single figure sitting at the back — just under the stained-glass windows depicting the Lamb of God, who didn't seem all that interested in what was going on below — an elegant, beautiful woman with red hair that flowed down her face like a fallen angel.

He knew that face. He had seen the woman in other circumstances, in other times: Jean Brash. Even at this distance, he observed that her face was composed and grave, looking back at him. A bawdy-hoose keeper in the House of God. Did this mean that all was lost?

However, there was hope, yes, there was hope, for at the front, on the right-hand side, sat his dearly beloved daughter!

Sarah, though, seemed to be busy sketching upon a pad, forming the likeness of a beautiful young female who sat beside her. The woman had a blue headscarf wrapped round her head to resemble a nun. Surely not a nun in the Greyfriars Kirk?

William hissed at Sarah, motioned her up beside the pulpit and whispered to her to bring *him trousers, shoes and socks at the very least. For a moment she moved to obey and then — oh most disobedient! — sneaked a look round the pulpit edge.*

The silence was now total. Young women, matriarchy, all looking towards them. Sarah turned to the watchers. Threw her arms in the air. And opened her mouth . . .

★ ★ ★

At that moment William Baines had woken up in a cold sweat, mercifully clothed in a flannel bedshirt and nightcap like Wee Willie Winkie.

What might it all mean?

Terrifying nakedness in front of a bawdy-hoose keeper and a nun?

One result of the dream was that he had most unusually slept late and Sarah had already departed for her work studio — she had also mentioned yesterday that she might entertain some like-minded artistic females at the place this evening and so might be late returning.

That had raised his suspicions and Baines fully intended to make an uninvited and unexpected visit.

He had nothing but deep distrust for the male wielders of brush, paint and pencil — he would make sure they were not lounging near his daughter, smoking like chimneys with thoughts that were nothing to do with decency and everything to do with moral decay.

Sarah did not know that he possessed a spare key to her studio door — usually he knocked out of politeness but tonight, should it even be locked, he would surprise them all. If the place was a haven of innocence, then he would excuse the intrusion, give them the Lord's blessing and leave; no doubt Sarah would be furious, but was he not her protector?

And fathers have a right to intrude, thus saving their daughters from ruin.

But what of this dream? Did it point to the future, the past or a fractured present?

He had in fact intended to base his next sermon upon the subject of original sin, quoting extensively from Romans and Ephesians — working on it the previous night — and these were the notes blown and scattered by the wind.

Yet something else was on his mind, a darker, deeper feeling of disquiet. A sense of foreboding.

Over the last few days, when walking in the streets musing, as was his custom, on the Almighty's ways and means, he had the odd notion of being watched.

Once he had turned sharply and thought to glimpse a small shape darting out of sight behind him.

Possibly some child up to mischief?

Possibly.

Baines shook his head in some irritation at the random tendency of thoughts and shuffled the papers of a Sabbath sermon back into some kind of order.

One of the passages on original sin caught his eye. Ephesians 2 verse 3:

And you were dead in your trespasses and

*sins, in which you formerly walked accord-
ing to the course of this world, according to
the prince of the power of the air, of the
spirit that is now working in the sons of
disobedience. Among them we too all
formerly lived in the lusts of our flesh,
indulging the desires of the flesh and of the
mind, and were by nature children of wrath.*

Was the nakedness to do with lust? Surely not
— libidinosity had never been welcome in his
bosom. Or was the lack of cover to signify some
unacknowledged guilt?

No matter the striven-for innocence, his life
had not been blameless — at times he had
lacked the strength to follow teachings from the
Lamb of God and defy the authority of man.

It still troubled him that all those years ago he
had allowed the death of that boy Finch to be
passed by at the wayside.

'Children of wrath,' he murmured, before
moving at the window to close off this interfering
wind.

* * *

Gavin Young looked up from the counter into the
man's eyes and knew at once.

His assistants busy with other customers, the
shopkeeper had retreated as was his custom to a
little nook of a side counter where he might
value the tobacco leaf and covertly make sure via
a carefully placed mirror that no one was passing
contraband to friends.

240

One can never be too careful.

The man was adequately dressed, a little shabby but the clothes of sufficient quality that he did not stand out from the clientele, yet there was a slight smell of — how to put it — unwashed flesh. And a curious mixture of stale and yet cloying sweet breath.

Beggars may not be choosers, however, though Gavin was scarcely a mendicant.

'Alexander Moncrieff passed me your name, sir?'

Not a rough voice and the fellow seemed intelligent enough to move further inside where he may not be easily seen or spied upon.

Young inclined his head in answer but no more than that — never does to look too eager. After all, was this not a mere sales transaction?

Yet his heart was racing as the man continued.

'A pity he died. So . . . unfortunate.'

'Yes,' Young replied simply.

'He gave me to understand that you . . . appreciated my humble efforts and might wish to witness the . . . creative process?'

Young caught up a breath in his throat. So, Moncrieff had passed on his earnest request.

Now or never. He was not a daring man and this might well be dangerous — who knows what could happen?

If these women were, say, diseased — even to be in the same room? And yet he must not flinch, he must be brave.

A quick glance at the concealed mirror — no one in the place had a head turned in their direction. When he looked back, there was a small scrap of paper lying on the counter.

'The address, sir,' the man remarked quietly. 'Seven thirty of this evening might, I trust, be . . . convenient?'

Young usually returned home round about this hour — that would be *most* convenient.

He could tell Martha he had his accounts to study and leave a decent interval for what might occur. And yet was it all too expedient?

Did this man know his habits? Know more than he should? Spy upon the righteous?

For, of late, he had a strange feeling that he was being dogged as he made his way home: however, when he glanced around, normality seemed in place. No, surely not — the offered time would merely be a happy coincidence.

Happy?

There was an almost uncontrollable urge of excitement in his nether regions, most unseemly, most — *uncontrollable*. None of this showed on his face, however, he was certain of that — absolutely certain.

His clean, well-kept fingers — a tobacco man must never have long fingernails; who knows what remnants of dead insects or native dust might accrue — closed round the scrap of paper and once more the head was inclined. Positively.

Then: 'There will be a cost, of course?'

'There is always a cost, sir. But I'm sure — on a regular basis — we may find mutual agreement.'

Another inclination from the shopkeeper.

The man took a deep breath as if inhaling all the scents and fumes at the one gulp, and then left. Gavin Young watched him go and then looked at his own face in the side mirror.

It was calm, untroubled. However, as yet another satisfied client left the establishment, a small jet of wind blew in from the open door and whisked up the few strands of hair that lay in precise lines across his scalp. Lifted, then laid them back in place.

But that was only a momentary disturbance. He looked around the gleaming brass and dark wood of his shop. Yes. Everything in place.

Serenity. Order. His watchword.

★ ★ ★

Whereas a current of icy blast had bullied its way in to the studio of Jack Burns as the workmen struggled to haul a large block of stone over the courtyard cobbles and then through the open door.

Jack had erected a small makeshift platform, and with much grunting and muttered oaths, the red sandstone was wedged into position.

Marble he could not afford, but from the Drumhead quarry not too far distant to Falkirk, this was affordable and perfect for purpose. The workmen had been paid and then departed, so now it was merely Jack and the goddess.

She was hidden in there somewhere but he would have much preparation before a beginning was embarked upon. He put his hand on the surface. It was cold.

Jean Brash's body had been warm and moved in ways that near defied description. He had

243

known some women in his time, but none with such oceanic tides at their command.

There was a moment when she had risen above and pinned him to the thin lumpy mattress, letting out a deep sound of pleasure that would have brought the nearest male out on the thrash like a rutting stag.

It was too powerful to be a moan and too deep to be a cry. Elemental — it resonated through her body like a bell ringing.

Not a church bell, however. Pagan. It would have terrified Saint Paul although John the Baptist might not have quailed.

For a moment her eyes had lost focus, and then they came back sharp again and looked down at him. She had smiled like a hungry tiger.

'Gird your loins, my mannie,' said the Mistress of the Just Land. 'This is just the commencement.'

★ ★ ★

Although Jean Brash did not much resemble a goddess at this same moment, as she tramped the wynds and byways of Leith — she could have found a driver for her coach or even hired a carriage, but for some reason she felt like being on the streets, where she had been raised.

Where she had watched Jessie and Nan ply their midnight trade; where she was bound to labour likewise until the fortune and misfortune of meeting Henry Preger.

This was her world.

Again she was wearing Hannah's old scabby

244

coat, but her people knew the woman inside and though there was no great fuss made, she moved through them like a queen.

The old woman had wanted to accompany her but Jean intended to shift quickly, and after Hannah, Maisie and Lily had passed out her messages to the street people, their mistress had left the messengers at the Just Land while she walked out to harvest any results.

On various street corners a nondescript man or two would arrive at her side to mutter a few words. So far nothing had emerged.

A few thought they might have witnessed someone of Jeb Summer's description near the Salamander area or down by the harbour, but it would be mostly in the dark of the night when drink had been taken and eyes blurred.

The conduits and sewer drains that ran under the surface of the parish — a rabbit warren of stench and slime — were not to be undertaken without risking life and limb. Too dark for safety, too slippery if assailed.

No. Better to find Jeb above ground — take capture there — hang the wee bugger upside down from a lamppost until the truth spilt out of him.

If indeed he still existed at all. For, apart from Lily's testimony, the most Jean could glean so far were moments that flickered on the edge of vision — out of the corner of the eye.

Only one auld besom, Mary Tibbles — a whisky mopper that slaked her drouth by sliding up to a tavern tumbler with the last dregs of raw spirit and God knows what spit and saliva

245

clinging to the bottom, then emptying it in the one gulp before the barman threw a beer-sodden towel or the contents of a bowl of dried peas in her direction — swore to have seen what might have been the man face to face. If face to face was indeed an accurate description.

'I wis emptying my bladder in a wee wynd off the harbour, Mistress, over a grating intae the sewer, when I heard a noise below. I looked down and there was a wee bugger underneath, in the depths, the street light caught him a wee toatie bit.'

Mary winced at the memory.

'My piss was dribblin' all down his face and he wis laughin'. Lik' a mad thing. Then he wis gone.'

Of course, Mary could have been spinning a tale for reward, but it seemed too outlandish not to be true. The old woman took the proffered coin, then left to buy a decent dram for a change while Jean continued on her pilgrimage.

One other approached her, a small, trim figure of a man — Archie Millar by name.

Archie ran one of the Half Uncles — the small pawnshops in Market Square: most of the men who ran these places would take advantage of their supplicants and rob them blind with no compunction, but Archie was an exception. He took profit for sure, but gave as good a possible price for the random pitiful possessions offered as surety. The interest charged was lower than others and he had the reputation of being a decent wee soul.

He also had a memory of Jeb — not an

immediate one, but he had come to offer what he could. A Queen must be honoured, especially since this particular one had provided Archie with what to his eyes was a bonny wife.

Margaret Reid now Millar had run out of steam and confessed to her mistress that the life of a magpie was no longer for her; what she desired was a quieter path. Jean knew of a certain solitary wee man who was looking for a companion he could trust.

Margaret was near twice his width, but as Hannah Semple remarked, 'Ye want someone ye can find in the dark, Mister Millar; thin women are a menace.'

So, for Leith, true love held sway. And Archie had a debt to pay that was not part of a pawnbroker's pledge.

A payment from memory. You cannot weigh memory, you cannot put a price on it, but you may slide it across the counter.

★   ★   ★

Wee Archie Millar had shivered in his bed and thought angrily of the pack of cards stolen from him earlier that week by that dirty swine Summers.

They had been his pride and joy, found on the street where some careless person had let them fall — maybe a gambler who counted them no longer lucky, maybe a player who lost a deal, maybe a child who had thrown them out of the window to spite a brother.

Jeb Summers had stolen them and laughed in

Archie's face like a monkey while Dirk Martins did the same. But they were nothing without Johnny Finch — he was the one everybody dreaded — even Jeb kissed his arse in deep fear.

One time, had Archie not seen Johnny gob right into the other's face, and Jeb stand there with a frozen evil grin while Martins and Finch laughed at the sight?

Mind you, Martins laughed to save his skin.

Then one night it all changed.

★   ★   ★

Standing on the street corner, impervious, it would seem, to a slanty cold rain that the east wind herded through Leith like a watchful sheepdog, Archie related the events of Finch's death to Jean Brash.

Of course, she had wrung some of this same story out of the craven tongue of Barton Laidlaw, but this was from the inside, from a man who had no reason to bend truth.

How the three had boasted about the bucket of filth they had poured on to Moncrieff — somebody had tipped the man off, yet only Finch had been named.

Why only Finch?

Who knows, but that was what had happened.

Archie's own tortuous path to the workhouse was another story, but he had managed at length to apprentice himself to one of the wee 'uncles' for he had a sharp mind and was trustworthy.

But to return to that night. Moncrieff had howled at them all in the kitchen after beating hell out of Johnny Finch, and then the boys had been thrown into the dormitory.

He had slept beside Dirk Martins's bed, so overheard the exchange between Jeb and Dirk when the dwarf went to see Johnny.

'How long,' asked Jean suddenly, 'had Moncrieff been away by then?'

'Maybe an hour or two.'

'D'you think he went back . . . to beat the boy some more?'

'No. We would have heard the screams. Anyway he said he was going back in the morning. To do some more damage.'

The remark produced a silence, and then Archie continued how he had keeked out from slit eyes to witness Jeb return with news that Finch was not moving.

'How long was Jeb away?'

'Twenty minutes. Maybe. Hard tae tell.'

Then Archie had seen them cut hands and swear vengeance.

He thus acquainted Jean with what had followed after Finch's death, how Jeb and Dirk had ruled the roost as if favourites of Moncrieff, the man smiling on indulgently. But then, out of the blue, the Smiler — for that was Dirk's nickname — was taken away by a couple of visitors.

He had watched through the window — nice folk, they seemed, English spoken, Dirk a' dressed neat, his fair hair combed flat and parted. Off went the carriage and that very night Jeb Summers had slid out a window, never to be seen again.

Jean nodded her thanks, reappraised her people to watch and be careful, then asked one other thing.

In the Just Land, she had gone back to look at the photographs. Not from any joy, for sure, but to look again at the particular face of one pinioned woman. It had to be — now that her eyes were not affected by the nausea in her belly — Nan Dunlop.

Search her out, Jean told them, find her and lead me to her. Don't seek high, seek low.

The mistress then returned to the Just Land. She had a feeling that come the night there would be some kind of resolution to all this.

What she did not anticipate, on moving the key in the lock and opening the door, was witnessing Hannah Semple's stony face while behind her rampaged the figure of Inspector James McLevy.

The man was raging fit to burst, and he let out a bellow that would have terrified the well-stuffed Septimus, next door in the main salon.

The bear spent its time looking up at the painting of the octopus — who knows what they thought of each other, especially now that the sea creature had a hole right between its eyes — but that did not concern the inspector for the moment.

'Jean Brash, I want a word wi' you!'

29

Little Polly Flinders
Sat among the cinders,
Warming her pretty little toes.
Mother came and caught her
And whipped her little daughter
For spoiling her nice new clothes.

What followed post bellow had all the elements of a French farce interspersed with the apocalyptic prospects of ruination and a long prison sentence.

Comedy and tragedy. Kissing behind the curtain.

An apoplectic McLevy marched the women into the kitchen in no way assuaged by offers of sugar biscuits or a Lebanese grinding, Hannah frantically trying to signal something at Jean that the mistress could not remotely fathom and such signalling cut short when the inspector turned a bleak and suspicious eye.

To say McLevy was disenchanted with the provider of his only decent coffee would be to understate the matter. Silence hung in the air like a thundercloud of mischance. Then the inspector broke it.

'Recognise this?'

He produced a note that Jean cursed herself for writing, and even worse signing her name, but when she looked closer, what proved black icing on the cake was the fact that Laidlaw had dated the damn thing — otherwise she could have claimed it to be from another time.

Long, long ago before a dead judge lay in the cheese room in the depths of the Just Land.

No time to worry about this. Now she would have to brazen it out though surely there wasn't too much harm done. The councillor would not dare to make official complaint, he believed that Jean had too much on him. So what in God's name was McLevy in such a fankle about?

Yet the one thing she did not know was what Hannah had been told by the inspector and had been trying to convey by dint of hauling graphically at her neck and sticking a tongue out at the side, mimetic persuasion not being the old woman's strong point, namely that . . .

'Barton Laidlaw was murdered last night,' announced McLevy with an evil glint in his eye. 'Strung up lik' a leg o' lamb on a flesher's hook.'

Jean schooled her features to betray nothing. Mind you, this disclosure was enough to turn even Pallas Athena's bowels to water and the goddess only had Medusa's hair to worry over, not James McLevy.

The man himself moved in close quarters.

'Ye were there last night, don't attempt tae deny it. The fellow is now dead. Explain yourself.'

The note itself precluded any decent swerving. It had read:

Dear Mister Laidlaw,
    I would be obliged if you might spare me

252

some time this evening. A matter of some
importance.
   Yours,
   Jean Brash

Of course, she could try bare-faced denial,
claim it to be a forgery, but some instinct told
her the attempt would be a waste of time.

Besides, if she was found out to have lied, that
would put a tin lid on it. As well as the black
icing.

'I needed some advice from . . . poor Mister
Laidlaw. Murdered — what a dreadful thing to
happen,' Jean responded slowly, while her mind
was racing fit to burst.

'Advice about what?'

Why not get as near some kind of truth as she
could, for when we run out of falsehood, what
else is left?

Murray Craddock, who was McLevy's over-
riding superior and a man the inspector heartily
detested, had been after Jean for years — nipping
at her ankles like a yappy dog.

'I had heard that . . . a certain chief constable
was moving to put a motion through the council
to close the Just Land under an official order.'

A grudging nod from the inspector. Craddock
had tried this once before and had been
outmanoeuvred by Jean. The man was an idiot,
but dangerous enough — and he lodged high up
in the Leith Masonic, way above Lieutenant
Roach.

'And I wanted to make sure Mister Laidlaw
would be on my side of the situation.'

'Tae bribe him, ye mean?'

Jean affected an enigmatic look with a slight trace of culpability, as Hannah weighed in with a lot less subtle support.

'Well she didnae go tae bliddy hang him by the neck, that's for certain sure.'

McLevy knew well that it had taken at least two people to effect the hanging and murder — but there was nothing to say that Jean couldn't have been one of them. He doubted that, of course, but would proceed as if she was guilty as hell because one way or another, the woman was in this up to her long white neck.

'So ye admit ye went to bribe the man?'

'Not at all. Merely to ask that I be offered a measure of protection.'

The inspector grunted and Jean hoped they had moved the discussion to safer ground, but you could never tell with James McLevy. As his next words proved.

'You were outside his house howling lik' a wolf. Why do so if you hadn't just made a kill?'

Hannah's eyes widened — this was news to her. Mark you, somebody who shoots an octopus is capable of anything.

Jean was rocked right back on her heels — was there nothing the man did not know?

'Says who?' she managed somewhat inelegantly.

'I have a witness.'

She sensed a missing beat in the words.

'You're bluffing.'

'The very fact you ask means ye did it.'

Hannah had drawn back. She had seen these

two lock horns before and it was best to stay out of the way. Besides, she had other things to worry about: the whereabouts of that lang dreep of a constable, for instance.

Jean moved in so that her face was close to the inspector's — equal and opposite.

They had been through many scrapes together, life and death, love and hate, and now existed at a wary distance from each other where a depth of feeling was balanced by realisation that a line had to be drawn — and not crossed over.

Neither expected any mercy. Mercy is a luxury in this world.

She was adjacent enough that he could smell her perfume, some French concoction, no doubt, and he was also aware that the mistress was probably breathing in the remnant fragrance of a hastily bolted meal of hairy tatties — mashed potato and dried saltfish.

Jean did indeed inhale that aroma. While it was not unpleasant, it was far from seductive.

'Let us suppose,' she said softly, 'that Mister Laidlaw offered me his . . . assistance in answer to my prayers . . . and outside his domicile, as the rain battered into my face, I . . . because I had achieved my desire . . . released myself to the elements.'

Green eyes looked into grey. The tiger and the wolf.

'Have ye never done that, James?' she asked. 'Or do you keep it hidden down too deep?'

'Release myself?'

'In joy and liberation.'

'I don't recognise these words.'

'What a pity.'

'And I know you're up tae something.'

'How come?'

'Ye sent Hannah tae question after Alexander Moncrieff. He and Laidlaw died similar, jist a different card.'

He snapped out the Queen of Spades from his top pocket and held it right before her eyes.

Again she kept her composure. And again he surprised her.

'Moncrieff had the Ten, Laidlaw the Queen and I'm wondering, Jean Brash, where is the Jack o' Spades?'

As if in answer a distant voice called from the lower reaches.

'I've reached the end of the line, sir. Not one step further can be accomplished!'

My God.

Mulholland.

In all the entangling furore and panic, it had totally slipped Jean's mind that the constable, usually like McLevy's shadow, was not on hand.

So where the hell was he?

'On my way, Mulholland,' bawled the inspector, and he set off out through the kitchen door.

As Jean and Hannah hurtled after, a hissed exchange took place between them.

'The constable jist ducked oot the kitchen door; I couldnae stop him, Mistress.'

'Ye should have cut the bugger's throat.'

'He'd jist arrest me.'

'McLevy!' bawled Jean, reverting for a

moment to a creature of the wynds. 'Ye have no right to let your damn constable run loose in my establishment!'

'He just likes tae wander,' was the cheerful response as the inspector tripped daintily down the stone stairs that led to the cellars, conveniently forgetting that it was he, in fact, who had instructed Mulholland to slide off and nose around.

And there was the man himself, standing in front of the cellar cheese room door, looking faintly aggrieved.

'I poked into most places down below, even where the girls leather hell out of those who desire such benison but' — to prove a point he rattled the door unavailingly to and fro — 'this one has refused me entry.'

'Whit's in here?' asked McLevy.

'None of your damned business,' replied Jean Brash.

'It's locked,' said Mulholland helpfully.

'Where's the key?' This from the inspector.

'Lost,' said Hannah desperately.

'I can solve that, Hannah, don't you worry your head. I am a policeman. We solve things.'

With the air of a prestidigitator, he produced an iron ring of lockpicks, a parting present from one of Leith's most skilful practitioners, Donnie Pettigrew, who, on becoming a cobbler, had said farewell to a life of criminal activity and gifted the implements to McLevy.

His wife Mary, in fact, was the one who had discovered Laidlaw's body — all roads lead to Leith.

'That's against the law!'

Jean's fury at this invasion was such that she thought for a moment of hauling out her derringer and shooting the man where he stood. But as she hesitated over this somewhat precipitous action, he deftly inserted the little rod, twiddled like a surgeon and sprang the lock to release the heavy door.

And that was it. Open sesame. They all looked in.

To discover an empty table.

The grey sheet was upon it, but nothing else. In a totally vacant room.

McLevy sniffed.

'Cheesy,' he announced.

'French fromage,' said Hannah. 'Doesnae half stink, eh? Worse than the dry boak.'

This word, a picturesque term for heaving up the innards till there was nothing left to heave, not only summed up Hannah's view of French fromage, but gave Jean a chance to think.

'We're about to clean out the room,' she added, trying to hold back a desire to shout *Stick that in your pipe and smoke it.* 'The crumbs get everywhere and the rodents go mad . . . frighten my girls.'

'Why lock the door, then?'

This logical question of the constable's brought a lightning and apparently common-sense answer.

'To keep the mice inside, of course.'

Such skewed logic cut little ice with McLevy but on that note the police took their leave, the inspector promising to return when he had *further investigated.*

He knew as sure as a dog had fleas that Jean was up to something rank as the French cheese. When he found a connection between Laidlaw and Moncrieff, he would know more.

How far back did the connection go? Was it possible Moncrieff once worked for Laidlaw?

And how had he been recommended for that workhouse in the Haymarket?

When McLevy asked at the place, the reason seemed beyond the present officials, lost in history, and he had left it there, having other avenues to explore.

'That may have been a mistake,' he said out of the blue to Mulholland.

'What might have been?'

'Never mind. I'll go back to go forward. And keep in your head, Constable. Every moment of this . . . we tremble upon the edge of disgrace!'

With that ironic echo of his lieutenant's words, he headed off, stubby little legs moving at twice the pace to match the loping strides of his colleague.

In the Just Land, Jean and Hannah had watched carefully in case the police suddenly turned round and came back howling blue murder that they had seen a dead judge stuck out on the roof amongst the chimney pots.

When this did not happen, they looked at each other.

'Either it was an act of God,' said Jean, 'or Maisie and Lily are in the frame.'

With that they sped upstairs to knock upon the girls' door, identifying theirselves to be who they indeed were and minus official invigilators.

A voice bade them enter. They did so.

Maisie and Lily sat primly inside on two small armchairs, hands folded in laps like a pair of maiden aunts at the seaside.

They looked up in silence at Jean and Hannah before Maisie cleared her throat.

'Lily saw them come in and knew the danger. So we sneaked doon the stairs and took the key frae the hook above the lintel where it is aye planked hideyways.'

Indeed, had McLevy known of this, he could have saved himself a fandango with the lock-picks.

'The body was stiff as a Sabbath corset,' continued Maisie. 'We shoogled him out of there, locked the place, replaced the key and then up the stairs intae the hall . . . Oh my God . . . we were praying that door wouldnae open and McLevy's big baw face stick itself out the kitchen!'

Lily suddenly did a remarkably accurate imitation of the inspector's gargoyle visage when on the trail of the unwary and Maisie broke into near hysterical laughter at the danger passed.

Hannah laughed as well but Jean's face was set. Too close for comfort, too near to home. It had to end.

'Where did you stash the judge?' she asked quietly.

'We got him up the stairs right enough,' replied Maisie. 'But then we ran out of notions. Didnae want tae stick him under the bed wi' the chamber pots.'

She gestured vaguely towards a largeish

wardrobe in the corner of the room.

Hannah marched over and pulled open the door.

There, wedged bolt upright amidst the various outfits of their trade — dresses of a shepherdess, leather-bound dominations, nurses attire and garments ranging from Egyptian bizarre to ordinary Leith street clothes — was the rigid form of Judge Hilton Abercrombie.

When first searching Abercrombie's house, Jean Brash had experienced a vision of John Knox looking out of the wardrobe. Perhaps she had been more prescient than she realised, for here was another visitation. Cheeks sucked in, dry flesh pulled tight, lips puckered up like a Halloween ghost, his sightless eyes hooded malevolently as if about to pronounce sentence.

Jean signalled to Hannah, who shut him back out of sight.

'It was all Lily's idea, Mistress,' Maisie said eagerly. 'She's a clever wee devil.'

Lily, however, was anxious that Jean's face was still hard to read as she stared at the now closed wardrobe. But then the mistress turned to her and smiled a little. All was forgiven. The past wiped clean.

'You did well, Lily.'

This had to end, Jean thought.

Tomorrow court sessions would start again and the absence of a hanging judge would be brought to notice.

The gallows rope would swing for nothing and folk would begin to ask questions.

One way or another, this night it had to end.

30

When I was a little boy,
I washed my mammy's dishes;
Now I am a great boy
I roll in golden riches.

He should kill Jeb and be done with it. A series of wild thoughts ran through Dirk's mind. Yes. Kill him.

He had noticed as he'd dressed to leave this night that one of his best cufflinks was lacking a coloured stone. Too late now to change, just keep it in place. But was it an omen? No, just an accident. And who knows, he might come across it again.

It would be easy. The dwarfie swine turns his back and then, in the pocket of his coat, Dirk has secreted a claw hammer. Bought this very day. New. Shiny. The claw itself razor sharp and ready for an instant kill, like a bear's talon. Except not the throat. No. Back of the head will do the trick.

The wee bastard trusted him — as much as he trusted anybody — he would turn his back — to tend the rat's grave, maybe — yes — to tidy up the earth, say, make sure the cross was straight as a die, and then — one crack.

He had an image of Jeb's head spouting blood, the albino falling on his face, and then another strike, and another, and another, and another. Till nothing moved.

Except maybe the blood, but that would be slow and he could shift his polished shoes — painstakingly cleaned by the hotel porter and already picking up dirty mud in the tunnel as he moved along — yes, shift them out of the way and leave the dead body to lie there till the other rats, not white but brown or even black, claimed the dead dwarf for their own.

Crawl over. Bite in. Welcome to the feast.

No one would ever go down there. No one would ever find him. Save the rodents.

After all, Jeb could not complain: had the albino not created the man who murdered him; given him the taste for blood and a feeling that throbbed all the way to his waiting gonads?

Filled the scrotum, true enough.

Dirk had been raised by adoptive parents — a decent, honest pair with a small grocery shop in Bristol. They had given him their name, changed his Christian one to that of his new father. A great honour.

Raised him to be a good boy, a fine boy, an obedient boy, a decent boy who smiled easy, who wore a white collar in the world of business, a sweet boy.

Look at him now.

Thank God they had died early, proud of what they had done, what he would achieve. Mind you, at times he had been a bad boy, with the local girls especially, and to hang a cat up by its tail, then stone it to death — well, all the boys did that, it was part of growing up.

You grew up, the cat hung down.

To be cruel is to be human. As long as it's

hidden behind a smile, what does it matter? Childhood glory.

Yet now he had to grow up all over again. Should never have come back here — but too late for that. Jeb had pulled him back into the dark, the past had taken root in the present — though he still had the chance to make a deal. A big deal. Make his name.

Tomorrow they would meet with Forbes Crichton and grease the wheels.

Business is business. Money comes first. Money was the Golden Calf.

It could all be shattered, though, if something went wrong, if the killers were caught. What if people were watching even now, waiting for them to make a mistake?

His whole life could be destroyed!

But Jeb would not give it up.

Dirk was sensible. Jeb was mad.

No more deaths. Except for one addition. He near laughed aloud at that.

'Ye're early.'

Jeb spoke the words from where he sat in a corner, chewing at a bone of sorts he had found in the scaffie bins behind the flesher's shop. A ham bone, bits of the meat still fresh and tasty. God bless the pig.

A small black rat that Jeb was feeding up to replace his poisoned pet scuttled off at Dirk's arrival.

The Smiler could now find his way to the cave even in the dark, for though it had just turned evening outside in the street, the light had already gone — anyway, down here it was never light. Save for the candles. Just like a church.

The dwarf sized up his visitor. In that hotel room, Jeb thought the man to have lost his nerve but now he seemed in better fettle. Smiling.

They stared at each other, each watcher with thoughts of administered death.

'The tobacco man comes first,' said Jeb with a sly grin. 'I watch his shop — he waits all by himself at night. You can chap the door, he'll trust your face.'

He giggled at that. His little joke. Dirk's mouth was dry.

'What . . . about the holy man?'

'He walks out late. We can take him in one o' the side streets. Hang him from a crossbeam.'

Jeb threw the bone carelessly into another corner for the rat to get later, and wiped his mouth across with a sleeve.

'Is that not . . . risky?' asked Dirk.

'God's on his side, we have the devil. In this world, devil wins out every time.'

Then Jeb grinned again and took out from the recesses of his monkish outfit two more playing cards, holding them playfully in his long, curved fingernails. King and Ace of Spades.

'As long as ye kiss the devil's arse, the game will never be lost!'

The dwarf roared with laughter at that idea. Dirk echoed the laughter but it was an empty noise. The man was mad. No doubt about it. Put him out of his misery, that would be the best thing.

One of the candles guttered and Jeb moved to replace it with another. His back was to the

Smiler. Jeb lit one candle with its fellow, and some of the hot wax dropped on his skin. Burned hot but only for a moment and then a skin formed.

Pain often hides behind a skin.

For some reason the dwarf's mind went back.

★ ★ ★

Jeb slid open the door to Moncrieff's room to witness Johnny Finch slumped face down upon the Pole of Correction.

Was he dead? Was he alive? Was he sorry for what he'd done?

The shirt had been stripped off his back and the welts were livid against the white skin, blood oozing from deep slashes where Moncrieff had laid it on with a vengeance.

The albino walked across softly and crouched a little so that his face was level with the other boy.

Johnny's head was to the side, mouth open, slavers dribbling down, eyes shut towards the other. The eyes flickered open.

The mouth drew in a small gob of saliva and with his remaining strength, Johnny spat it into Jeb's face.

★ ★ ★

Now, thought the Smiler. Do it now.

The dwarf was still hunched over, head silhouetted by the fitful candlelight. Dirk had taken out the hammer, raised it high.

Now. Do it now!

But he could not.

In his mind's eye he saw the hammer descend, the blood gush, the figure crumple, but it was as if something had frozen inside him, as if he could not move.

Then Jeb let out a whimpering noise and Dirk quickly hid the hammer behind his back. He could still do it, though. He could still do it!

Jeb turned and his eyes were full of tears — they ran down his white skin like so many streams down a sheer chalk face when a hard rain falls. But a man can cry for many different reasons.

'Johnny,' he muttered brokenly. 'I saw him. In the room. I saw him — dying.'

He fell to his knees in front of Dirk, head bowed to the floor like a sacrificial victim.

The Smiler put the hammer back into his coat pocket. He could not do it. Paralysed by old times. Too late now.

The die was cast.

31

My mother said that I never should
Play with the gypsies in the wood;
If I did, she would say,
Naughty girl to disobey.

Sarah Baines lay naked in her studio bed. Not Pallas Athena naked, more the human variety.

The meeting had been a strange affair. Jack Burns and two of his more shady companions had turned up and, to their surprise, had been welcomed by Louisa Lumsden.

But welcomed as what? Patriarchal exemplifiers?

At first the men had sat somewhat awkwardly amongst the all-female audience, because although at least a pair of them had come with the idea of causing mischief, they were also curious as to what might be discussed.

And though they paid some attention to the idea that women might one day be granted an equality of sorts, that day was far distant. Until then, they would look on with a kindly eye but also an eye that might note the contours of a female colleague and hope for a sidelong glance denoting her desire for more than just equality.

Perhaps even this night, in this gathering, for there were many young ladies that might never have met such dashing louche lads the likes of them.

The male is ever hopeful that the female will wish to improve the race through his beneficial blessings.

Jack, however, had recently experienced the power of a goddess in full flow and had had his eyes opened to a plethora of sexual drive and forceful intelligence that had left him — as it were — flat on his back.

So while his two companions might hide a sly smile, his feeling was more one of wondering if something might be coming their way in tackety boots.

Louisa spoke for two hours without hesitation, with passion, and a heartfelt fire that pinned back the ears.

The young women who had come to Sarah's studio were social acquaintances with a certain education and an intellectual bent towards independence of thought — mind you, the idea of politically augmented self-sufficiency and sexual determination might faintly alarm at this very moment.

The militancy that was yet to come could well have terrified them, but by that time their muscles would have strengthened, eyes and teeth sharpened, so who is to know that amongst these refined and delicate creatures a different breed of combatant might not be already in formation?

They were informed by Miss Lumsden, in case it had passed them by, of the discrepancy as regards the looming Municipal Franchise for women and the fact that although they might vote for a councillor, they would yet be denied the vote for a member of parliament.

'They throw us seeds,' expostulated Joanna, 'as if we were canaries in a cage.'

She also forecast a healthy rise in the divorce rate now that the Married Woman's Property Act had restored women to their own legal identity.

'You may own, sell and buy property, you may sue and be sued; you may even be made bankrupt!'

Laughter at that but a hard truth was embedded in these words. The canary could leave its cage . . .

All this was delivered with great authority, for Miss Lumsden was a headmistress. She ruled the roost. Most decidedly not a cagebird.

At her school, St Leonards, in the town of St Andrews, she emphasised physical development, team spirit in games, academic application of mathematics and the classics — all right in a boys' academy, perhaps, but were not little girls made of sugar and spice?

Of course, the words *sugar* and *spice* may have many different meanings — sugar might be sublimely seductive, and did not Richard III refer to a certain royal pudenda as a *nest of spicery*?

As regards the academic qualities, her girls had minds sharp as Hannah Semple's cut-throat razor.

Louisa herself was tall, willowy, with a clear complexion and lush chestnut-coloured hair that, though pinned up, tumbled to her shoulders if unleashed. She had a thrilling low voice, which when charged with emotion, sent a pang of pleasure through Sarah's impressionable secret parts.

Her finishing words were exalted, uplifting, but contained an underlying note of warning that might be summed up in the old Scots phrase *Wha's not fur us, might weel be against us. Gardyloo!*

She fixed her audience with an unwavering eye and remarked the following formal statement of intent:

'We do not wish to usurp, but we will not bow the head any longer. We will reform the world to all that is wise, humane and holy. With a woman's power, in a woman's way. But we will bow the head no more.

'Those who stay in the house will not hear the call; those who ignore it will pay a price.'

Though willowy, she was fulsomely endowed and her proud bosom heaved to emphasise the point.

As the audience left with slightly dazed murmurs of thanks and the two other men sidled out to head for the nearest tavern, Jack Burns was one of the last to leave. He thought for a brief instant of asking Louisa about the possibilities of posing, but after a warning flash of fire from Sarah's eyes, decided against it.

The headmistress extended her hand and Jack found the grip strong — it reminded him of a different clasp, for a different reason, from a different woman, who had soared above him like a hunting eagle. And then swooped.

Mister Burns closed the door in farewell.

That just left Sarah and Louisa Lumsden. Face to face.

So while murder and mayhem were breaking

out all over Leith, while folk hung from beams by the neck and every narrow wynd pulsed with sin and danger, while blackest treachery waited to leap out from an alley, love's beginnings joined in the dance.

Sarah thanked the lecturer politely and tried to halt a certain anarchic tremble that had set itself going in the upper thigh of her left leg.

Louisa replied even more politely that it had been a pleasure and she must now leave to catch the last train back to St Andrews — a long journey via Leuchars.

Of course there was an early train one could take the next morning, but she had carelessly forgotten to ask her friends in Edinburgh for a bed where she might lay her weary head upon the pillow.

She had thrown on a long dark blue travelling cape with a hood that set off her striking looks and gave her the appearance of a heroine in some romantic novel.

Sarah Baines was rather petite and gazed up at this dashing creature with the hazel eyes and chestnut hair.

The creature waited. She was a headmistress, after all — and they never make the first move.

The trembling in Sarah's leg had now become a hammer jolt, to match a certain pounding in the heart.

Miss Lumsden could stay here, though it was a small bed in a side alcove behind a rose curtain that had been rigged up to provide a decent modesty. If such was needed.

And what about Miss Baines?

She ... she ... Was that a squeak in someone's voice? Miss Baines would go home to her father.

'That would be a pity,' murmured Joanna. 'I do so enjoy your company.'

Sarah closed her eyes as the other moved towards her, so near she could smell a perfume of some kind. The artist never wore any herself for fear of provoking her father to religious reprimand or inciting her male colleagues to unbridled lust, but now she wished she had dunked herself in a vat of violets.

However, when she opened her eyes again, Louisa had moved away to pick up the recent drawing Sarah had made of the old woman with the sad, bruised countenance.

'This is yours?'

Sarah nodded, not wishing to risk another squeak.

'It is very good. You have real talent.'

The headmistress unexpectedly slid the cape from off her shoulders and draped it over an empty easel.

'I believe I've missed that train.'

It was as if she had, in the one action, shed all her clothing. To Sarah's eyes, as if completely naked.

And Louisa?

She saw a young tender girl, exquisite, with an erotic vulnerability that was irresistible. And Louisa never resisted temptation.

'Might you, perhaps — may I call you Sarah?'

'Please.'

'Sarah ... lower the lamps. I find candlelight

more conducive to . . . communication.'

The artist did as she was bid as if hypnotised — the whole scene had taken on a hallucinatory quality as if something from the *Arabian Nights*.

'It might also be conducive to lock the door.'

This was also accomplished by Sarah.

'Come here,' was the next command and, like a good pupil, Sarah obeyed her teacher.

Joanna tilted Sarah's face with an extended index finger under the chin and then kissed her. Softly at first, but then more demanding, with a long, sweet tongue that tasted like honeycomb.

'It is cold in this place,' she whispered. 'Let us seek out . . . a little warmth together.'

Joanna divested.

Sarah divested.

One more kiss, the shivering not all due to a bitter climate, the taller woman leaning over, the more petite up on tiptoes, and then the pair tumbled into bed with a whoop of laughter and longing.

The lovemaking was fierce and tender by turn, curves of bodies entwining, tongue and touch, a passion that rose and engulfed both. Finally Sarah shuddered and let out a most unladylike yell of triumph and release.

The candles dimmed their lights in tribute to the power of such sensual explosion.

Sarah was breathless, her head buried into the neck of her lover, Joanna's long fingers, index and fore, resting quietly inside the artist like brush strokes.

'Your hymen remains intact,' murmured Joanna. 'Still a virgin, I'm afraid. But don't despair, there's more to come. Mother Nature is rich and bountiful.'

Sometime later, Sarah Baines woke up naked in her studio bed, snaked herself closer to the headmistress of pleasure and then went back to sleep.

And some time after that, a key moved softly in the outside lock, the studio door opened, and a respectable and religious head poked itself inside.

William Baines had come to protect his daughter from the ravening artistic predators of Leith. His eyesight was not all it could be and only one of the candles had survived the previous erotic shockwaves, so the man of God was not all seeing.

The room appeared empty and he advanced a little timidly into the space to find the drawn face of an old raddled woman staring at him bleakly from a corner.

There was little piety in the regard and so William averted his eyes to seek greener pastures. At least no hirsute arrant rogue painter was to be viewed, and for that relief, thanks be to God.

Then he heard a contented sigh from the side alcove where he knew a small bed had its place. Another sigh.

The rose curtain had been drawn across and his fingers were clumsy and fumbling as he inched the material back to gain admission of sorts.

The light was still feeble and flickering behind him but enough that he could make out two shapes under the blankets — blankets that he recognised as favourites of his dear departed wife.

One of them even had her initial embroidered large — M for Mary — sacred mother of our Redeemer.

One of the shapes moved restlessly and threw back the covers.

William was stricken to the core as he viewed his own daughter's naked breast, shameless, with one little hard nipple pointing up at him like an arrowhead.

He shook his head in horror. What was he doing? A nipple — his own daughter's. This must not be allowed. This must not be . . .

Then a hand came across and covered the breast. For a moment he was relieved and then even more horror-stricken. Another hand must belong to another body. Another *naked* body?

He could not restrain a high-pitched yelp like a dog with its tail trodden underfoot, and that other body must have heard this noise.

A hand drew Sarah protectively away from William and into . . . Another breast — naked — larger, from what he could see. The holy man stood there like a pillar of salt. A woman's head raised up.

From Joanna's point of view, she had feared that this was one of Sarah's wild artist friends who had blundered in for some wayward reason.

But then she saw the smooth round face, the gasping, parted lips and a stout neck that bulged over the stiff, unmistakable collar of a Presbyterian minister.

The man's mouth opened and shut but no sound emerged. Unusual for a preacher.

William tried to form words — words of anger, of retribution, of outraged betrayal, of patriarchal shame and just revulsion. But all he could manage was a croak.

The woman was handsome, striking, as Jezebel must have been, or Delilah. A sinful seductress. With his own daughter beside her naked body.

Was that a look of pity on her face? How dare she extend pity to a man of such deceived rectitude? He pointed an accusing finger, to shout like Moses on the mountain, to tell her of the rank offence, to damn her forever to the flames of hell . . .

For what said Romans 1: 26?

For this cause God gave them up unto vile affections: for even their women did change the natural use into that which is against nature —

But once more nothing emerged, the devout struck dumb by immorality upon Earth.

A rising in his gorge caused William Baines to flee this den of iniquity, crashing the door shut behind him. The noise partly woke Sarah and she whimpered in her sleep. Joanna drew the girl in closer.

It would be a long passage — the morrow could be quite another matter — but she aimed to relish every living moment of this night, every living moment that held the sweet scent of love.

32

There was an old woman
tossed up in a basket,
Seventeen times as high as the moon;
Where she was going no mortal could tell
For in her hand she carried a broom.

The broken woman sat in the Rusty Nail and tried to still her trembling fingers as they hooked around a small cracked tumbler that still contained a drib of the cheapest raw whisky.

Legend had it that a sheep's head skull had once been left in its barrel overnight and by morning had dissolved into nothingness. Hence the name Ramsheid Dip.

She had nursed it for near two hours, purchased with the last coins the wee lassie had given her for sitting like a lump of coal while her face, ugly as the sin of Judas, was scratched out on a big sheet of paper.

At the end the lassie allowed her to look at what had been achieved. A ruin.

Ravaged like a cornfield.

If the sitter had sighted close enough, she could have traced a reason for every line, every crack, every deep gouge. But one keek was sufficient, thanks.

A midden of bones and skin.

Another wee sip. At least it was warm in here. Soon she'd drain the glass and head off for a colder place, a cruel place. Was this what she deserved for a wicked life?

She had been wild, vicious even. But not any more. Now she was beaten. Broken.

Wiser too late.

That drawing didnae know the half of it. The trouble with these folk was they aye looked in from the outside.

Artists be damned. Jist gawking in through the window.

'Hello, Nan,' said a voice.

And there she was. Jean Brash. Once a wee girl in a dirty yellow dress and now, resplendent in a lilac coat and a neat French bonnet, the Mistress of the Just Land.

A fine lady, her appearance had reduced the threadbare tavern to an awed silence. A queen amongst them. Like Victoria Regina. Even Shug the barman folded his beer cloth into a tidy square by way of skewed veneration.

From Jean's point of view, she looked down at a wrecked, withdrawn figure, as if the vital juices had been drained out of the woman.

And Nan had once been vital. Elemental. Dangerous. Long ago. In another time. Another life.

★ ★ ★

The one thing Henry Preger loved above all things was to have two women fighting over his favours.

The older one, Nan Dunlop, was a bit of a wild animal. He liked that trait in a woman, but

279

this time she had gone too far. Spitting in the face of the other young bitch, a girl she'd brought to Henry — a virgin, Nan had claimed.

Henry took care of that on the first night but there was something in the girl he could not reach, could not bring under his heel, could not fathom, could not enslave or subdue. So he kept her for himself.

It was never in him to be afraid, but though he was aching to own her and had made her his mistress; though he crushed her in his arms and made her watch while he beat hell out of other people, both men and women, even with all that he sensed she was waiting — for a moment — in time.

Nan had been his other fancy trallop for a while but she had no class. Henry liked class in a mistress so he could destroy it — made it all worth the while. This girl — Jean Brash — was like something he had never met before.

Would she be the death of him? he wondered, and then laughed at that thought. He would live for ever.

Nan's claws were out and she screamed blue murder — no class, right enough. She put them right up against the girl's face. All she had to do was rip them down.

'You took me in when I had need,' said Jean Brash. 'I owe you that much. Scrape away.'

The older woman had turned to stone. Jean left the room — a dirty wee room at the back of the Foul Anchor tavern.

Henry wrenched Nan round and slapped her hard across the face — she liked that often. It *roused her. But this time it was not a precursor to violent penetration.*

'On your way,' said Henry Preger. 'If I see you in here again, I'll cut ye deep, frae low tae high.'

★ ★ ★

Both women now faced each other in a different tavern and recalled that last time they had met from very different angles of memory.

Preger had nearly broken her, Jean Brash recalled; that evil, insidious imprint Moncrieff had shafted into her childlike psyche was always there, like a devil out of hell, tugging at the faded yellow dress, hauling her down into a black pit of submissive addiction.

Dependency upon a cruel and callous depravity. A need for inflicted pain as a token of affection. She fought it from the depths of her soul but the sheer bestial ferocity of Preger was like a storm beating in at her, night and day.

And then one evening in the Foul Anchor a young constable had appeared. Like Jean, he seemed on the point of defeat. But then she had smiled at him, winked an eye, and Henry Preger was smashed down, never to rise again.

Now the sum of her life, all of her memories, had brought her to this one moment of time. In another tavern.

The mistress had been prowling restlessly in the Just Land, when word of Nan had been brought in — the woman who had sold her into whoredom, but since the seller knew nothing else, she could hardly be blamed.

No time like the present; no time to waste. So Jean got to it. Moncrieff had sold these vile images and the man who made them must know something, someone. It was a long shot. She had her people watching both Gavin Young and William Baines in case of a happenstance, but until then she could either scratch her behind or repeat a test of bravery from the dirty wynds of childhood.

The boys would kick over a wasp's nest and then run like hell. The slowest got stung or sometimes one of them was tied up and left nearby. For fun.

Jean was not tied up, but this night she would kick over the wasp's nest and stand her ground.

Even if it meant confronting all the demons from the past — the time with Preger had been a hellish torment and to go back there was to relive that emotion.

The deeper you buried it, however, the stronger it became.

'I believe I saw you in a photograph not long ago,' she remarked to Nan. 'In agony. Pinned to a wheel. A dirty business, I would think.'

'Aye,' Nan muttered. 'But a girl has tae live.'

For a moment there was a flash of humour in the pain-racked face and Jean was transported back to that first moment when they had met.

Nan's bright green bonnet dancing in the air.

Jessie's wise, creased face with eyes that had seen eternity and not blinked.

'I'll try to help you if I can,' Jean offered. 'But you have to help me.'

'Nothing for nothing, eh?'

'I can give you money. Find a clean room. I owe you that much, at least.'

An echo of words from long ago. Life is often nothing but a series of echoes.

'Ye owe me nothing,' the woman replied. 'I treatit ye worse than bad wi' that bastard Preger.'

The mistress nodded acceptance of that truth.

'I owe you anyway. You saved me.'

'I sold ye.'

'Business is business.'

Nan tried to straighten up and caught a glimpse of herself in one of the tavern mirrors. 'Mind you,' she said. 'See where it's got me, eh?'

'You can make amends,' replied Jean. 'With some information.'

Nan's turn to nod.

'These . . . images. Who takes them and where?'

The other woman's lips twisted in a tired smile.

'I'm due tae haul my battered auld body there this very night.'

'Well, you will not. Just give me the name of this man and where to find him.'

Nan told the name. The address. And Jean closed her eyes. What an idiot. She should have known.

Hannah was waiting at the bar. Jean had asked her to wait — the meeting with Nan might be a touch delicate. Jean crossed back to the old woman and gestured to where the other still sat with the empty whisky tumbler clasped in her mottled hand.

283

'Take Nan to Mrs Dewar's and make sure she's settled.'

Minnie Dewar — a kindly soul — ran a boarding house for waifs and strays — she would take care of Nan till Jean found a better solution.

'Whaur are you heading out for?'

Jean looked at Hannah's concerned face and smiled almost gaily as she fingered the derringer that lay snugly in a hidden pocket of her lilac coat.

'I'm going to get my photograph taken,' said she.

33

Away birds away,
Take a little. Leave a little,
And do not come again;
For if you do,
I will shoot you through,
And there is an end — an end of you.

Jeb giggled to himself as he heard the Smiler cursing under his breath while his nice shiny shoes got planked into yet another oily dank puddle.

They were in complete darkness save for a stump of candle the dwarf carried before him. He had many such stumps in the various pouches of his covering habit — needed because he traversed far and wide under the streets of Leith and knew these tunnels and cavern sewers like a rat knows its hidey-holes.

The dwarf had recovered himself; that bad passage when he had remembered the spit in his face and everything it raised up in his guts had vanished like a dead memory.

And were they not presently on the last trail?

Two more to go and then — and then — what?

What would he do then? What fine vengeance could he follow? He had come to enjoy death. He would miss it. And where would Dirk go? Would he leave Jeb in the lurch? That could not be allowed. Blood brothers, eh?

He felt under his clothing to where the garrotte was secreted and also the needle-sharp chisel fashioned with such loving care.

He had used it recently to scratch another hanged man on to the sooty wall of the cave but the implement had yet to be plunged in, to draw deep blood, to take a life, and so was still a virgin blade. Surely the devil would be merciful and supply a nice piece of flesh?

For some reason, female flesh appealed in that respect. The bitch Jean Brash, for instance — all fancy clothes and fine skin — sticking it into her belly would be a pleasure. He still remembered that kick she gave him, and it would be just the thing to watch her face collapse as the blade penetrated and then ripped up.

All prepared for that eventuality. All prepared.

He also had the King and Ace of Spades — the last two cards — tucked away until the need arose.

Dirk made a snuffling noise at the back. He'd got too soft — too soft — not like Jeb. Aye, should the Smiler take one backward step — the man would be lost without him. Stone blind. What about Jeb, though?

Would he be lost the other way?

That was the trouble when you let people into your world; you grew to depend upon them. Unless they were rats.

For a moment he felt a weird panic. But then more practical matters took over as he stopped and pointed upwards at a grating.

'This will do it.'

Dirk wheezed, a hankie spread over his face to rebuff the virulent smells and stinks that surrounded them like ghosts tugging at the sleeve. It had been a noxious, germ-ridden journey.

They had been about to emerge at Salamander Street when Jeb had sniffed like an animal sensing danger. He had raised the grating a little and peered out, pale eyes like a rodent in a cage.

There was nothing to see except the ruined walls and battered door that hid the grating from sight, but Jeb was not comfortable.

'Too many people,' he muttered. 'I can smell them.'

Dirk had looked out also but could see nothing.

'Nobody hindered me.'

Jeb sniffed again.

'You werenae the target mebbye.'

It now bothered him the way that lassie had looked at him during the slaughterhouse rampage. She had not turned her head away, but watched him out of sight.

As if she recognised him. That female face he glimpsed in the window at the Just Land; was it her?

That's what ye get for a kindly action — betrayed every time.

What if she had told somebody? Anybody would do. The world is full of enemies.

Not taking chances, he had therefore led them in another direction to find their destination. And this was as near as he could get.

Jeb prised up the heavy street grating and looked out. Darkness — that was good. He loved the dark.

They scrambled out and then he scuttled through the back streets and wynds, with Dirk on the outside to shield him from the regard of any curious passers-by, until they reached a corner of George Street.

There was a heavy biting wind beginning to blow so folk kept their heads well down, holding on to hats and bonnets — that was a blessing.

The tobacco shop was dark and looked deserted like the street itself — people heading home for supper not on the point of committing a merited strangulation.

'No one at home,' said Dirk hopefully. 'Too late.'

'He'll be in the basement,' replied Jeb with certainty. 'I've watched these many nights. He'll leave at half past the hour — we'll chap the door jist before — you at the front. An upright citizen — nothing to fear — *in ye come, sir — dear me yer shoes are a wee bit manky.*'

The dwarf cackled away at his little joke and Dirk shivered in the brattling wind that was now scouring the streets. His feet were soaking wet and he felt an abrupt surge of killing rage.

'All right,' he said tightly. 'Let's get it done.'

'Wait!'

As Dirk made to move Jeb hauled him back with a strong wiry arm — the strength in these arms and clawed hands was always a surprise, and had been especially so for those necks round which he had slipped the wire.

A knee in their back for good measure.

Moncrieff had soiled himself. A coward tae the end.

Another sniff. Something still bothered him. The dwarf had, over the years, developed an instinct for danger as an animal senses the presence of a predator. He couldn't spot them out but . . .

'Folk are watching,' he muttered. 'Watching close.'

He peered out again down the street. There in a doorway, a lighted stub of a cigarette — Wild Woodbine, no doubt. He looked on as the stub fell to ground and was extinguished under a heavy boot.

'Why would folk be watching?' asked Dirk.

To this worried question Jeb shook his head.

'Folk are aye watching.'

Dirk wasn't convinced by that; observers meant suspicion and suspicion meant discovery. Tomorrow he would be in clover, but one mistake tonight and Dirk might be the body swinging on a rope.

He felt exposed on this windy street corner and was relieved when Jeb muttered something and dragged him away in another direction.

However, relief changed to more disquiet when he found himself being propelled into a dark alley that ran behind the rear of the tobacco shop — it had rubbish and earth underfoot and was obviously used by the scaffie wagons.

'I've had my eye on this bastard Young for a while,' said Jeb sagely. 'I know his back and front.'

There was a flight of stone steps that led down to a basement door. A dim shaft of light came through a small window where the blind did not hold together.

'He'll be in there. Get him in there.'

'How?'

'He willnae answer a knock at the back. Pick the lock, mebbye.'

'And if you're not able?'

'Kick the door in.'

'You're demented, man.'

'That's the plan.'

'There must be another way!'

As if in answer, the light was quenched and moments later, the back door itself opened and a figure slipped out, up the steps and off along the alley.

The two killers pulled back into the shadows.

Gavin Young was leaving by the rear, just to make sure none of his employees might be loitering out front to follow their master in prurient pursuits, or anyone else for instance see him taking a different route from his usual way home.

And, of course, in the process losing the men Jean had stationed out the front to keep him safe and sound. Thus deception breeds destruction. In life the only person you ever really fool is your gullible self.

For a moment the man turned, coat buttoned, muffler to the neck, a large top hat oddly positioned on his small head and the wire-framed glasses glinting from a stray shaft of lamplight.

Like a hobgoblin.

Then he was off.

'We follow,' hissed Jeb. 'Then we make a kill.'

'Where?' Dirk tried to keep a plaintive note out of his voice, but the more the evening progressed, the more disturbed were the thoughts in his mind. This was madness and he was part of it.

'Where?' echoed Jeb and sniggered. 'A man that leaves by the back door is going tae a secret place. And a secret place will be quiet. Quiet as the grave.'

He set off and the Smiler had no option but to follow — and regret the fact that he had not hammered down upon his boon companion when he had the chance.

Young kept to the back streets, heading down towards Leith, and Jeb was in clover.

'Home sweet home,' he crooned, but to Dirk Martins it was more like a journey into hell.

34

I married a wife on Sunday,
She began to scold on Monday,
Bad was she on Tuesday,
Middling was she on Wednesday,
Worse she was on Thursday,
Dead was she on Friday,
Glad was I on Saturday night,
To bury my wife on Sunday.

Those who live near the sea are used to a kind of climatic violence that can arise out of nowhere and strike like a charging bull — a tempest of wind and rain.

The sharpening wind that Dirk Martins had felt freeze his bones on the corner of George Street was mere precursor to a storm that had whipped up in the unruly North Sea and decided to celebrate the arrival of a new year by unloading a hellish brew of rain, gale and whatever else could be picked up on the way upon the city of Edinburgh and the parish of Leith in particular.

Such outbreaks are known in local parlance as *scuddering Nancy* and have no mercy upon man or beast.

The east wind was a babe in arms compared to this unleashed power of nature, and though the participants it deluged upon might conceivably have reflected upon the relative fallibility and frailty of the forked human worm, quite a few found themselves concerned with an even more murderous activity.

Death by strangulation and its consequences.

And as Jean Brash left the tavern to disappear into the night, other characters and events moved and suffered under the same sky.

★ ★ ★

Gavin Young was buffeted by the rising storm even as he stayed close to the buildings of the ancient Kirkgate.

The address he had been given was a number in Coatfield Lane, which ran off the larger thoroughfare, and as he turned to pick his way down, the precise Mister Young was wondering if he had made a mistake.

What if the man who had come to his shop was a fraud? Or worse, a thief of some sort who would seek to rob him. But then why would he supply an address?

No. The fellow had breeding. All would be well.

A wind-propelled slate clattered into the road behind him and Young turned sharply. Just a slate, though.

He was on edge, of course, only sensible to be on edge, and he had experienced an uneasy feeling of being followed on his journey — so much so that, even though not far from his destination, he had hailed a cab, in fact the only cab to be seen on the streets since horses were no more keen on this fierce inclemency than humans, and been happy, for once, to pay high price for a short journey.

Anyone following would be lost. Some of his employees were overly inquisitive and a man cannot be too cautious.

The cab had dropped him at the Kirkgate, which made the ride even shorter, because he did not intend the cabbie to know the true destination either, for who knew what the man might tell, and now Gavin was safe travelled except for this damned wind and rain.

Yet all the time there was that feeling of nervous excitement — an undercurrent that trembled the blood. He was a careful man and was going against a lifetime of prudence. As Mister Young walked on, a jumble of thoughts ran through his mind — images from the past.

★ ★ ★

His father had been a flesher. He was a jovial man with a purse-lipped wife who ruled the house with an iron hand. Gavin was meek, passive, clever at school, mean with money like his mother, but every Saturday as a penance, the small boy had to help his father in the shop.

One time, when his father had gone to the tavern for what he considered a well-merited draught of beer at the end of the day, the two other butcher's boys, for a laugh, had shoved the son and heir into the cold slaughter room and locked the door. Everywhere he looked there was a carcass. Sheep, cows, fat pigs with open mouths and drooping ears, hung on hooks

294

like a picture gallery.

One massive body, splayed open, a bull perhaps, the ribs hanging raw; he had stuck his head inside. The smell made him gag but he prised the body further apart and climbed in to hide from view. What was he hiding from? Death, perhaps?

When the boys finally relented and opened the door, they found him blue with cold, crouched up amongst the bovine innards. He looked out at them and then screamed. Not for a laugh.

Afterwards, his mother made sure that her beloved son never worked in the shop again. The bull had no opinion on the matter.

★ ★ ★

Thirty-nine. The number given.

A small house, heavily curtained, but no different to others in the lane. The paint on the door was peeling a little and the lock was hanging a little loose on its hinges. Was that a worry?

He could still go back.

Gavin lifted the knocker and rapped. The door opened and it was indeed the same man, a polite expression of regret upon his face.

'I am afraid, sir, the . . . subject for my art and your diversion has not yet arrived.'

The man stepped back a little and beckoned Young into the gloomy hall, out of the storm. This Gavin did, but only enough to avoid the battering rain, no further, and he had made no response while the man continued.

'She will receive due . . . reprimand. But I

have taken the liberty to lay out for your edification many of my most treasured depictions and I think you will find the experience . . . most rewarding.'

Gavin Young hesitated; was it a trap?

'They await you down in my cellar room — that is where I also . . . practise my trade, sir.'

The man still sensed a certain reticence and played what he hoped was a winning card.

'The various implements and accoutrements have also been laid out for your inspection and approval. The subject will no doubt arrive shortly — perhaps the bad weather has delayed her — but when she does, I shall make sure she receives a most . . . rigorous censure.'

He stepped further back in invitation.

'If you would do me the honour?'

A sudden image of his wife Martha, hung up on a butcher's hook, clamped and pinioned, invaded Young's mind and at the same time a fierce storm blast blew the door shut behind him.

It would seem nature had made the decision.

Boreas. God of the North Wind. With purple wings.

★ ★ ★

William Baines bowed his head in prayer, yet he was not in church. The study surrounded by his holy books was where he had sought the most immediate solace.

He could have sold this house in Pilrig Street, off the Leith Walk, and occupied the manse at

Greyfriars, but this was where he had shared a life with his beloved Mary and he could not bear to leave the place.

He could hear a frantic rain beat upon the windows and torrents of water cascading down from the roof above to splash uncontrollably on to the streets. Not unlike his own thoughts.

William feared that had he gone to his church to address the Lamb of God for comfort and advice, the action might cross paths with one of his congregation.

Someone such as Martha Young, for instance, who may have seen the naked despair in his face and somehow divined or intruded upon the cause. For make no mistake, if word of this spread through the Greyfriars flock, he would be pitied, yes, but there would also be an attendant sly casting of aspersions.

A minister must be above all sin and he could just imagine the sleekit smiles, the innuendos, the talk behind his back, judgement in the eyes and the shaking of holy heads.

A daughter from his loins, depraved and abandoned to sin. And who would pronounce a verdict from on high?

The unco guid. The rigidly righteous. The high exalted.

Would he count himself amongst them?

No. Not so much. William had always tried to see the best in his fellow humans, but he was not a fool or hypocrite and was only too aware of his own limitations. At times he followed the rules of church and state and lacked compassion for those who did not obey these strictures. Now he was lumped in with the misbegotten.

The shock and anger he had felt at first was like a sword through his soul, but in a strange way it had faded and left wounded confusion in its wake.

All certainty fled.

He tried to banish from his mind the images of his daughter's and another's naked breasts — nipples like sentries on duty — but the pictures kept creeping back inside as mice would after cheese.

What could be done?

His wife would have known the path. Mary. A compassionate soul.

She would have forgiven. Could he?

Or his congregation?

No. They would and could not.

So that just left William Baines, minister, father, brought up against a reality he had never before experienced.

He had tried to interest Sarah in the teachings of the Bible but other than — in his opinion — a somewhat morbid interest in Saint Sebastian, the girl had only paid lip service.

Lip service. For some reason these words upset him.

One passage, though, had interested his daughter. Ruth 1: 16–17:

And Ruth said,
Intreat me not to leave thee, or to return from following after thee: for whither thou goest, I will go; and where thou lodgest, I will lodge: thy people shall be my people,

and thy God my God: Where thou diest,
will I die, and there will I be buried . . .

Addressed to Naomi. Woman to woman.

Perhaps he should have paid more attention?

He bowed his head again in prayer and the light of his downstairs study burned bright — the curtains not being drawn — to send a signal down the front garden path out into the dark, drenched street, of a life within.

A signal that would resonate with the death that would soon be waiting without.

★　★　★

McLevy's low-brimmed bowler was blown off by a gust as he entered the station, to be neatly trapped but unfortunately crushed by the boot of Ballantyne.

As the inspector, without a word of thanks, grimly punched his hat back into shape, his bounden superior, Lieutenant Robert Roach, emerged from the office, where he had been communing with the portrait of his dear Queen Victoria, to demand what news and progress.

McLevy had hoped to nip in off the howling streets to collect his old beaten-up service revolver, which had seized up a mechanism and been left at the gunsmiths — the mender had promised to repair the beast and been as good as his word — the inspector about to pick the gun up where delivered at the station desk and to depart on the instant, when the gust of wind struck.

Time was of the essence and he would have planned to brief his lieutenant later on that night, but now he was pinned by the circumstance of a foul rainstorm.

Mulholland would be no help at all, lurking at the back like a municipal lamppost.

'Well, McLevy, what is your report? I have just had a note hand-delivered from Chief Constable Craddock, to ask this very question.'

All the other men in the station became very busy with various oddments but their ears were flapping, as was often the case when this pair got to public grips.

To be fair, Roach was not necessarily a stupid or selfish superior, but Craddock had been sending hourly demands for up-to-date bulletins as regards the murder of Barton Laidlaw and the lieutenant was at his wit's end.

McLevy moved in closer and beckoned Mulholland over to join them.

'We found a link between the victims,' he stated quietly. 'And I must be on my way accordingly.'

He hefted up the revolver and slid it into a special pocket sown inside his overcoat by his own fair hands. His mother had been a skilful dressmaker until she cut her throat with her own shearing scissors.

'I may have need of this.'

Roach blinked.

This was serious — that was a rare tone he had just heard from the inspector.

But Craddock needed a bone to chew.

'I have to tell the man something, James.'

'A long time ago, a boy died in one of the Charity workhouses — it was rumoured Moncrieff had beaten him to death.'

'And?'

'It was covered up, sir. The governors of that workhouse put it to bed; even promoted the bugger to another place, where he disgraced himself with a young girl and was booted out on his ear.'

Mulholland, lamppost or not, made a contribution.

'Barton Laidlaw was one of the governors. He and Moncrieff die the same way. Same kind of playing card on the dead body.'

'We got a' this frae one of the old gadgies who used to manage at the boys' workhouse. On his last legs but his memory was clear enough.'

McLevy jammed his bowler back on.

'One other on the board was Judge Abercrombie.'

'Good God!'

'We tried his house on the way back but it's all locked up. Could be he's away on a holiday, but the court starts tomorrow and if he's not there, I'll need official entry papers.'

What McLevy did not say was that he had been tempted to pick the lock at the judge's house. But it was an old-fashioned curly key job and even the inspector baulked at the thought of breaking physically in through the window.

'I'll make sure you get them,' said Roach firmly. 'If at all needed. Are there others on that board?'

McLevy started to edge away.

'Young the tobacconist and the Reverend Baines — we're on our way to warn them. Jist in case. Might not be worth the while but better safe than sorry.'

'Baines? I play golf with the man!'

'That's nice.'

'Do you have suspects?'

'The auld fellow said the dead boy had two friends, Jeb Summers and Dirk Martins. A rumour in the workhouse said the boys had sworn vengeance, but that was a long time ago, sir. And time waits for no man!'

With that, the inspector was out of the door and into the howling gale, and Roach knew better than to ask if he needed manpower to support — McLevy might have to move fast; he and Mulholland would do better on their own.

He sighed, sat down at the nearest desk, and started drafting a note to Craddock. To be truthful, he shared McLevy's low opinion of the fellow, even if they did inhabit the same Masonic lodge, but as the inspector was stuck with him, so his lieutenant was tethered to the Chief Constable.

As the hymn would have it, *You in your small corner, and I in mine.*

'Ballantyne?'

The constable stiffened proudly. Yet again he had been picked out from the herd.

'Aye, sir?'

'Take this note to the Chief Constable — post-haste, if you please.'

Ballantyne's heroic status shrunk a little.

'It's a gey wet night, sir. Skelpin' down out there.'

'Are you a man or a mouse?'

The constable thought about it for a moment, and then went to get his coat.

Roach sighed once more. William Baines was a decent soul — a fair striker of the ball — but sadly shared with Roach the affliction of a wayward putter.

Now the poor man might be a target for murder.

Another sigh.

Only two days into a new year, and Roach was already facing an eternity of crime.

35

This is the maiden all forlorn,
That milked the cow with the crumpled horn,
That tossed the dog,
That worried the cat,
That killed the rat,
That ate the malt
That lay in the house that Jack built.

The intrepid investigator was drenched with a deluge of icy rain as she slipped and slithered her way over the uneven, cracked flagstones of Coatfield Lane.

The lilac outer garment provided fair protection against this onslaught, but even so, the Scots word *drookit* most perfectly described her appearance; the plumed hat that had so impressed the denizens of the Rusty Nail, a petite French Gem with feathers, now looked as if a dead pigeon had landed upon her head.

'Buggeration!'

This unladylike exclamation, which hearkened back to a young girl lost and running in the lower wynds of Leith, had been caused by her foot slipping into a deep puddle and the water slopping over fashionable boots to render the feet inundated and saturated.

Nan Dunlop had supplied Jean with the name and number of the man she sought. The name she had known from another life; the number was . . . she was guessing here because it was so damned dark and wet, the doors being a hidden mystery and half the numbers had fallen off in any case.

Or was she on the wrong track? No. Lo and behold. There it was. Thirty-nine.

There was a doorknocker as well, and for a moment Jean hesitated before putting out a soggy gloved hand. But to her surprise the door swung back under touch to disclose a long and narrow hall.

The lock itself was flimsy and hanging away at an angle. Had the violent winds perhaps blown the thing off its hinges?

Should she call out?

Jean decided against that idea and closed the door behind, but as she moved down the hall she slid the wet glove of her right hand into her coat to pull out the derringer, which was held to the side.

Total silence, save for the howling wind behind that rattled and jolted the rickety door. Halfway down the hall was a grubby curtain that she pulled aside to reveal a small kitchen.

An oil lamp shone fitfully on the table but the room was deserted and the table itself was littered with the remnants of a meal, if you might call scraps of bread and a few crumbling lumps of cheese a meal.

The place had a grimy, unkempt appearance not improved by unwashed dishes in the sink and an empty whisky bottle lying alone like a dead soldier amongst plates that were piled to the side.

She went back into the hall and saw another door at the end and to the left. It disclosed a flight of steps leading downwards but at least there seemed a pale source of light seeping through at the bottom.

Out of the blue came a weird high-pitched noise, part-way between laughter and pain.

Silence. Then it came again. Laughter and pain.

Jean gripped the gun tighter and slowly made her way downwards. The stone of the steps had an oily, mossy feel underfoot, the walls dank with a strong smell of mould. There was a brooding menace to this passage, and was it her imagination or were the sides narrowing in on her as she descended further into the depths?

Claustrophobia. The fear of enclosed spaces. To suffocate, buried alive, the earth fill your nostrils and eyes blacked out, wedged tight like a coffin in a grave, every turn a hostile blank wall.

It took her back to that moment when she had hurtled sightless and terrified through the wynds as if the devil himself were on her trail.

But now the sense of evil was looming ahead.

At the bottom of the steps was another door. She moved the handle with her left hand, gun in the right. Her heart was pounding, a feeling of primitive fear. Was Lucifer himself on the other side?

Again the high-pitched sound, fainter this time, like an animal caught in a trap. The feeling of fear was palpable, like a block of ice — spreading through the limbs like a cold disease.

But she was Jean Brash. Queen Bee.

The Mistress of the Just Land pushed further open the door and looked in on something like a vision out of hell. Grotesque and terrifying, in a silence that was broken only by the diminishing sound of death.

The walls of the room were bare save for various iron rings embedded in the surface trailing heavy links of chain — these ended in padlocked manacles — she had seen their usage from the photographs in Abercrombie's safe.

Scattered wildly around on the floor were items of photography equipment and lamps, one of which, on its side, was supplying light for this nightmare scene.

Implements of torture, vices, clamps, cuffs and blindfolds had been hurled to all sides, and strewn all over these obscene trappings and thrown to every corner like confetti at a wedding, were photographs — captured images of torture that made up an unholy gathering.

Hanging above, swaying gently in the draughts that the storm outside had brought to bear upon the hellish chaos, was the body of Gavin Young.

Neat and tidy no longer, a rope round his neck, suspended from an iron ring that was embedded into the ceiling — no doubt intended for other purposes.

'A pretty sight, is he not?'

Jean near died of shock and whipped round with her gun pointed, but there was no need.

In a far corner that she had not yet noticed, sitting up against the wall, was the origin of the sound that had accompanied her visit and the

307

purveyor of images to chill the soul.

The photographer. Tam Drayton.

His grubby pale shirt was stained dark with red and fingers fumbled as he tried to lift a cracked shard of Meerschaum pipe to his lips — the bowl intact, stem broken, a spilt box of matches at his feet.

As he tried to speak, a thin rivulet of blood ran out of the corner of his mouth and found a resting place in the tobacco-stained yellow beard.

'If you would be so kind.'

He pointed to the matches — from where he sat to where they lay was obviously an unfeasible journey.

Jean stooped without thinking, struck a match upon the bare wall to light the flame, and held it over the bowl of the pipe, cupping her hand to shield it from the whirling draughts of wind.

The sweet smell of hashish rose in a cloud as Drayton inhaled, held in the smoke, and then blew it out. The action set off a fit of coughing and more blood, which spread over the lips and chin.

Jean motioned as if to part the shirt to see the extent of the damage, but Drayton shook his head.

'Too late. All gone.'

Another suck of the pipe at the embers of hashish, but the face was deathly white as if the body had already given up the ghost.

A *deid strake* — a death wound.

She spoke for the first time.

308

'How did it happen?'

'They just — appeared. The dwarf. He cut me. To the gut. Then — choked — the tobacco man. Hung him up. I had to sit and watch. He cut me deep.'

'The other killer. What did he look like?'

'Very — respectable.'

Drayton laughed at that idea then let out a cry as his body shuddered in pain. He tried to draw again at his pipe but the bowl was now empty and charred.

'Pity that,' he murmured, eyes vacant, mouth slack.

Jean became aware that one of the photographs was under her foot. She kicked it to the side and saw the face of Nan Dunlop looking up, a rigid smile of agony on her face as she hung from the chain.

'Why do this, Tam?'

'Money.'

'Hatred, more like.'

'I don't really know. I fear I am a lost soul, Jean Brash.'

With that his head fell forward, the breath ceased, and what spirit he had left . . . departed.

Jean lowered her own head for a second and the body above creaked in its chains — for Gavin Young had been hung post-garrotte by the very implements he had come to witness in action. The bitter bitten.

She had no time to take him down — Mister Young would have to wait until the quest was over. He would not be lonely — there was a playing card, no doubt the King of Spades, wedged into the wire-framed spectacles to keep him company.

This man was dead.

But one other was still alive.

36

And when the door begins to crack
It's like a stick across your back
And when your back begins to smart
It's like a penknife in your heart
And when your heart begins to bleed
You're dead, and dead, and dead indeed.

William Baines looked mortality in the face and tried not to flinch. To show fear now would be to lack belief.

The sharp point of the chisel was sticking into his neck and he could feel a trickle of liquid down his skin, no doubt blood, which would stain the clerical collar.

Thank God Sarah was not here — in fact, of course, she was in bed with another woman, but at least that meant not embroiled in her father's nemesis. And possibly, were she a witness, sharing his appalling fate. No. Better tucked up in the arms of — he would assume someone who loved her?

A better choice by far. What strange thoughts to have on the point of a heavenly departure.

A knock at the street door and he had moved to answer — perhaps his daughter come to throw herself at his feet and beg forgiveness, he had thought, or perhaps some poor wretch stranded by the storm and looking for refuge.

It was a man, standing on the small garden

path that led to the street, respectable from his clothes, a heavy coat drenched, of course, by the rain, but his face concealed somewhat in the dark.

'May I assist you?' asked William.

'You certainly may,' answered the other, but then a goblin shape sprang out from his side, as if he had given birth like the rib of Adam, and the minister was hit back and assailed by this demonic troll.

A needle-sharp blade jabbed in under the chin and he was forced backwards into the house, into his study, shoved down into his own armchair — unable to move while a face out of hell grinned an evil grin and chattered its teeth together like a simian familiar.

'Ye don't know me, eh?'

To the troll's question, William shook a careful head — too much movement might be fatal. The other man stayed in the shadows of the room as if not part of this, but the next words belied any thought that he might be on the side of the angels.

'For Christ's sake, Jeb, get it over!'

'Nae hurry, nae hurry,' said the new-named troll. 'A man is entitled tae enjoy himself.'

He pressed the blade tip in so deeply that Baines could not move — as if impaled. Nailed to the cross.

'Johnny Finch. Remember that name?'

The minister blinked acknowledgement — a nod could have had lethal consequences — but a sickening feeling of guilt crept out to join the dread within.

The Charity workhouse.

Baines had allowed himself to deny his own teachings; failed that boy and let the cause of his death be buried with the body. All these years it had troubled his soul and now he would suffer retributive justice from a demon out of hell, perhaps, but deserved nonetheless.

Jeb giggled at the thrawn, haunted look on Baines's face.

'Comes back now, does it not?'

One more blink as another squall rattled the window that looked out on to the street — perhaps the storm wanted to come in and watch the show.

'Ye turned your back upon him, and now ye pay the price.'

The troll with his left hand, the right being otherwise occupied, took what looked like a playing card out of the folds of his monkish garment, and turned it so that Baines could discern the Ace of Spades.

'A wee present, Minister — frae Auld Nick — he'll be waiting for ye in hell.'

The card was slid into the top pocket of the minister's neat and sober suit and, as he did so, Jeb pursed his lips and spat straight into William Baines's face.

While the target could not refrain from reeling back and wiping a hand at the mess, the dwarf deftly pocketed the chisel to slip round the back of Baines's armchair.

Like a snake he moved and there was a reptilian cast to his features as he unleashed the garotte and slid the wire in place around the

313

minister's neck. One firm wrench backwards and Baines was pinioned.

'Any last wishes?'

After asking this, the troll giggled again and the man in the shadows cut in angrily.

'Just do it, Jeb!'

Dirk's nerves were shredded; usually the dwarf managed the job at a vicious speed — speed was of the essence, and it was over in moments. So why the talk?

Even with Gavin Young it had been swift and lethal — cut the other fellow in the guts, leave him to die in his own blood, strangle and hang the wee dribbling tobacco man who was still pleading for his miserable life at the very end (the man had no dignity) and then the dwarf had gone into a frenzy, throwing the manacled bits and pieces all over, howling with glee as he stamped and ripped, scattering the manky photos to every corner of the room.

Yes, even then it had been quick and to the point, save the scattering. Plus, to be truthful, Dirk had joined in with that as well. Madness is catching.

Earlier, they had chased after the hansom-cab that Gavin Young had hailed in the street, Dirk puffing out of breath, Jeb not even bothered by such, both like drowned rats in the driving rain. But luckily the cab had not gone far — not far enough to escape pursuit.

Then follow, watch Young enter a house, and after, take their turn. The street door was easy, hanging near off its hinges in any case, then in and down, and then . . . Madness.

Now, though, while Dirk was still soaking wet he was yet possessed of stone cold sanity — and he knew that the longer they stayed in this house the more dangerous it became.

Also, he felt uneasy about the killing of Baines; the man had been kind to the boys when he visited, so Dirk had no desire to meet his eyes or be seen by him.

However, for his part, Jeb would not be hurried — he was king now — he was the one who gobbed in your face. And Dirk had better realise that it would not end here — there would be other times, other deaths.

The world was full of people that deserved to die and the Smiler had to play his part. And not ever leave his one true friend.

To Jeb's delight he had perceived a narrow full-length mirror opposite, possibly to let the minister check his holy attire before going out to spread the word of God, but now perfect for Jeb to view himself and the rooted form he had at his mercy. A plaything.

He pulled harder and the man let out a strangled cry yet still did not resist. Guilty as charged.

'A last wish. I asked ye!'

Finally the preacher managed a word or two.

'I — I — would wish to pray.'

'Don't make it too long, eh?'

Jeb nodded agreement at his image in the mirror — they would both enjoy the spasm of death to follow.

William Baines bowed his head as a psalm of David came to his mind.

The Lord is my shepherd; I shall not want.

He maketh me to lie down in green pastures: he leadeth me beside the still waters.

He restoreth my soul: he leadeth me in the paths of righteousness for his name's sake.

Yea, though I walk through the valley of the shadow of death, I will fear no evil: for thou art with me; thy rod and thy staff they comfort me.

Thou preparest a table before me in the presence of mine enemies: thou anointest my head with oil; my cup runneth over . . .

As the minister murmured the words at first and then his voice rose a little in volume, Jeb began to fidget uneasily and the scar he had cut into his hand long ago started to throb, as if on fire.

His image scowled at him. Get on with it.

Dirk also was riven by the words; for some reason they cut into his blood-guilty soul. And, like any self-respecting member of the lunatic planet, he reacted accordingly.

'Kill him, for God's sake!'

Jeb heaved back and the wire cut through.

Baines choked hard and committed his soul to eternity. But the animal within had other ideas: not while there was breath in the body.

A coughing roar and the minister threw up his hands to pull the wire away from his throat.

Jeb grinned like a madman — this was what he lived for; this was his exaltation.

He hauled back once more and, despite the fierce resistance, felt the wire begin to cut deeper. Soon it would be all over; soon he would be the king of death; soon he would hang the man high . . .

A crash and the glass of the study window shattered as a large garden stone struck it into a splintered mess. Another hard blow split the glass completely and a huge shard fell into the room like a bolt of lightning.

A doeskin-gloved hand extended through the gap. It held a derringer.

William Baines could see all this reflected in the long mirror before him.

A shot and Jeb Summers howled in pain as a bullet went straight through the flesh between neck and shoulder to embed itself in the King James Bible that had pride of place upon the bookshelf.

As it should in a decent Christian home.

The dwarf dropped to the floor, leaving the deadly garrotte to drop behind, scuttling on his hands and knees towards the open study door. The shadowy figure of the other man also ran for his life and there was a grotesque, near comical moment as they collided in the gloom of the doorway.

Another shot. Another howl. And then they were gone from sight.

A pale rain-streaked face, a face seen earlier appearing ghostlike at the window had the killers deigned to glance that way, a face splintered into myriad images by the cracking of the glass, was in sight for a moment then it too was gone.

William Baines struggled mightily for breath and tried to staunch the flow of blood from his flayed throat with a white handkerchief, which immediately stained red.

He reflected, though, that it could have been worse — a great deal worse — he owed his existence to a doeskin glove and a derringer.

Hammering upon his front door.

The minister staggered back down the hall to see a woman's figure outlined through a narrow stained-glass segment of the portal.

William, coughing the while, opened the door, a mite cautiously given the experience of the last time, and saw a tall female in the pouring rain with a small smoking gun in her hand.

She wore a lilac-coloured coat that, despite its saturation, seemed to glow in the dark. Red hair was plastered to her face — the green eyes blazing. A face he had seen and recognised in his dream.

'You — you're Jean Brash,' said William Baines. 'I've seen you at the racecourse.'

Though he would never wager money, a sinful pastime, William enjoyed the races at Leith Links. Mistress Brash enjoyed them also — though she bet a plateful and hated to lose.

'Where did they go?' snapped the female.

'The — the back door probably — that would make sense — yes.'

The minister winced, his wits somewhat scattered with pain as he dabbed the hankie.

'Are you able to hold on?'

'I will survive. Just a — scratch.'

Jean smiled suddenly. 'I met your daughter,

318

Sarah. She has a deal of honest grit. Now I know where she gets it.'

As she moved to brush past him, he tried to form some sense out of all this.

'Where are you going?'

'Off tae the slaughterhoose!'

With that she was gone through the house to follow the killers out the back door for a final reckoning. The minister held the cloth in place round his neck and looked out at the hellish cacophony of wind and rain.

For some reason the words from *Tam o' Shanter* came into his mind.

> *And sic a night he taks the road in*
> *As ne'er poor sinner was abroad in.*

Then William closed the door, turned and leant back upon the stained glass.

Honest grit, eh — what was he to make of that?

37

Here comes a candle to light you to bed,
Here comes a chopper to chop off your head.

Jean battled down Leith Walk as the wind howled up to give her a far from welcome greeting. And while it tugged at her clothes like an unruly child, she reflected that when you are stripped back to the bones, then and only then does the real self emerge — the rest is just pantomime.

She was no longer a bawdy-hoose keeper, no longer the woman of fashion, no longer even Mistress of the Just Land — that was her last bulwark, the final mask she wore to protect herself, but even that was gone.

Now she was just Jean Brash. Elemental. An essence distilled.

Throughout this night, as she had stumbled and fallen in the rain, grazed her knees and arms, French hat whirled away in the wind, face scraped clean, she had been taken back to that moment all those years ago when a terrified wee lassie found herself abandoned and lost.

And that same fierce will to live, not to bow the head at the implacable workings of fate, the voice that said *there will be always one moment*, had risen up from the depths and filled her with an iron resolve.

When she got to that window and looked in, saw Jeb Summers (could not make out the other

320

man in the shadows; Dirk Martins it had to be, but the face hidden yet from view) saw the murder in progress like a nightmare — it only took a matter of moments to lift the heavy garden stone, crash it through the glass and then fire the gun.

Back to the bones.

The minister must have been through something similar, for there was a deal of gumption in his face and that was only ever found with a back to the wall and the devil's pitchfork at your throat.

And now? Now it was Salamander Street — had to be — where the killers would go.

A gust blew a mixture of dirty puddle water plus icy rain smack at her face in agreement, and Jean gave vent to a primitive howl that matched the one she had let rip outside Barton Laidlaw's domicile.

All her people, she would assume, had been driven off the streets by the battering storm, though presently it might be dying down a little.

On her own now. She ducked into a shop doorway to draw breath.

The side streets had brought her out halfway up Salamander — way towards the top was the slaughterhouse, ominous and dripping like a monster waiting to be fed.

From what Lily had said, Jeb Summers had appeared from lower down. But where exactly?

Some of the lamplights had been blown out by the storm and the few left were working fitfully. Well, nothing for it but to trust in her instincts and hope that God was on her side.

Not that she'd ever witnessed evidence of that particular leaning — especially when in the hands of that bastard Henry Preger.

Again from Lily — though the girl's recollection was jumbled from events — it had been an alley off to the left. Of course, it could have been just a detour to somewhere else, far away and out of sight, but ye have tae start somewhere, eh?

Even Satan had to make a beginning. Lucifer falling to Earth.

She smiled at that notion.

Hannah Semple would be in a fine old state — what a worrier the woman was — born tae rack herself over a wee thing like a dead judge and a pursuant mistress.

Jean had tried two narrow alleys already and found nothing to indicate a pair of killers in flight. One more to go and then she'd just have to call out Jeb's name in the night — wait for him to pop out with a bouquet of roses and a knife between his teeth.

The storm was suddenly a spent force — it had tried to huff and puff and blow the house down, but the Edinburgh castle still stood and so did the domicile of slaughter. A weird dead calm had descended like a funeral service, and it seemed the whole world was dripping with water.

Then out of it came — a voice that near jumped Jean out of her skin.

'Mistress Brash?'

She spun round, hand at the derringer pocket,

and then gasped in recognition and disappointment.

Plookie Galbraith.

At his feet was a small mongrel dog that looked twice as drookit as its master.

She might have known that of all her people, he would be the last one standing. Never had the sense tae get in out of the rain.

A young, gangling, awkward soul whose face was covered with pockmarks and acne — hence the name *Plookie*. He shivered in the cold night air, his thin body and thinner clothes no protection — soaked to his threadbare skeleton — God knows how he had lasted outside this long.

But here he was and was he of use?

'Have ye seen anything, Plookie?'

A regretful shake of the head.

'Nothing, Mistress.'

She sighed.

'Until a wee bit ago.'

'Whit?'

The boy would drive her to distraction.

'Two men came doon the street. One was near the ground. Like ye said. Couldnae see them well, right enough but . . . like a wee dwarf.'

Jean, via Lily, had supplied a rough description of Jeb Summers.

'Where did they go, Plookie?'

The youth pointed a long dirty finger at the last alley to the left.

'In there. I thought tae follow, but then thought tae wait.'

Just as well or he would probably have joined

the list of corpses. The dog whined and Plookie gave it a last morsel of food.

'He likes raggie biscuits,' said the youth.

Jean left him out there like an attendant scarecrow, with a warning to keep watch and not budge. He was her guard. Her sentry.

Plookie stood up proudly at that and she left him under one of the few remaining working streetlamps.

Into the alley.

Nothing to be observed. Had the young man been mistaken? He was not overly gifted with brains. Then she saw the sign.

Almost passed it by, when a sixth sense stopped Jean in her tracks.

An old broken door that had been sheltered by some narrow crumbling walls and on the reasonably dry but cracked framework — a smear of blood. Halfway up — around the height of her waist — just about as high as a wounded dwarf might lean his neck upon to rest a moment.

She stripped off her glove and put a pinkie against the smear. It was still damp — even a little blood came off on to her skin. Recent, then.

Jean squeezed past, in fact had to wrench open the door to do so, cursing under her breath as part of her coat ripped off on a protruding nail — that was an expensive coat, lilac a hard colour to find — but there, there, on the saturated ground, tight up against the crumbling wall, was a rusted wire grating.

Little wonder no one had found it, accidentally or otherwise.

She hauled at the grating, which was not as heavy and immovable as appearance dictated, and it pulled away with a slight metallic creak to disclose a dank-smelling hole plus a gully of sorts that sloped steeply downwards.

That much she could discern by a shaft of streetlight that had strayed up the alley from the road opposite where Plookie stood on guard, but after this there was little more to be seen.

Ah well. Nothing ventured, nothing gained.

Of course it could all lead to nowhere, but she doubted that. A hunter's instinct.

Jean carefully peeled off her other glove to lie neatly by its companion at the side of the shifted grill. The material was now soaking and might well slip on the sludge she would no doubt encounter when she searched for a hold of sorts. The deeper you go in life, the slimier it gets. Might play merry hell with her fingernails, but sacrifices must be made.

She cautiously lowered herself into the gulley. Thank God her fashionable boots were sturdy enough, recently heeled and soled by Donnie Pettigrew because the Edinburgh cobblestones had knocked the original Italian leather for six. Her coat and skirts clung to her like a second skin — no chance of them catching on anything, so no worries there.

The only concern was the prospect of what might await at the bottom.

In fact, as she groped downwards, she found there were some narrow iron rungs hammered into the brickwork — slippy and treacherous but enough to gain a purchase on.

The darkness, however, was a different matter — pitch black in the descent.

It took all Jean's nerve to penetrate further for she hated the dark. A fear of being interred within a Stygian pit, swallowed whole by the giant maw of an infernal monster — this had haunted her from infancy.

Other childhood images of loss, one after another, broke upon her like waves upon a black sea. One in particular: Margaret Brash's open mouth as the old woman lay back in death, jagged shadows on the wall as Jean shook the body, its head jerking to and fro like a marionette.

It is easier to be brave for a brief and glorious moment than to confront the icy block of panic. To force yourself downwards into the abyss when a part of you is screaming not so to do.

But at last, with a jolt, her feet landed on solid ground — if you could call the ooze and clinging mud that squelched under her feet in any way a secure surface.

She felt her way along the wall, praying that bare fingers would not encounter something alive and slimy, like a leech or slug or . . .

Her face hit a spider's web and Jean struggled to control a childlike fear as she scraped the clinging gooey mess away from her skin.

When would the nightmare journey end?

Then she saw the faintest glimmer of light ahead and as she inched towards it, heard the murmur of voices.

She had reloaded the derringer, her last two bullets — one for each killer if necessary — the gun now in her right hand as the light grew a little stronger. The sounds now formed themselves into words and the words were charged with rage and panic.

Jeb and one other — the voice oddly familiar. She had heard it before, but where?

The Just Land. She had heard it in the Just Land!

But who . . . who was Dirk Martins?

Jeb's voice came first.

'That bitch — Jean Brash, it must have been. Took the top right off my ear!'

'You'll live.'

'Big hole in my neck.'

'The bullet went through. No harm done.'

'Still bleeding. See?'

'It will stop, Jeb. Just — calm yourself.'

Dirk did not sound calm — his voice was tight.

An angry mutter from Jeb indicated the dwarf was not of a peaceful persuasion either, and Jean almost had a weird fit of giggles at the damage she had wrought.

Pure tension on her part, because she was now so near to the source of light that she would be on top of them in a moment . . . And then what?

Shoot them down in cold blood?

Then she would be no better than a killer herself. But if alive, how could she get them back along that tunnel and out on to the surface?

That might not be possible. Oh well. First things first.

Now Dirk spoke.

'You think she saw me?'

327

'Who cares?'

'I care! She could tell folk. I'd be finished.'

Jean Brash stepped out.

'As a matter of fact, I didn't see you clear,' she announced evenly. 'But now I do.'

38

Baby baby, if he hears you,
As he gallops past the house,
Limb from limb at once he'll tear you,
Just as pussy tears a mouse.

And there they were by candlelight.

But it was not a romantic liaison.

Jeb was hunched over, sitting on a box of some kind, a chunk taken out of his ear right enough, raw and red. He had a piece of dirty cloth clamped over the wound on his neck as a makeshift bandage, but from the way his eyes popped open and the dwarf sprang to his feet, not too much damage had been done.

And also facing her, rigid with shock, was none other than the man she had encountered that night in the Just Land — the Bristol boy who had cavorted merrily with the magpies. Fat, bald and smiling. Now, just fat and bald.

The man known as Sammy Deacon.

Something had nagged at her from that night, something inside her had known, remembered, recognised, but it had been too deep to be brought to a conscious reference.

'Dear me, but you're well beyond the pale, Dirk,' she said. 'All that bonny hair. Gone tae hell.'

He had indeed changed almost beyond recognition but had she not been so hectic on the murder night, Jean might have seen something familiar.

In the eyes, perhaps. Especially in the mouth. But then again, possibly not.

Dirk Martins had been a handsome, smiling, treacherous boy with a full head of straw-coloured hair. Like a beacon.

Now only the treachery remained.

The man himself had still said nothing — it would seem that Jean's appearance had struck him dumb.

As if she were an angel fallen from heaven: mind you, that could be either Gabriel or Beelzebub.

She noted that Jeb's similar silence might also be due to the fact that his hand was sliding inside that strange covering he wore.

'Just keep the fingers steady, Jeb Summers,' she told him. 'Elsewise I'll have to shoot you.'

Jeb grinned like a rat, his white skin livid against the red trickle of blood.

'Ye already did that, Jean Brash.'

'Always room for one more.'

Dirk's mind was in a frenzy. All he feared had come to pass. His life was over. There would be no deal tomorrow. No money to pocket. The bastard dwarf — it was all his fault. He had led Dirk astray — Dirk was a good boy.

'I never did a thing.' His first words to Jean were a lie. 'I only watched.'

'Liar,' said Jeb, grinning all the more. 'Ye did for Laidlaw and I'll tell the world.'

'Liar yerself!'

Dirk shot a look of pure hatred at the albino,

330

who seemed unaware of this and sniggered to himself. The whole time Jean was aware that Jeb would be looking for an opening. If he could distract her — just for a moment — that was all he would need.

She saw that there were some ends of rope in the corner — maybe kept for the next hanging. They might come in useful. What was it McLevy had told her once, filtering the coffee through the gaps in his teeth?

I aye offer the guilty party an opportunity tae make amends. At least until I can get the restrainers on and throw them intae jail. Then they can go tae hell.

'If you help me, Dirk,' she promised. 'It will go well with you. The judge will be merciful.'

That is providing he's not stuck inside a wardrobe or lying in the cheese room.

'Pick up the rope in the wee nook there, then tie his hands behind — and lash them tight!'

Dirk moved to her command. Whether he believed Jean or not, better his hands were free than Jeb's — he might get a chance to run for it.

The dwarf sniggered to himself again but this time there was desperation in his eyes. As Dirk walked behind him, Jeb made a sudden dart to the side. Jean moved and stepped back to cover him with the derringer, but then nature took a hand.

To replace the white rat, Jeb Summers had been feeding another, smaller, black skittery wee beastie, and on hearing raised voices and hoping for a bite to eat, the rodent came scampering out

— only to be stood upon and squelched by Jean's newly soled boot.

It squealed like a soul in torment, a hellish and unexpected noise that startled her into falling back, and at that moment Jeb launched himself. His head butted her in the midriff, winding her completely, the gun flew backwards out of her hand into the gloom of the passage behind, and Jeb had her at his mercy — his knees pinning her to the ground, the needle-sharp chisel at her throat.

The rat crawled off to recover, its insides in a terrible state — all the beast had wanted was a bite to eat.

'Well,' said Jeb Summers. 'This will be a pleasure, eh? Ear to ear, Jean Brash, but nae prayers this time.'

Jean gasped for breath; she could see Dirk's face over the dwarf's shoulder — still harbouring resentment towards Jeb, a conflict of emotions.

How could she use it?

There will come a moment — one blow, one chance — but where the hell was it?

'Would you kill a woman?' she croaked.

'Easy,' replied the dwarf.

'And you, Dirk Martins?'

The man averted his face and did not answer.

'I kill everybody,' crowed Jeb and began to move the point of the blade. Ear to ear he had pledged.

'Even Johnny Finch?'

A desperate throw — not a spade, perhaps, not even a court card, but the only one she could play. It had occurred to her before as a possibility, but now she had to make it stick.

'Whit?'

At least the blade had stopped.

'The boy that had his bed next to you, Dirk. Archie Millar. He told me.'

'Eh?' from Martins.

The fact that she even knew the name startled both men and Jean took the moment to lie at a rush.

'Moncrieff aye swore that Johnny was alive when he departed the room. You go in, Jeb Summers — middle of the night. Come out. Leave him dead.'

'Liar!'

Yet Jean saw something in Jeb's eyes and when does a lie become the truth? Although what followed was total deceit.

'Archie told me. You bragged tae him. That you'd done it. Killed poor Johnny. Told him. Bragged it deep!'

Jeb swore an oath and went to slice the blade but Dirk Martins came up quick and gripped the hand tight.

'That's whit happened, right enough. Ye went. Ye came back. Left him lying still, ye said.'

'So what? She's a liar, I never told a soul.'

'Told what?'

This lightning intervention from Jean just to fuel the flames almost cost her dear as Jeb screamed back, 'Shut up, dirty bitch!'

He went to finish it but Dirk had gripped his hand hard.

'Told what?'

'Nothing!'

The two men had almost forgotten Jean now; it was as if they had gone back to a lethal childhood. Eyes locked, teeth bared.

'Did ye kill Johnny Finch?'

No answer.

'*Did ye kill the poor bastard?*'

A howl in response.

'*Who cares?*'

The dwarf's mind had snapped.

What he'd kept secret in the recesses of his soul — it had come back not that long ago and had caused him tears of a twisted remorse, but those he had brushed away. Now the secret had returned once again.

★　★　★

Johnny had gobbed on him, laughed at him, treated Jeb like a bad thing. So he had told Moncrieff that Johnny had dropped the pee — that he'd done it all by himself.

And the man had promised that Jeb and Dirk would be kings. Johnny would be beaten bad and put tae another place. A hard place. And no one would ever know that Jeb had told. But Johnny knew. Somehow. Saw it in Jeb's eyes, maybe, or Moncrieff had let it out somehow. But Johnny knew.

Spat in his face. He would tell Dirk. Jeb's only friend. So Johnny had tae die. It was easy. Moncrieff had a big, fat cushion. For his bony arse. Johnny was near out of it anyhows. Shove his face down on the cushion. Shove. Hold.

Shove. Till he stops. Then put the cushion back.
  Easy.

★ ★ ★

'He deserved it,' Jeb added simply.
  'Why, for Christ's sake?'
  'I did it for you, Dirkie.'
  'Eh?'
  Jean watched them — sadly the blade had not
deviated from her flesh — as Jeb continued.
  'So that you'd be my friend. Jist us two, eh?
But then ye went away tae another place. Bristol.
Left me.'
  Jeb looked disconsolate for a moment, and
then cheered up once more.
  'But then ye came back. That was good.'
  The dwarf gently moved Dirk's unresisting
hand from his and nodded in content — felt
right tae get that off his chest. Holding it too
long. Dirk would understand. His friend.
  'But — but what about the scar we cut? The
vengeance?'
  'That was jist tae keep you close. Alongside of
me. Brothers.'
  'We killed these men for nothing!'
  'They deserved it. They pissed on all of
us. Ruled us lik' kings. They deserved it.
Anyhows.'
  Jeb smiled as if what he had said made perfect
sense. Dirk could go nowhere without him. He
turned back to the body beneath.
  'Now, jist finish the job, and we're back where
we started. Friends, eh? Forever.'

Jean almost shouted the words at Dirk — last chance:

'He fooled you, Dirk. All the time. All that vengeance. For nothing. Played you for a fool!'

Jeb whipped his head back round again to see Dirk's reaction and as he did so, as she created that diversion, Jean Brash struck the blow.

One chance.

Both knees came up sharply and hammered into the back of the dwarf's head. Jeb had been sitting right on her shoulders and there was just enough room to nail him.

One of the knees connected with the damaged ear — agony and surprise tumbled him away. Jean rolled off to the side, her hand flung back into the shadows.

And then Dirk saw his chance. How to get free.

As he had thought before with Laidlaw — two birds, one stone.

While Jeb shook his head in pain, Dirk unloosed the claw hammer from his coat pocket — he had failed to use it before, but not now. Now it was justified.

Up it swept and down it came, spattering out the bones and flesh of the albino like a burst rotten apple. Then again — up and down. One more for luck.

Jeb died hardly knowing what had hit him.

Had he been able to speak, he might have said *I thought you were my friend. My brother.* But he said nothing.

The dwarf just died.

It had happened so quickly, the woman was

still twitching backwards on the ground.

Dirk took a deep breath.

'I'm sorry, Jean Brash,' he said. 'But if you stop breathing as well, I'm in the clear. No one will ever know.'

With luck William Baines had never glimpsed his face — Dirk had kept to the shadows. Of the two that knew his identity, one was now dead — and the other?

'I'm sorry,' he repeated and hammered down.

But the damned woman was too fast. She rolled away and the claw of the hammer stuck into the ground. Dirk jerked the weapon back out — she was on her hands and knees scrabbling around in the shadowy passage that led to the cave.

A perfect target. This time he would not miss.

He would be safe forever and make his fortune.

The Smiler.

The hammer.

Up it swept. Down it came.

Except for the fact that Jean finally found what she was searching for — that damned wee derringer; next time she'd bring an elephant gun — and shot Dirk right between the eyes.

He staggered back.

She shot again. Aimed for the heart. God knows what she hit, but he fell forwards like a dead man. And stayed that way.

His body draped grotesquely over Jeb's unmoving corpse.

Brothers at last.

Jean hauled a harsh mouthful of fetid air into

her lungs and pulled herself to her feet — shakily, but she made it. Just about.

As she leant against the wall, beside her face, scratched into the surface, were three depictions. A man stabbed in the back, two others hung high. A charnel house. Two fresh bodies on the ground, one of them dead by her own hand.

Jean had never killed a man before, at least not from close range. Her body trembled from the aftermath of that event.

Time to go.

She somehow found her way back along the darkened passage to where the gully led upwards.

How could she possibly make that climb in this dark?

Then a light shone downwards upon her. A hurricane lamp. And behind it, the concerned face of Constable Martin Mulholland.

Another face appeared.

'Well, Jeanie,' said James McLevy. 'Fancy meeting you in this neck o' the woods.'

39

I do not like thee, Doctor Fell,
The reason why I cannot tell;
But this I know and know full well,
I do not like thee, Doctor Fell.

Hannah Semple sneaked a look at her mistress and marvelled at the composure shown on this third day of a new year.

True, the face was pale, but no trace of the white-knuckled happenings from the previous night could be read on that serene countenance.

Never mind the deid body that had been laid out by her wee gun. No. When the woman finally returned to the Just Land, did she not just announce that she'd found a perfect solution to the problem of Hilton Abercrombie?

Now transferred back to the cheese room since the wardrobe had not suited his honour, the costumes not to his liking.

Jean had spent near to three hours closeted with James McLevy at Leith station — God knows what he had put her through, but she had came back looking like a dishrag and had then brought Hannah, Maisie and Lily up to date with events.

And what events, eh?

Prevention of murder, lawful execution — well, lawful in Hannah's reckoning — and what a story to unfold.

Lily watched Jean's lips, her own mouth open in sympathy, Maisie's eyes were out on stalks, while the old woman herself shook her head like Doubting Thomas.

But then, then, just when you might have thought the adventurer be off to her bed, Jean Brash slugged back another cup of coffee (the stuff on offer at the station not fit for human consumption, one thing upon which she and McLevy could agree upon), made her announcement as regards the judge (this, by the way, being well past midnight) and the helter-skelter began all over again.

Maisie, who had some ability with harness and whip, was persuaded to don an old coat and hat of the absent coachman Angus, get into position atop the vehicle, gee up the cuddies, and rattle the resplendent cream carriage through deserted dark streets with four passengers inside.

It came back with three.

Then they all went to bed.

Now Hannah and the mistress were seated in the office of Lieutenant Roach in front of two harbingers of doom — Roach and Chief Constable Murray Craddock — and it had been at this precise moment that Hannah chose to marvel.

Both authority figures, especially Craddock, were, to put it mildly, sceptical to the point of outright disbelief at the written statement extracted late last night by one James McLevy and signed by one Jean Brash.

The inspector himself had waited impatiently for official papers to enter a certain judicial residence and, on reception of same, had shot off with Mulholland to effect a lawful intrusion — some time before the women arrived at the station for Jean's further questioning, to be greeted by a pop-eyed Ballantyne.

Jean had once made a kind remark to the young man — taking pity upon his shyness and affliction. He had never forgotten such, and led her through the station like royalty.

However, McLevy's exit and the young constable's escort had left Jean to the tender mercies of Craddock.

The chief constable was a ramrod, straight-backed martinet who should have been in the army where he could have caused upheaval and distress in foreign lands.

Out of everyone's way.

Instead he had brought his mistaken ideas of discipline and rigorous rules of hidebound morality to Leith, which could have done perfectly well without them.

James McLevy laid down the law in Leith.

Jean Brash ruled the other world.

Craddock had failed to learn this lesson.

He had a bony, hooked nose and beady eyes that gave the appearance of a buzzard — eagle, the chief constable would have preferred, or peregrine at least, but in the eyes of a possibly prejudiced onlooker, buzzard was the best fit.

He had cross-examined Jean on the contents of the statement for a fair while now and had arrived nowhere. His sandy hair with severe side parting was brushed to an undeviating rectitude as fingers tapped with a deal of contempt upon the statement.

'You expect me to believe all this?'

'It is the truth,' was her calm reply.

Roach, sitting under a severe likeness of his beloved Queen Victoria, was more sanguine of response. He had experienced a few jousts with Jean in the past, come out worse every time, and so consequently held his fire.

'Every fact you have alleged,' Craddock leant forward, a hawk-like persecutor in his own eyes at least, 'will be scrupulously checked. One mistake, one lie, and you will feel the full majesty of the law.'

Whit a nanny goat.

Hannah's thought might have found echoes in Jean's own mind but no trace showed in that imperturbable face, and it irritated Craddock all the more.

'You killed a man!'

'Self-defence.'

'A reputable business-person.'

'An accessory to murder, at the very least.'

'Your proof?'

Roach made a mild intervention — after all, the woman might be a bawdy-hoose keeper and in the past, an alleged Queen of Crime, but if scrupulosity was to be the watchword, then it worked both ways.

'McLevy has interviewed the Reverend Baines and has received confirmation of the man's identity.'

Indeed, William Baines, despite what Dirk Martins had assumed, had glimpsed enough of the man in the shadows to offer a decent stab for distinguishing the features.

'Plus the fact,' Roach continued a mite doggedly, 'that McLevy examined the dead man's cufflinks and found them to be missing a small jewel stone.

'This stone, in fact, was found by the inspector in Barton Laidlaw's carpet weave. Circumstantial evidence to be sure, but not without power.'

Craddock grunted at these, in his opinion, pallid suppositions, and resumed his indictment.

'You could have come to the police sooner with your suspicions and prevented a murder!'

'I *did* prevent a murder and all I had were, as you say, suspicions — nothing more. Proof is everything.'

Roach could scarce forbear to nod — something he was forever telling a certain inspector.

This fruitless exchange was interrupted by a sharp rap upon the door, the lieutenant called permission to enter his office, and James McLevy took the stage.

40

The hart he loves the high wood,
The hare she loves the hill;
The knight he loves his bright sword,
The lady loves her will.

If Jean looked pale but composed, the inspector appeared as if recently run over by a newfangled steam-roller.

He rarely cut a dashing figure, but his head had not touched the pillow all night, dealing with the corpses of Gavin Young and Tam Drayton when later directed by Jean to the address, plus, earlier, the missed by a whisker corpse of Baines, and the stone cold certainties of Jeb Summers and Dirk Martins.

His face was pouched with fatigue. How many bodies does it take to weary a man? One more, it would seem, as Mulholland slid in behind with a polite nod to one and all.

McLevy made terse report.

'Hilton Abercrombie is dead in his house. Strangled — garrotted — but no' strung up.'

'A stab wound in the back,' Mulholland added. 'For good measure.'

'We found him lying on the floor in front of his desk. Body rigid. Stiff as a board.'

'Hard to tell, but been there for three to four days,' estimated the constable. 'The police surgeon will have a better notion.'

Naethin' o' the sort. We shoved the miserable bugger in place not seven hours since.

Again the mistress was placid while Hannah shivered; a hair-raising time even though Jean had the key for the door lock — the judge wouldnae fold worth a damn and just getting him round corners into the study was a nightmare.

But somehow they'd done it. Unseen, in the dead of night.

Craddock looked as if he had just swallowed a poisonous toadstool.

'This is — this is — iniquitous. How many bodies does that make?'

'Six by my reckoning,' said Mulholland, who looked as fresh as a daisy and quite cheerful considering.

'Six?' asked Roach. 'Dear God.'

'Could have been seven,' muttered McLevy. 'One for every day of the week.'

He nodded to Jean Brash, who nodded coolly back.

A feeling of flat calm, as if everyone had run out of outrage, but Craddock summoned up his reserves.

'You are dismissed for the moment, Jean Brash,' he announced coldly. 'But I must warn you of one thing.'

Here his eyes glittered with a far from concealed malevolence and Hannah felt a gut wrench of fear.

'Although Barton Laidlaw has suffered a sad demise, his most able deputy Forbes Crichton will be in charge for the foreseeable future. I have already discussed with him the closure of your bawdy-hoose and he is in full agreement that, under his command, the council will move heaven and earth to shut you down!'

A hellish surge of panic in Hannah Semple's heart — this was what she had sensed and feared all along. Not a direct result of the judge's murder, but a devastating side effect.

Her mistress did not alter her expression.

McLevy was thoughtful. He knew that poker face. She had something up her sleeve.

Jean had changed her clothing, of course, and wore a lavender-blue coat with a matching confection of hat. She was, in addition, equipped with a rather large reticule which she now unclasped to bring out a red ledger.

'Barton Laidlaw not long ago entrusted this to me. Perhaps the poor man had a premonition of approaching death. Who knows?'

A complete and utter falsehood; she had squeezed this ledger out of the fellow by dint of threat and — not to put too fine a point on it — blackmail.

Laidlaw had grovelled at her feet in abject surrender and raised no objection.

It always does to keep something in reserve.

'This is a record of various . . . transactions of the council, not necessarily of an official nature, and enumerates details of financial exchanges for, how can I put it . . . contractual favours given.'

McLevy and Mulholland flicked a glance at each other as Jean continued.

'It seems that the man who enabled these

transactions to be . . . accomplished, was none other than Forbes Crichton.'

Indeed, Barton had been crafty enough to keep his name out of the negotiations, but Crichton's was all over the ledger. He had been used as a messenger and should have read more Greek plays where the bringer of news is often shown to suffer a grisly fate.

Jean slid the ledger across towards Lieutenant Roach, who looked down as if it was an unexploded bomb.

Craddock now definitely resembled a turkey more than a buzzard.

'I think you'll find it interesting reading. I have a witnessed and notated copy of all the contents at my lawyer's office, in case you might need . . . confirmation.'

That much was true and Jean smiled for the first time.

'I assume you will remove the man from office; there are some other names mentioned that I am sure would interest the newspapers. Good day to you, gentlemen.'

Hannah grunted some kind of farewell and the two women left in state.

In the dazed silence that followed, the face of James McLevy could have matched Jean's in the poker stakes.

Mulholland looked down at the floor as if he'd found something very interesting there.

A stern Queen Victoria stared down at Roach, who stared down at the ledger.

In the lieutenant's mind he could see a putt on the fifteenth green heading straight as a die, and then disappearing into the hole. Which reminded him. Once William Baines's neck was mended, they must have a game. Been too long.

Craddock saw nothing — face blank, mind likewise.

'I came back in a rush tae tell you this, sir,' said McLevy to his lieutenant. 'I'll need tae pick up some men and return to the scene of the crime.'

Roach nodded in the affirmative.

McLevy and Mulholland left. Craddock was silent, chewing a bitter cud.

'I wonder,' asked Roach with a concerned look on his face, 'if you would care for a cup of the station coffee, sir? I can recommend it. Fit for a king.'

On the other side of the door, McLevy sent Mulholland off to round up some constables and walked out of the station, where Jean Brash, as he had hoped, was waiting for him in the street.

Hannah was stationed by their cab, a discreet distance away.

'I have to thank you, James.'

To this remark McLevy grunted and shook his head a trifle wearily.

'On your next visit, I promise to find you sugar biscuits freshly baked, and brew you up a cup of the best Lebanese.'

Some compensation for his labours at least.

He and Mulholland had been on the go all night, given up at the tobacco shop and then Gavin Young's house, but no wonder they couldnae find the man since he was hanging from a beam in Coatfield Lane. They had then made for Baines's residence and been told Jean was heading for a slaughterhoose — knew that must be Salamander Street.

Battled down there, caught up with Plookie Galbraith, scared him into further direction, seen the scrap of lilac coat on the door, then the doeskin gloves by the grill. And then?

'Ye owe me right enough,' he said.

But not as much as he owed her in this case.

'I always pay my debts,' said Jean. 'You're welcome any time.'

They nodded farewell and she started to walk away.

'Oh, Jeannie?'

She turned.

'Funny thing,' remarked McLevy. 'The judge's body. It smelled of cheese. Very . . . cheesy.'

For a moment their eyes met, a sardonic look to the inspector's, innocence personified in hers.

'Cheesy? Now there's a mystery, eh?'

And with that response she was off to the carriage.

The constables split out of the station and McLevy was surprised to see Ballantyne amongst them.

In response to the raising of an eyebrow, Mulholland shrugged. 'Can't do much harm, can he?'

'No. Don't suppose so. The harm's already been done,' muttered McLevy, and then raised his voice.

'Ballantyne, you lead the way. Our destination is Niddry Street.'

The proud young man marched off at the

front, Mulholland beside to keep him on the right track, while McLevy trudged off at the rear, whistling tunelessly through his teeth.

But at least ... at least the promise of a decent cup of coffee. That stuff brewed in the station was pure poison. And fresh-baked sugar biscuits? Manna from heaven.

As that reflection took place, the door to Sarah Baines's studio was knocked upon and the young woman opened it to find her father on the doorstep.

'May I come in?' he asked somewhat huskily.

She noted that, unusually, he had a large woollen scarf wrapped around his neck, the face very pale.

'Are you all right?'

'A long story. Some other time.'

She stood aside and in he came, the door was closed and they stood somewhat awkwardly together as William noted that the same old woman was still propped up in the corner giving him the evil eye.

'I — I had just finished a letter to you, Father. I — may as well — give it now.'

Sarah crossed to a table, picked up the epistle and handed it over. He glanced through the paper swiftly.

It informed a certain William Baines that his daughter had been offered a post as Art Teacher at St Leonards School for young ladies and would be moving to St Andrews as soon as possible.

Short and to the point. Not a trace of apology. Or guilt.

'Good,' he said.

'Good?'

'You love art. You may continue your work, make a fine teacher, and this study will be kept so that . . . should you wish to return for a visit, here it is.'

This was not what Sarah had expected. Joanna had told her of the — as she put it ironically — *heavenly visitation.*

'And if I am — accompanied?'

'That is your concern.'

A firm statement, the eyes a trifle bloodshot for some reason but steady enough.

'You don't — disapprove?'

'I neither approve or disapprove. I have run out of — moral firepower.'

He smiled suddenly.

'He that is without sin among you, let him first cast the stone at her. John eight seven. My next sermon.'

Sarah was transported back to a father she once knew. Her eyes filled with tears and she ran to give him a fierce hug, which elicited a yelp of pain.

Passion can be such a painful business.

The weather had stayed fine all day as Jean, Hannah, Maisie and Lily watched carriage after carriage arrive to disgorge the magpies. They chattered and shrieked with laughter, God knows the mischief they had caused and experienced.

But they brought life, and there had been too much of the alternative recently.

Which reminded Jean:

'How did Nan get on at Minnie Dewar's?'

'Famous,' replied Hannah. 'They knew each other, frae long ago.'

Minnie had her own chequered past.

'Maybe Nan could settle down there. Help round the place?'

'As long as she stays off the whisky.'

Jean nodded at this inconvertible truth.

One of the younger girls, Jenny Cox, a Dundee damsel, called across.

'Mistress, I hae a message frae Teenie Donnachie: she's no' coming back. Gettin' buckled up.'

'Who's the lucky man?' asked Hannah caustically.

'He's a scaffie.'

'That'll keep her busy.'

In fact, the only thing Teenie had ability towards was washing and cleaning, so a midden man would keep her well occupied. No great loss because she was beyond hope at her chosen profession.

Nearly everyone had returned except the Dalrymple twins and their father Angus — Aberdeen being a long haul away — they aye came back last.

'That reminds me,' murmured Jean as they watched the throng flood through back garden gates towards the house, 'I was just wondering. Angus, the coachman, he could use a stable hand? For the horses.'

'Such as who?'

'Plookie Galbraith.'

'We jist get rid o' one misfit, ye bring in another!'

'Plookie likes animals.'

'How would ye know that?'

'He has a dog.'

Hannah shook her head, and then spotted something else from the animal kingdom.

'There's that bliddy cat again.'

Horace had appeared on the garden wall and was peering cautiously in the direction of the pool. It reminded Jean of some unfinished business.

'I wonder how Pallas Athena is getting on?' she pondered.

'Whit?'

'Never mind.'

She looked around. The place was suddenly empty, Maisie and Lily gone to catch up on the gossip, inform everybody what a quiet time it had been and explain how the painted octopus had a bullet hole in its head.

Only Horace remained, and he disappeared once Hannah chucked a stone in his direction.

'Come on,' said Jean. 'We have a bawdy-hoose to run, Miss Semple.'

As they were about to vanish from view, Hannah mused upon something.

'Ye know, I aye wonder who put me up for Keeper of the Keys?'

'A mystery, Hannah; life is full of them.'

A disappointed grunt and then Jean could resist it no longer.

'Would you really like to know?'

'Damn right.'

'James McLevy.'

'Whit?'

'I asked. He recommended.'

'How come?'

'I think he just got tired of sticking you in the penitentiary.'

A look between them. Had Hannah gone down for the third time, that would have been a long, long sentence, especially if she'd come up before the late Judge Abercrombie.

'McLevy did it?'

'No less.'

'That bliddy man. Can he no' mind his own business?'

'He's a policeman, Hannah. Nosy as hell.'

She ushered the old woman in ahead of her, and then before following, looked back out on to her world.

Three days in, and six dead bodies later.

But she was still Jean Brash.

Mistress of the Just Land.

Acknowledgements

I'd like to thank my wife Lisa and daughter Maddy for putting up with the strange crabbed creature in the attic, the loyal and supportive readership and listeners of the McLevy canon, Siobhan Redmond for her portrayal of Jean Brash which has granted me so many insights into the character, Brian Cox for his equal and insightful performance as James McLevy, Tim O'Grady for his shrewd and canny observations on receiving the first four chapters, Lisa Highton for her unflagging encouragement and intelligence, my copy editor Hilary for her unflinching bravery in the face of my bizarre punctuation and, on a domestic front, thanks to Cisco the cat, and Daisy the dog for their simplicity of being which has often kept me on the straight and narrow. To wit, Cisco — 'Where's the grub?' And Daisy — 'Is anyone going to play with me?'

I have good friends, good wine, good food, good neighbours and, if I wasn't such a Greenockian, I'd count myself a lucky man.

My one sorrow is the absence of my great friend Michael Cameron who can't be here to raise a glass but I always have my other friend Graham, who'll raise two.

There's a line of Bob Dylan's always runs in my mind. 'I've got nothing but affection for all those who've sailed with me.'

David Ashton

The nursery rhymes preceding each chapter are part of the traditional canon.

We do hope that you have enjoyed reading this large print book.

Did you know that all of our titles are available for purchase?

We publish a wide range of high quality large print books including:
Romances, Mysteries, Classics
General Fiction
Non Fiction and Westerns

Special interest titles available in large print are:
The Little Oxford Dictionary
Music Book
Song Book
Hymn Book
Service Book

Also available from us courtesy of Oxford University Press:
Young Readers' Dictionary
(large print edition)
Young Readers' Thesaurus
(large print edition)

For further information or a free brochure, please contact us at:
Ulverscroft Large Print Books Ltd.,
The Green, Bradgate Road, Anstey,
Leicester, LE7 7FU, England.
Tel: (00 44) **0116 236 4325**
Fax: (00 44) **0116 234 0205**

NOR WILL HE SLEEP

David Ashton

1887: The streets of Edinburgh seethe with anarchy as two gangs of students rival each other in wild exploits. After a pitched battle between them, an old woman is found savagely battered to death in Leith Harbour. Enter the Thieftaker — Inspector James McLevy. Robert Louis Stevenson, author of *The Strange Case of Dr Jekyll and Mr Hyde*, is in the city to bury his deceased father, and the two recognise each other as observers of the dark side of human nature and hopeless insomniacs. But glimpses of the murderer indicate a slender figure with a silver cane — a dancing killer not unlike Mr Edward Hyde. Is it just a coincidence that Mr Stevenson is back in town?

A TRICK OF THE LIGHT

David Ashton

Halloween, 1881. Edinburgh. And the dead are restless. Inspector James McLevy is called to action when Muriel Grierson, an outwardly genteel widow, is robbed at home. Her knight in shining armour — one Arthur Conan Doyle, recently graduated from medical school — is keen to learn from such a master of detection as the renowned inspector, but McLevy is less sure that he requires a new acolyte. When a vicious murder occurs with evidence of supernatural strength, all roads lead to Sophia Adler, a beautiful young American spiritualist, and the inspector becomes involved with one of the most dangerous women he has ever encountered . . .

FALL FROM GRACE

David Ashton

A burglary and murder at the home of Sir Thomas Bouch, the enigmatic architect of the ill-fated Tay Bridge, sets Inspector James McLevy off on a trail of brutal killings, lethal liaisons, and a double suicide that leads to a violent encounter with an old enemy, Hercules Dunbar. Caught up in a terrifying storm as he tracks his foe to Dundee, McLevy watches the rail bridge collapse and plunge into the icy depths of the Tay. The aftermath brings the destruction of reputation and love, as the inspector uncovers the secret passions that have led to murder . . .